The Three Bı

Vol. 2

Mrs. Oliphant

Alpha Editions

This edition published in 2023

ISBN : 9789357945905

Design and Setting By
Alpha Editions
www.alphaedis.com
Email - info@alphaedis.com

Contents

VOL. 2

CHAPTER I.

PLAY.

IT must be admitted that the counsel thus bestowed upon Laurie in respect to his work had rather a discouraging than a stimulating effect upon him. It disgusted him, no doubt, with Edith and his big canvas, but it did not fill him, as it was intended to do, with enthusiasm for Clipstone Street, and his other opportunities of legitimate work. He made it an excuse for doing nothing, which was unfortunate, after so much trouble had been taken about him. Perhaps, on the whole, it would have been better to have let him have his way. The padrona herself thought so, though she had not been able to refrain from interfering when she had the opportunity. The Square, and the adjacent regions, had pronounced almost unanimously that the sketch was a very clever sketch; but, notwithstanding, deprecated with one voice the big canvas, and the ambitious work. 'I did it, and you see I have not made much of it,' said Suffolk. 'If I thought I could make as much of it as you have done, I should go in for it to-morrow,' cried Laurie, with an enthusiasm for which the painter's wife could have hugged him. 'But, dear Mr. Renton, if you would but advise him to take simpler subjects!' Mrs. Suffolk said, with her pathetic voice. Suffolk was a man of genius, as even old Welby admitted, and slowly, by degrees, the profession itself was beginning to be awake to his merits; but as for the British public, it knew nothing of the painter, except that up to this moment he had been hung down on the floor, or up at the roof, in the Academy's exhibition, and sneered at in the 'Sword.' This was what came of high art.

Mr. Welby paid Laurie a visit in his rooms, to enforce the lesson upon him. 'If we had room and space for that sort of thing, it would be all very well, sir,' said the R.A., 'but in a private collection what can you do with it? The best thing Suffolk could hope for would be to have his picture hung in some Manchester man's dining-room;—best patrons we have now-a-days. But it would fill up the whole wall, and naturally the Manchester man would rather have two or three Maclises, and a Mulready, and a Webster, and even a Welby, my dear fellow,—not to speak of Millais, and the young ones. There's how it is. A dozen pictures are better than one in our patrons' eyes,—more use, and more variety, and by far more valuable if anything should happen to the mills. Though it's a work of genius, Renton,—I don't deny it's a work of genius,—whereas this——'

'Is nothing but a beginner's attempt, I know,' said poor Laurie. 'That is all settled and understood. Let us talk of something else.'

Mr. Welby, without heeding the young man, got up, and gazed upon the white canvas, which still stood on the easel like a ghost, with the white outlines growing fainter. Laurie had not had the heart to touch it since that evening in the Square. 'I don't understand how you young men can be so rash,' he said; 'for my part, I think there is no picture that ever was painted equal to the sublimity of that blank canvas. Why, sir, it might be anything! Buonarotti or Leonardo never equalled what it might be. It is a thing that strikes me with awe; I feel like a wretch when I put the first daub of vulgar colour on it. Colour brings it down to reality,—to our feeble efforts after expression,—but in itself it is the inexpressible. I don't mind your chalk so much. It's a desecration, but not sacrilege,—a white shadow on the white blank,—and it might turn out anything, sir! Whereas, if you put another touch on it, you would bring it down to your own level. The wonder to me always is how a man who is a true painter ever paints a line!'

'It is well for the world that you have not always been of that opinion,' said Laurie, forcing out a little compliment in spite of himself.

'But I have always been of that opinion,' said Mr. Welby. 'Unfortunately, man is a complex being, my dear fellow, and whatever your convictions and higher sentiments may be, the other part of you will force itself into expression. But the thing is to keep it down as long as possible, and subdue and train it like any other slave. That is always my advice to you young men. Never draw two lines when you can do with one. Don't spoil an inch more of that lovely white canvas than your idea will fill. Keep within your idea, my dear Laurie. You should no more tell it all out than a woman should tell out how fond she is of you. Art is coy, and loves a secret,' said the old man, warming into a kind of enthusiasm.

These were the kind of addresses which were made to Laurie in this his first attempt to stumble out of his pleasant amateur ways into professional work and its habits. He could not but ask himself, with a tragi-comic wonder, whether it was anxiety for his good alone which wound up his friends into eloquence, or whether there had ever been a novice so overwhelmed by good advice before. He had done what he liked in the old days, when what he liked was of little consequence; but it was clear that he was not to be permitted to do what he liked now. He was affronted, disgusted, amused, and discouraged, all in a breath. Work in cold blood for work's sake, to lead to no immediate end, was something of which Laurie was incapable. It seemed to him that the way to become a painter was by painting pictures, and he did not give the weight they deserved to his friends' counsels when they adjured him to work at smaller matters, and to postpone the great. 'I shall never satisfy them,' he said to himself; and accordingly the spur being thus removed, his natural habit of mind returned upon him. He had no tendency to extravagance, being simple in all his tastes, and it seemed to him that he could get on very well on his two hundred a-year. 'I shall never marry,' Laurie said to himself, with a sigh, 'nor think of marrying. That sort of thing is all over; and there is enough to keep me alive, I suppose. And why should I go worrying everybody about pictures which I don't suppose I am fit to paint? But I may be of use to my friends,' he added in his self-communion. So he took to play instead of work, which he found to be more congenial to his ancient habits, and he fell back into it as naturally as possible. It would have been better for him, so far as his profession was concerned, had they let him have his own way.

But if he could not be a great painter himself, it was possible enough that he might be of use to those who were so. Though he had been momentarily absorbed by his abortive project, and momentarily thrown off his balance by all the opposition it met, yet he had not forgotten his promise to Mrs. Suffolk. If there was anything he could do to open the eyes of the British public, and show it what a blunder it was making, that would always be so much rescued from the blank of existence. Laurie's Edith, even had she come to the first development which he once hoped for her, could never be,—or at least it was not probable that she would ever be,—equal to that scene in the Forum, which hung neglected on the wall of Suffolk's studio. To bring the one into the light of day was perhaps a better work than to paint the other. It was the first thought that roused Laurie out of his own mortification. He bore no malice. He was too sweet-hearted, too easy and forgiving, for that. Indeed, on the contrary, he was very grateful to one at least of his hardest critics. The padrona had uncovered her heart to him by way of pointing her objection. He had seen into her mind and spirit as perhaps no one else had ever done. He was sorry for the pain it must have given her to speak to him,—even more sorry than for himself; but Laurie could not, though Mrs. Severn would have wondered, speak what people call 'a good word' on her behalf when he got Slasher in his power. The words would have choked him. Ask any man in ordinary Art-jargon and common print to applaud the woman to whom his own heart began to give a kind of wordless, half-unconscious worship! Ask for praise, public praise, for his padrona. He would as soon have thought of leading her upon the stage to have garlands thrown at her feet like a prima donna. Here was a disability of woman which nobody had ever thought of before. It did not matter much, from Laurie's point of view, whether they blamed her or praised her. To name her at all was a presumption unpardonable, the mere thought of which made his cheek burn. And yet it would have done Mrs. Severn a great deal of good had the 'Sword' taken an enthusiasm for her. And Laurie had no objection to her work. He knew that he could not have done it for her had he tried his hardest. Her independence, and her labours, and her artist life, were all part of herself. He could not realise her otherwise. But to have her talked of in the papers! Laurie's private feeling was, that instead of influencing Slasher in her favour, he would like to knock down the fellow who should dare to have the presumption to think that she could be the better for his praise!

But Suffolk was a totally different matter. And Laurie, having turned his back upon the studio, and turned himself loose, so to speak, upon the world again, set to work at the club and elsewhere, to cultivate Slasher with devotion. Slasher was understood to be the special art-critic of the 'Sword;' and he had qualified himself for such a post, as most men do, by an unsuccessful beginning as a painter, which had, however, happened so long ago that some people had forgotten, and some even were not aware of the fact. Though he was not ill-natured, it must be admitted that Laurie commended himself to the critic by the want of success which the young fellow did not attempt to disguise. 'My friends are a great deal too good to me,' Laurie said, with comic simpleness; 'they have all fallen upon my picture so, that I have given it up. What is the use of trying to paint with every man's opinion against you? I have not stuff enough in me for that!'

'Poor Laurie!' Slasher said, with a laugh which was not unkind. 'If you had persevered, probably I, too, should have been compelled, in the interests of art, to let loose my opinion. So it is as well for me you stopped in time.'

'But I want you to let loose your opinion, and do a service to the nation,' said Laurie. 'I want you to come to my place and meet a friend of mine,—the cleverest fellow I know. All he wants is, that you should speak a good word for him in the "Sword."'

'Ah!' said the critic, with a groan of disgust; 'I am tired of speaking good words. I don't mind walking into anybody to do you a favour, my dear fellow. There's always some justice in anything you like to say against a picture,—or a man either. But if you knew the sickening stuff one has to pour forth for one's own friends, or one's editor's friends! I am never asked to give a good notice in the 'Sword' but I feel that it's for an ass. Instinct, Laurie! I dare say your friend is everything that's delightful, but if his pictures were worth twopence you would never come to me for a good word.'

'I should not ask you to praise him, certainly, if I did not think he deserved it,' said Laurie, with a little offence.

'Ah! if you were as well used to that sort of thing as I am,' said Slasher, with a sigh. 'I don't mind cutting 'em all up in little pieces to please the public. A slashing article is the easiest writing going. You have only to seize upon a man's weak point,—and every man has a weak point,—and go at it without fear or favour; but when Crowther comes and lays his hand on my shoulder in his confounded condescending way, "My dear fellow," he says, "here's a poor devil who is always pestering me. He is a cousin of my wife's;" or, "He's a friend of my brother-in-law's;" or, "He was at school with my boy," as the case may be. "I suppose his picture's as weak as water; but, hang it! say a good word for him. It may do him good, and it can't do us any harm." That's what I've got to do, till it makes me sick, I tell you. I'll pitch into your aversions, my dear Laurie, and welcome; but don't ask me to say good words for your friends.'

'But my friend is a man of genius,' said Laurie. 'I don't want you to speak up for him because he is my friend; but because his pictures are as fine as anything you ever saw.'

Slasher shook his head mournfully. 'I don't know anything about his pictures,' he said; 'but that's how criticism gets done now-a-days. A man speaks well of his friend, and ill of the fellows he don't like. And, as for justice, you know, and appreciation of merit, and so forth,—except, perhaps, once in a way, in the case of a new name, that nobody knows,—you might as well look for snow in July. And it's just the same in literature. I said to Crowther the other day: "That's a nice book, I suppose, as you praised it so." "No," he says, "it's not a very nice book; but the man that wrote it is a nice fellow, which comes to the same thing." No, Laurie, my boy, I'm sick of praising people that don't deserve it. That's why I go in for cynicism and abuse, and all that. It may be hard upon a poor fellow now and then, but at all events, it isn't d——d lies.'

'I don't want you to tell lies,' said Laurie, half-affronted, half laughing. 'Come with me on Thursday to the Hydrographic. It's Suffolk's night for exhibition, and you shall see him, and see his work——'

'Suffolk!' said Slasher. 'That fellow! By Jove! I like your modesty, Laurie Renton, to come here calmly and ask me to praise a man's pictures whom I have cut up a score of times at least.'

'But I don't suppose you ever saw them', said Laurie, standing his ground.

'I've seen them as well as anybody could see them', said Slasher. 'I remember there was one in the North Room down on the floor one year, and one over the doorway. My dear fellow, I've seen the kind of thing,—that's enough. Heroic figures, with big bones, and queer garments—red hair, that never was combed in its life—and big blue saucer eyes, glaring out of the canvas. I know;—there are two or three fellows that do that sort of thing. But it will never take, you may be sure. The British public likes respectable young women with their clothes put properly on them; in nice velvet and satin, that they can guess at how much it cost a yard.'

'The British public ought to be ashamed of itself,' said Laurie; 'but you may come with me on Thursday all the same.'

'I don't mind if I do for once,' said the critic. And so the matter was settled. Laurie was a very busy man until Thursday came. He was as busy as he had been when his mind was full of Edith, but, on the whole, in a more agreeable way. After all, to shut yourself up all day long in a first floor in Charlotte Street, with a terrible litter about you,—for when there is nobody to keep you neat but a maid-of-all-work, and you have no time for 'tidying' yourself, litter is the inevitable consequence,—your windows shut up, and the light coming in over your head, as in a prison, is not a seductive occupation. Now that Edith was pushed aside out of the way and the windows were open, the room was more bearable. And why a man should make himself wretched by pursuing high art in direct opposition to all his friends? But Laurie betook himself, without entering into any explanations, to Suffolk's house, and devoted himself to the task of collecting together his friend's loose drawings. They had grown intimate by their frequent meetings in the Square. And Suffolk, who was in danger, as his wife feared, of getting 'soured,' and who was busy, and did not care to exhibit himself at the Hydrographic, gave in to Laurie with a half-sullen acquiescence. 'What's the good?' he said. 'But, Reginald dear, it may be a great deal of good,' his wife said, turning wistful eyes upon him. And Laurie went and came, bringing his spick-and-span new portfolios to receive the drawings, which were huddled up in all sorts of dusty, battered, travel-worn receptacles. In such matters amateurs are safe to have the advantage over the brethren in the profession. He mounted, and trimmed, and arranged all day long, with his mouth full of dust, and his heart full of hope; and confided his anticipations to the padrona in the evening, having established a right to the *entrée* at that moment of moments which she spent with her children over the fire. It came to look natural that Laurie should take his place on the hearth, in the firelight, along with little Frank and Harry. 'A curious taste,' the padrona said, and laughed; but not without a little wonder rising in her mind as to how this fancy was to be accounted for. 'The boy likes to feel as if he were one of the family, I suppose,' she said to Miss Hadley, who looked on sometimes, with her knitting, and did not approve;—'for he is only a boy.'

'He is boy enough to be fond of women a dozen years older than himself,' said Miss Hadley, with a significant nod. To which Mrs. Severn, with her eyes fixed on the fire, made no immediate reply.

'After all, it is quite natural,' the padrona continued, after a pause; 'he is separated from his own family by this strange business;—and such an affectionate, soft-hearted fellow!'

'Well, I think it is chiefly affectionateness,' Miss Hadley admitted: and she added after a moment: 'It cannot be for Alice, as I thought!'

'The child!' cried Mrs. Severn, in alarm. 'She is but a child. Don't talk as if it were possible any one should dream of stealing her from me. What should we do without Alice?' cried the mother, with a sudden pang. 'Jane, I hope you will not do anything to put such ideas in any one's mind.'

'Such ideas come of themselves,' said Miss Hadley. 'She will be sixteen in summer. She is of more use than many a woman of six-and-twenty. She must marry some time or other. Why, what else could you look for when you refused to bring her up to do anything? A girl who has no fortune in this world must either marry, or work, or starve; and I don't know,' said the strong-minded woman, with energy, 'which is the worst.'

'Hush,' said the padrona, with a smile, 'infidel! and here is the child going to her music. Alice, come and look me in the face.'

'Have I been naughty, mamma?' said Alice, bending over her mother. For a moment the two looked into each other's eyes, with the perfect love, and trust, and understanding which belongs to that dearest of relationships. If it gave a pang to the heart of the woman looking on, who had no child, I cannot tell. The mother lifted her face, still warm with all the vigour, and softness, and beauty of life, and kissed the lovely, soft cheek, in its perfection of youth. 'It would be no wonder if any one loved her,' she said softly, when the child had disappeared into the soft darkness in the next room, her heart wrung with a premonitory pang of tender anguish. That was the night on which Laurie brought his brother Frank,—splendid young Guardsman, who had run up to town to endeavour to arrange the exchange he wanted into a regiment going to India,—to introduce him to his friends in the Square.

But on the Thursday he rushed in breathless for five minutes only in the gloaming, to keep the padrona *au courant* of affairs. 'We have placed the picture, and it shows splendidly!' he cried. 'The only thing I fear is that Suffolk will be sulky, and not show as well as the picture. Could not you send for him before he goes, and put him in a good humour? If he were out of temper it might spoil all.'

'I will send for them,' said the padrona, 'and keep his wife with me till you come back. It is very good of you to take all this trouble. I wish you had a picture to show splendidly too.'

'How inconsistent some people are,' said Laurie. 'After making an end of my poor picture! No, padrona, that is all over. Let us now be of some use to our friends.'

'But it is not all over,' said Mrs. Severn. And then she paused, seeing, perhaps, some signs of impatience in him. 'Heaps of people can paint pictures,' she said; 'but it is not everybody who can serve their friends,—like this.'

'If it but succeed it will be something gained,' said Laurie, with a sigh of anxiety; 'and you will think me, after all, not useless in the world?' he went on, holding out his hand. Miss Hadley was looking on, with very sharp eyes; and she saw that the young man stood holding the padrona's hand much longer than was necessary for the formality of leave-taking. 'Slasher is to dine with me at the club,' he continued. 'He will be in good humour at least. And you will think of us, and wish us good speed.'

'Surely,' the padrona said, withdrawing her hand; and Miss Hadley sat glancing out of the darkness with her keen eyes; knitting for ever, and looking on. When the young man was gone a certain embarrassment stole over Mrs. Severn,—she could not tell why. 'He is as eager and excited as if his own fate were to be decided to-night,' she said. 'What a good fellow he is!' Miss Hadley made no reply. No sound but that of the knitting-needles clicking against each other with a certain fierceness came out of the twilight in the corner. In this silence there was a certain disapproval, which made the padrona uncomfortable in spite of herself. 'I am afraid you have changed your opinion of poor Laurie,' she said, after a pause. 'I thought you used to like him?' The children had not yet come down from their game of romps in the nursery up-stairs, and the two were alone.

'I like him very well,' said Miss Hadley. 'I like him so well that I can't bear to see him making a fool of himself.'

'How is he making a fool of himself?' said Mrs. Severn, quickly.

'Or to see other people making a fool of him,' said Miss Hadley. 'There, I have said my say! I don't know if it be his fault or yours; but the young fellow is losing his head, my dear, and you must see it as well as I do.'

'I see nothing of the kind,' said the padrona, with dignity. 'I am surely old enough to be safe from such nonsense; and you are too old to talk like a school-girl. You are as jealous as a man,' she added, after a pause, relapsing into easier tones. 'Would you like me to forbid the poor boy the house?'

'It might be best,' said Miss Hadley, stiffly;—'certainly for him. I don't know about you.'

'What folly!' cried the padrona, with momentary anger; but the children rushed in at the moment, sweeping away all other thoughts. Mrs. Severn, however, was more silent than usual as she sat in the firelight with Edie's soft arms clasped round her neck. She told but one story all the evening, and that an old one. Her mind was pre-occupied. The governess sitting in the corner grew bitter as she gazed at her. 'A woman with every blessing of life,—a woman with all those children,' Miss Hadley said to herself; 'yet a young man's silly love is enough to draw her mind away from them,—at her age! What fools we are!' Thus another little drama sprang into life in a corner, with actors, and accessories, and spectators, all complete. There was Alice in the great dim drawing-room, as usual, playing softly, till the very air seemed to dream and murmur with the wistfulness of her music. 'This romance should have come to the child,' Miss Hadley mused, with anger; 'with the child it would have been natural. With the mother——' She could not trust herself to realise what she thought about the mother. She had held so different an opinion of her at all former times; the padrona had shown herself so entirely unmoved by such vanities! And now, good heavens, at her age! Such were Miss Hadley's thoughts as she sat in the twilight, while her friend played with her children. She forgot her sister, who was waiting for her, and all the comforts of the little parlour in Charlotte Street. She would have liked to stay there all night, to keep at her post without intermission, to save the padrona from herself. 'She cannot realise what she is doing,' Miss Hadley said in her self-communion. And probably Mrs. Severn was aware of her friend's inquisition. She had a little flush on her cheeks when she received the Suffolks, for whom she had sent. She went into all the arrangements of the Hydrographic for that evening with an interest which was a little nervous and overstrained. 'I trust some illustrious stranger may be there to be of use to you,' she said, with a smile; and took no notice of Miss Hadley, who kept immovably in the background. And when Suffolk, in his best humour and his evening coat, went out to the Hydrographic, where his pictures were being exhibited, the two women, whom he left behind, talked a great deal about Laurie. Poor Laurie! He was very happy, and excited, and in earnest at that moment, believing himself in the fair way of serving his friend. And they both liked him with tenderness, such as women feel for such men. But yet they said 'Poor Laurie!' even in their commendation and gratitude; and did not well know why.

CHAPTER II.

WHAT CAME OF IT.

WHEN Laurie left the Hydrographic in company with his friend Slasher, he had still a hope of being able to present himself for a few moments in the Square to report how he had sped. But his companion, as it turned out, had no such idea. The Hydrographic held its meetings in the artists' quarter,—in that region which, but for art, no man of fashion would think of visiting. But being in it, for once in a way, Slasher, who considered himself a man of fashion, had made up his mind to make the best of it. He went with Laurie to his rooms, talking all the way of Suffolk's pictures. That the critic had been shaken by the sight of them, there could be no doubt. He had been moved by the admiration of so many men who knew better than he did. The mere fact that the painter had been invited to make such an exhibition showed that he was becoming known to his own profession, and had been owned by it. There was light, and space, and leisure to look at the pictures. There was the comfortable sensation,—in Slasher's case,—of a good dinner and pleasant company, and just such an amount of deference to himself as soothed and glorified his self-esteem. He insisted on going with Laurie to finish the evening, letting his tongue loose as they walked along. 'There is something in it, I don't deny,' he said. 'The contrast between that fair group of children and the dark Romans is very well done, and the monk's figure is full of expression. Let us see what you have yourself, Laurie. I, for one, am more interested in that. Welby is such a friend of yours, he might have found a place for something of your own to-night. It is not a bad room for showing a picture,—and all sorts of men go to the Hydrographic. It would be as good a thing as you could do to make Welby exhibit you there next time he has a chance. Yes, I don't deny there's a good deal that's fine about that picture. The light is very well managed. It sets one thinking of Rome, you know, and how the air all smiles and glows about you on a spring morning. It's not a bad picture. Is this where you live? It is not so nice as Kensington Gore.'

'No,' said Laurie, 'it's not so nice; but it's better for work;' and he ushered his companion into his room, where the contents of his portfolios, which he had carried off for Suffolk's sketches, lay about, all mingled with books and studies in oil and a great deal of litter. The big canvas, thrust back into a corner, a pale shadow of what might have been, presided over the confusion. It was not so nice as Kensington Gore; but to Slasher, who liked to feel himself a man of fashion and superior to professional persons, the disorder of the place was not disagreeable. Laurie Renton had once been 'a cut above him,' and it was not unpleasant to feel that Laurie Renton was now in circumstances to appeal to his patronage. They sat down together over the fire, and lighted their cigars; and what with the smoke, and what with the liquids that accompanied it, and the witching hour of night which makes men confidential, and the old associations, Slasher's lips were opened, and he unfolded to Laurie many particulars of his life. 'You would not think it, but I began the world in much such a place as this,' said the critic. Laurie, of course, knew all about the manner in which his companion had begun the world; for everybody does know all about everybody else, especially in respect to those circumstances of which everybody else is the least proud. The listener in this case had the embarrassing privilege of contrasting autobiography with history, which is always a curious process. But, notwithstanding this difficulty, Laurie was, as always, a good listener,—not from policy, which seldom deceives any one, but because he preserved that tender politeness of the heart and regard for other people's feelings which make it impossible for a man to contradict, or doubt, or sneer at his neighbour. 'I suppose he thinks it all happened so,' Laurie said to himself; and Slasher was grateful to him for the good faith,—a little puzzled certainly, but genuine,—with which he listened. In the breaks of his story he would get up and saunter about the room, turning over Laurie's sketches, and now and then he would interject some remark upon the special subject of the evening.

'Some of those studies of your friend's were fine,' he said, suddenly. 'I hope they'll do him justice next year at the Academy. I'll speak to Sir Peter, if you like; and if the picture he is doing now is as good as the one we saw to-night——'

'One bird in the hand is worth two in the bush,' said Laurie, oracularly. 'And half a loaf is better than no bread.'

'Hang it, what can a fellow do?' cried Slasher. 'You are the most pertinacious little beggar I ever came across. Do you think a man can go and eat his own words and stultify himself? Look here, I'll tell you what I'll do. You shall write a notice of the Hydrographic for the "Sword." Blow the fellow's trumpet up to the skies, if you like; say there's never been anything like him since Titian. And I'll take it to Crowther. Now I don't see what more a man can do.'

'I write the notice for the "Sword!"' cried Laurie, laughing,—'that is a little too strong. I never put a sentence together in my life.'

'As if that had anything to do with it!' said the critic. 'Why that's the only good thing I can see in this blessed trade of literature. You can go at it off-hand. Put a sentence together! Why I've heard you put twenty. It's nothing but talking, my dear fellow. A practical writer like myself, you know, goes off at the nail, and talks of fifty other subjects before he touches the right one; but I can fancy that the public, by way of a change, might prefer to hear what you wanted to say at once. Of course you can do it; and I'll take it to Crowther. A man cannot make a fairer offer than that.'

'It is awfully good of you,' said Laurie, in a ferment. The proposal went tingling through his veins like wine. It had seemed supremely ridiculous to him when old Welby had suggested that he should take to writing, just as he might have suggested shoe-making or carpentry. But from Slasher, to whom the doors of the 'Sword' were open,—and in Suffolk's interest,—the idea changed its aspect. Though there are no labourers of any description who so systematically underrate their trade as do professors of literature, yet it is astonishing how pleased every outsider is who is invited to enter that magic circle. Laurie felt that Slasher in his turn had paid him the most delicate compliment. Though he might have laughed at the 'Sword' and the critic, and at newspapers and critics in general, at another moment, no sooner was he asked to strike in, in the *mêlée*, than the craft and all its adjuncts became splendid to Laurie. What a power it was! How a word in the 'Sword' thrilled through and through those regions where artists congregated, filling some with boundless satisfaction and others with despair! When he cried out, in modest delight and surprise, 'I write a notice for the "Sword!"' thinking it too grand to be true, he already felt himself ever so much more important, so much cleverer and greater a person than he had been five minutes before. Perhaps, it is true, the smoke and the beverage that accompanied it, and the fact that it was two o'clock in the morning, had something to do with Laurie's pleasure in the proposal, as it had with Mr. Slasher's liberality in making it;— but still there it was. Laurie Renton, whom everybody had snubbed, down to Forrester,—whom everybody had interfered with and advised and ordered about 'for his good,'—might now become, all at once, an authority before whom they would tremble in their turn,—who would dispense justice, or favour, or vengeance, from his high-placed seat. It was when he looked at it from this point of view, and not out of any disinterested love of literature, that he jumped at the idea. Laurie leaned over the fire with his eyes glowing, and revelled in the wonderful thought. He was a little particular about his drawings in most cases, preferring to show them himself, and give what elucidation he saw necessary; but this time he permitted Slasher to make his own investigations undisturbed. All he had hoped for in his most sanguine moments had been to extract from the critic some grudging word of praise which should rouse public curiosity about Suffolk's picture. But to have the organ in his own hands, to say what he would,—to secure in his own person that art should be spoken of with understanding, commended without fear or favour, condemned with impartiality,—this was something beyond his highest hopes. Such a critic as he himself would be was the thing of all others wanted in the world of art. How often had the painters round him,—how often had he himself,—asked each other if such a thing were possible? And here was the possibility placed within his reach,—thrust, as it were, into his own hands!

Suffolk had gone home hours before, calling at the Square for his wife. He gave the ladies the very scantiest account of what had happened, but suffered the particulars to be drawn out of him, bit by bit, as he walked home through the dimly-lighted streets. Though he was too proud to make any demonstration of satisfaction before Mrs. Severn, yet his wife read in the eyes, whose expression she knew so well, that for once in his life the sense of general approbation had warmed him. 'It is all Laurie Renton's doing,' she said, in the candour of delight, with a generosity which was not so easy to her husband. Suffolk himself had never made any appeal to Laurie, and did not see it in the same light.

'I don't think Laurie Renton has so much in his power,' he said, 'though he has taken a great deal of trouble. It was Welby's affair chiefly, of course; and then, after all, a man who has been labouring a dozen years surely does not need to be grateful to anybody if he gets a bit of recognition on his own merits at last.'

'Of course it is on your own merits, Reginald,' said his wife; but the woman was more grateful than the man. She knew very well that it was not her husband's merits,—which, indeed, had met with but little recognition hitherto,—but that wistful word she had once spoken to Laurie, and his soft heart which had not forgotten it. Suffolk went on, quite unconscious of her thoughts and of her interference, to set down poor Laurie at his just value.

'Renton was there with a friend of his,' he continued;—'Slasher, Helen,— that confounded snob who has the impudence to give us all our deserts in the "Sword,"—as shallow an ape as you ever saw. Laurie's a very good fellow, but he's too general in his friendships. After feeling really obliged to him for his handiness, to see him arm in arm with a conceited ass like that——'

'Did you speak to him?' cried Mrs. Suffolk. 'What did he look like? Reginald, of course it is natural that you should be affronted; but if you consider how much influence the "Sword" has——'

'Oh, I was civil; don't be frightened,' said Suffolk. 'Deadly civil we both were; and he had something complimentary to say, like the rest. Trust those fellows to see which way the wind's blowing. But what disgusts one is to find Laurie Renton,—a fellow one likes,—hand in glove with a snob like that.'

'He does not mean it, Reginald, I am sure,' said Mrs. Suffolk, driven to her wits' end, and feeling at once disposed to assault her husband for his stupidity, and to cry over poor Laurie, thus cruelly belied.

'Oh, no, he doesn't mean it,' said the painter; 'it's only that confounded friendliness of his that likes to please everybody. If he had more stamina and less good nature——' said his critic, severely.

But he never knew how near his wife was to shaking him as she clung to his arm. And Mrs. Suffolk said no more on the subject,—reflecting, first, that when a man takes a ridiculous idea into his head, it is of no use reasoning with him; and, secondly, that Laurie should never know how little gratitude had attended his efforts. That at least she would take into her own hands. If Reginald did not know what his friend had done for him, she at least did. And so did the padrona; and the chances were that their thanks would be more congenial to Laurie than any gruff acknowledgments that might be made from another quarter. Thus the pair walked on, excited by the faint prospect of better days, through the glimmering, silent streets, when most people were in bed—the husband making his report in snatches, the wife drawing it forth bit after bit, and piecing the fragments together with an art familiar to women. She knew about as well what had passed as he did by the time they reached their own narrow, dingy door. And after one peep at the children, sleeping up on the fourth floor at the top of the house, Mrs. Suffolk joined her husband in his studio,—where he had gone to smoke his final pipe,—and drew forth further his bits from him, and added her words of assent or advice to the deliberations he fell into, standing with a candle in his hand before his half-finished picture. 'Please God, you shall have your comforts like the rest, if this comes to anything, my good little wife,' he said at last. 'Oh, Reginald, it is for you I wish it most,' she cried, with tears in her pretty eyes. That gleam of a possible brightening in their lot went to their hearts. Ah, hard, happy, chequered life!—so hard to bear while it is present, so sweet to look back upon when it is past!

But everything was hushed and asleep in the house of the Suffolks when Laurie shook hands with the critic, and stood at his door in the raw, chilly air of the winter morning to see him go. Laurie had not been keeping late hours for some time past, and the excitement had roused him out of all inclination for sleep. He went back to his fire and pushed away the *impedimenta* from his table, and with his nerves all thrilling, and his brain in a feverish commotion, began to write. Perhaps the soda-water had affected him slightly too—and the hours of talk, and the novelty of what he had in hand, had undoubtedly affected him. He sat till his fire burned out and his lamp ran down, making his first essay at composition. It seemed to him very easy in his excitement. 'If this is all they make so much fuss about!' he said, feeling himself not only capable of the 'Sword,' but of greater things. The street was beginning to wake to the first sounds of the morning when he threw himself on his bed, chilled and exhausted, yet full of content. Surely, after all, this rapid art, which could be caught up without any study, and the effect of which was immediate, was more to the purpose than the labour of months upon one piece of canvas, which might affect nobody, not even the Hanging Committee. New prospects seemed opening before him also,—prospects more vast and boundless than those which flickered before the eyes of Suffolk and his wife.

What if this were now that tide in the affairs of men, which it behoved him to take in its flow! He left his sketches lying about,—paper, and chalk, and canvas, all muddled together,—to be dealt with, in the absence of the portfolios, by the maid-of-all work; but he took his little writing-desk, with his new production in it, to his bedroom with him, where it might be in safety; and fell asleep when the milkman was going his rounds, feeling himself, as it were, on the edge of an altogether new career.

His composition, however, did not look so hopeful when he got up a few hours later, and read it over in the calm of noon as he ate his breakfast. Miss Hadley over the way had seen that his room was vacant all this time, the windows open, and papers fluttering about in the chilly air. She could not understand why he lost so many hours on such a bright morning, or what had become of him. It was nearly one o'clock before he had done dawdling over his tea, reading and re-reading his criticism. After all, it was not quite so easy. He made a great many emendations, and then took to doubting whether they were emendations; and grew querulous over it, and sadly disturbed in his confidence. Then he folded it up and put it in his pocket, and, snatching up his hat, rushed down-stairs. 'He is going to the Square,' Miss Hadley said, as she saw him dart round the corner; and she stood for a long time at her window pondering whether Jane could be right about that matter. 'She will never be so silly, and he will never be such a fool,' said the old lady; and sat down again, with her mind quite excited, to watch when he should come back.

The padrona, for her part, was standing at her easel, troubled with many uncomfortable thoughts. She had looked at herself in the glass that morning longer than usual, and had decided that there were a great many lines in her face which she had not thought of noticing. 'I am getting old,' the padrona said to herself, and laughed; and then, perhaps, sighed a little. She laughed because she felt as young as ever, and age seemed a joke as it entered her thoughts; and she sighed because—— who can follow those subtle shades of fancy? And then she began to think. Laurie Renton was but a boy,—not more than four-and-twenty at the outside, she calculated, reckoning as mothers do. 'Harry was beginning to walk when I saw him first, and Harry will be eight in March,' said the padrona; 'and Laurie was but a schoolboy then, not more than seventeen.' Four-and-twenty! He could not be more,— nothing but a boy. And Jane Hadley is an old fool;—that was the easiest solution of the difficulty. Mrs. Severn liked Laurie, she said frankly to herself. It was pleasant to have him running in and out, with all his difficulties and all his wants. He was such a good fellow,—so frank, so natural, so willing to help everybody, so transparent about his own affairs, so——affectionate. Yes, that was the word;—he was affectionate. Half banished as it were from his own family, he had linked himself on to hers, and she was pleased it should be so. And as for any folly that might enter any one's head! 'These old maids!' Mrs. Severn said to herself,—though it was not like her to say it; and thus she tried to dismiss the subject. If he came too often, she might perhaps suggest to him that it would do him a great deal of good to go and study in Italy for the winter. 'And I should miss the boy,' the padrona said to herself with candour. But in the meantime there was nothing she could say or do. It was simply ridiculous to think of taking any other step. At her age! and such a boy!

She was still working at the picture which Mr. Welby had commended. It was a commission from her patrons, the Riches of Richmont, and was to be hung in a spot chosen by herself in the bright country-house, full of light, and air, and flowers, and everything sweet, to which they sometimes invited her. Edith's little 'wooden sister' was standing to her at the moment, draped in great folds of white. She was working hard at the folds of the dress, and studying with puzzled anxiety the position of the limbs, which, Mr. Welby had declared, had no joints in them. And she was anything but grateful to Jane Hadley for throwing, just at this moment, an additional embarrassment into her mind. It was while she was thus occupied that Laurie rushed in breathless with his tale of last night's proceedings and his paper to read to her. Any prudential thoughts that might have entered her mind as to the propriety of keeping him at a distance vanished at the sight of him. It was all so perfectly natural. Whom else should he go to, poor fellow, to tell his doings, to communicate all his difficulties and his hopes? Mrs. Severn blushed to think that she could have allowed herself for one moment to be swayed from her natural course by such absurdity. Jane Hadley must have lost her senses. Should the boy go to old Welby and tell him? Should he confide in his landlady? Who was there that he could come to in his difficulties but herself?

'I have brought it to read to you,' said Laurie, 'if you can take the trouble to listen. I am afraid it is dreadful trash. The truth is, I was a little excited about it last night; and now, this morning——' He was abashed, poor fellow, and explanatory, and very anxious to impress upon her all the excuses there were for its imperfection. Somehow, everything had a different aspect in the morning! He went on, playing with the paper; and then, making a dash at it, began to read. It was not very good, to tell the truth. There was an attempt to be funny in it, which was not very successful, and there was an effort after that airy style which so many young writers attempt unsuccessfully; and then there was a rather grand conclusion, full of big words, which Laurie had risen into just as he heard the first cry of the milkman, and felt that it was necessary to come to an effective close. The padrona went on painting very steadily at her easel. She had the notion, which women so often entertain, that a young man, with all those advantages which a man has over her own sex, could do anything he chose to do,—and especially Laurie, her own *protégé*; and yet here, it was evident, was something he could not do. The writing in the 'Sword,' though it was said to be nothing remarkable, was not like Laurie's writing. Poor Laurie's narrative, instead of the sober little history it ought to have been, read like a bad joke. He might have been sneering at Suffolk for anything the reader could have made out, and patronising him oppressively at the same moment. Never woman was in a more uncomfortable position than was Mrs. Severn standing at her easel. Laurie himself was so conscious of its weakness and flatness that he attempted, by dramatic tricks with his voice, to give it effect. 'Good heavens! Suffolk will go mad,' the padrona said to herself; and then there was a word or two about Mr. Welby. And the author sat breathless, trembling, yet with a smile of complacency on his face, to hear her opinion. Poor Laurie! whom she had already driven to the utmost bounds of patience in respect to his picture! She shivered as she stopped to arrange the drapery on the little lay figure. Certainly, to be Laurie's adviser-in-chief was a post which had its difficulties as well as its pleasures.

'Is that all?' she said, when an awful pause of a minute in duration warned her that the moment to deliver her judgment had come.

'All!' said Laurie, flattered by the question, and beginning to take courage. 'I should have thought you had found it quite long enough.'

'Well, perhaps it is long enough,' said the trembling critic; 'but still I think there might be another paragraph. You have not said anything about the German sketches, for instance, which were so clever; and you know, if I am to be a critic, you must let me find fault. There are one or two turns of expression. What is that you say about Mr. Suffolk having lived out of the world?'

'"This young artist has little acquaintance with the ways of the world,"' read Laurie. '"He loves nature, which is open to high and low. Instead of conciliating the critics and picture-dealers, he has satisfied himself with the models on the steps at the Trinita di Monte. Perhaps we ought to warn him that this is not the best way to please the British public."'

'Mr. Suffolk will not like that,' said the padrona. 'It looks as if you meant something against his character. It looks like a sort of accusation——'

'Why, it is a joke!' cried Laurie; 'every one must see that at a glance.'

'But people are stupid,' said his critic, taking courage. 'I think you should change it. And then about Mr. Welby. Don't you say he has almost given up painting? There is nothing he hates to hear said like that.'

'"Our veteran master in the art,"' read Laurie, '"feeling his own strength decay, has called upon a younger brother to fill his place,—a substitution at which artists will rejoice." I mean, of course, that everybody will be pleased to find he is spared the trouble.'

'But he will not like it,' said the padrona. 'I think I would say, instead of that about the Trinita di Monte, that he has spent a great deal of his time in Rome, and has caught the warmth of the atmosphere and brilliancy of the colour, and so on; and Mr. Welby,—I would say how graceful it was on his part to lend his aid to a younger man, and how ready he is to appreciate excellence. You told me to say what I think. And don't you think if you were to begin just plainly by saying Mr. Suffolk's works were exhibited at the Hydrographic, instead of that about the gem that is born to blush unseen——?'

'In short,' said Laurie, with a flush on his face, 'you don't like any part of it,— beginning, or middle, or end.'

'Yes, indeed I do,' said the treacherous woman. 'I think it is very nice; but I am sure you could improve it. Don't be offended. You could not expect to turn out a Thackeray all at once.'

'Nor a Michael Angelo,' said Laurie, desponding; 'nor anything. I shall always be a poor pretender, good for little;—and this attempt is more ridiculous than all the rest. Well, never mind. If it were not for poor Suffolk's sake——
'

'For Suffolk's sake you are bound to do it,—and do it well,' said Mrs. Severn; 'and for mine,—I mean for everybody's who cares for you. To begin at three o'clock in the morning, after a night of talk and smoke, and then to be melancholy because you are not pleased with your work! There are pens and paper on that table, Laurie, and I will not so much as look at you. Go and try again.'

'Do you mean to say you care?' said Laurie; and he went and stood by her, while she continued to work.

He thought it was a little hard that she never turned, never looked at him, but went on painting faster than usual, making false lines in her haste. He had no thought that she was afraid of him, and of any foolish word or look which might change their position to each other. He stood wistfully with his heart full of unspeakable things, yearning for he knew not what, longing for a little more of her, if it were but a glance from her eye, a touch of her hand. She had wounded and mortified him, and then she had bidden him try again; but would not spare him a glance to show that she cared,—would not stop painting, and going wrong. He stood and looked on, watching her in a kind of fascination. She had been hard upon him, and he had felt the sting, and forgiven her; and now he might make reprisals if he would. He put out his hand suddenly and took the brush from her hand. 'I am not going to be trodden on for ever,' he said; 'I am the worm that turns at last. I am going to put in that elbow; you are doing it all wrong.'

The padrona never said a word. She gave the brush up to him, and stood looking on while he carried out his threat,—looking at the canvas, not at him. He did it, and then his heart failed him. He had not an idea how much alarmed she was, and terrified for the next word. He had not made any investigations like Miss Hadley's into the state of his own feelings. He did not want anything,—except to be near her, to have her attention, her sympathy, and do whatever she wanted. Now he became alarmed, in his turn, at his own boldness, and humbly laid the brush out of his rash hand.

'Padrona mia, I am a wretch, and you are angry with me!' he said. Then Mrs. Severn laughed, and broke the spell.

'We are quits,' she cried, with a nervousness in her voice which Laurie could not account for. 'You have given me the upper hand of you, Laurie. Now go and sit down yonder, and write your paper all over again from the beginning. I accept your elbow. You are bound to do what I tell you now.'

'As if I did not always do what you tell me!' said Laurie, and he went and sat down at the writing-table, eager to please her. As for the padrona, she took up her brush with a little shudder, feeling she had escaped for this time, but that it might not be safe to trust to chance again. The foolish boy! And yet with all his folly there was so much to like in him! Perhaps even the folly itself was not so despicable in Mrs. Severn's eyes as it was in those of Jane Hadley, who had never been fluttered by alarms of this description, the good soul! But this sort of thing, it was clear, must not be allowed to happen again.

The paper, however, was written, and much improved, and at last, toned down by repeated corrections, was declared ready for the 'Sword,' and worthy of that illustrious journal. By that time it was dusk, and there was no choice but to let him stay to tea. The padrona sent her attendant from her to listen to something new Alice was playing, with a genuine horror of Jane Hadley's comments, and annoyed consciousness of which she could not divest herself. But the young man stayed only ten minutes by Alice, fair though the child was, and sweet as was her music in the soft wintry gloaming, and came straying back again to the little group on the hearth-rug, to share Frank's foot-stool. 'He says he is to go to the pantomime, mamma,' said Frank, whose whole being was pervaded by the sense that Christmas was coming. 'And I say he is to go to the pantomime. Mamma, I love Laurie,' said little Edith. 'But my pet, I am not Laurie's mamma to take him to the pantomime,' cried the padrona loud, so that Miss Hadley could hear. Alas! Miss Hadley did not take the trouble to listen. She looked, and saw Laurie half on the stool, half-kneeling, with the fire-light shining on his face, and that turned upwards to Mrs. Severn who sat back in the shadow, with an expression, as the governess thought, which nobody could mistake. Was it the padrona's fault?

CHAPTER III.

A PATRON OF ART.

NOTHING could be more satisfactory in every way than the notice in the 'Sword.' It was not eloquent, nor too long, and Slasher was pleased. 'By Jove, Laurie, I was afraid you'd go in for fine writing, or for chaff, which is as bad,' he said, with an air of relief. And it was very clear and distinct as to Suffolk's merits. It made such a commotion through the whole district round Fitzroy Square as has seldom been equalled, except just at the opening of the Academy. The paper was lent about almost from house to house. 'Have you seen what the "Sword" says of Suffolk's picture?' one would say to another. 'I hear it was all through Laurie Renton.' It almost seemed to Laurie as if people looked at him more respectfully in the streets. At all events, the fellows at Clipstone Street showed a difference in their manner; and yet there were some even there who shook their heads. 'He would never have made much by art,' said Spyer, who went now and then, and drew for an hour or two, by way of keeping himself up, 'or I should have been sorry; the pen and the pencil don't agree. But it's a good thing for Suffolk. The dealers are beginning to look after him. It's enough to make a man sick, by Jove! years of work go for nothing, when a paltry half-dozen words in a newspaper—— ! If I was a young fellow like the most of you, I'd do something to put a stop to that.'

'What can any one do put a stop to it?' said one of the young men. 'We have no private patrons now-a-days. We have only got the public and the press, to do our best with them. Laurie Renton draws very well for an amateur; I hope he will not end in the "Sword."'

'Laurie Renton was born an amateur,' said Spyer; 'he never was anything better, and couldn't be. Let him take to writing. That's what heaps of people do after coquetting with art. He may make something of that; but he never will paint a picture that has any chance to live.'

'He draws very well, all the same,' said Laurie's defender. But on the whole, though it gained him an amount of respect and importance among them, his little attempt at literature did not raise Laurie's reputation. It looked like a defection to the painters round him. Though it was but for once, and took up but two columns in the 'Sword,' he was given up as having gone over to literature, which, in the opinion of the Clipstone Street fellows, was a very easy and well-rewarded trade. Suffolk himself did not quite know what to think. He lost not a moment in going to see his critic, and thanking him for the good word he had said for him. But yet he was a little unwilling to acknowledge that it was Laurie's paper which brought that picture-dealer to see him. The very next week after, the 'Looker-on' had a notice of the Hydrographic, and followed Laurie's lead, praising the picture with still greater effusion than he had allowed himself; and even Mrs. Suffolk, when she saw this, was moved in her heart by a momentary feeling that Laurie had been very measured and even cold, in his approbation. She was grateful, and so was her husband,—but——. There was a degree of pleasure in their satisfaction with the 'Looker-on,' which was wanting in their gratitude to Laurie. Gratitude is a cumbrous thing to move about with. And Laurie felt that even the padrona expected him, now he had begun, to go on writing articles. One morsel of print implied to all these innocent people an engagement on the 'Sword' at least, and ready entry into literature in general. If he had gone on writing, and stood up like a man for his friends, the society which surrounded him would have felt that he had done his duty. But there seemed to all his comrades a certain cowardice in contenting himself with one effort. That he should have exerted himself on Suffolk's account was quite comprehensible; but to stop there, and do nothing further, and say no good word for anybody else! It was that he did not choose to take the trouble, people thought,—not even for the padrona;—for nobody suspected that Laurie would have been torn by wild horses rather than have put her sacred name into profane print. This was a refinement of sentiment which no man could be expected to enter into. Mrs. Severn herself was perhaps a little disappointed too. It would have been but natural that she, his closest friend, to whom he came with all his troubles, should reap the benefit of the pains she had taken in getting him to write; but never a word in celebration of the padrona's pictures came into the 'Sword.' 'He does not care for them, I suppose,' she said to herself with a little sigh, not taking it unkindly, but with a doubt which clouded her sunny sky sometimes,—a secret suggestion in her mind that her pictures did not deserve admiration. She sighed, poor soul, because she could not make them better, not because it was not in her heart to conceive of higher things. But then she could not afford to wait and think, and collect her full strength, and do her very best. Sometimes she pulled at the tether that bound her, with that impulse towards excellence which is in every sensitive nature. But she could not stop long enough in her ordinary work to achieve anything beyond it. She thought Laurie did not consider her pictures worth talking about, and contented herself without any bitterness. He was not doing what in the merest commonplace way he might have done for her; but the padrona, who was fond of Laurie, did for him what few painters are disposed to do for one another,—she offered him a share in the one special piece of goods which no artist likes to share;—she had the magnanimity to send him a note to Charlotte Street, in the end of March, on one of those coldest of spring mornings, to come and meet her patrons, the Riches of Richmont, at lunch.

The padrona was not given to the writing of notes, nor indeed had she much occasion so far as Laurie was concerned, who seldom was absent from the Square for an entire day. But he had felt, without knowing how, a certain difference in his reception since the day on which he wrote his paper at Mrs. Severn's writing-table. Not that she was less kind or less interested in him;—perhaps it was, though the young man did not think of that, that there was always somebody there, and that the third person, instead of keeping in the background, was brought into the conversation, and spoiled it. Perhaps Mrs. Severn, too, thought the interloper spoiled it. Talk is pleasant, a *quattr' occhi*; but then the interloper was needful. This depressed Laurie's spirits in spite of himself. There was not much that was exhilarating in his prospects generally. Nothing more had come of his literary ambition after that one paper, and his work as an artist went on by fits and starts, with no particular aim in it to spur him on; and his friends, who were all in the heat and fervour of their work for the exhibition, naturally felt that a man who was not preparing for the Academy, who had no share in their white heat of excitement as to the decision of the Hanging Committee, was still something of an outsider. And a cloud had risen on his intercourse with the Square. Laurie was low, and felt despondent about affairs in general. And the chilly spring and the east winds affected his—temper, he said. Probably it was something else besides his temper that was affected. He had begun to say to himself that he was a useless wretch, and not good for much, and that it was ridiculous to hope that he could ever make any mark in the world; and would come home from seeing his friends of nights, who were all so busy, with a certain sensation of misery. The padrona's pictures had been put into their frames, though she was still working at that one for Mr. Rich, and her studio was beginning to get freshened up and decorated in preparation for the private view, which every painter affords to his or her friends and patrons. Even old Welby had taken down the white canvas and the Angelichino, and placed two of his own pictures to have the final touches given to them and to be exhibited before they went to the Academy. As for Suffolk, he was working with a kind of passion at the big picture which had been so unsparingly criticised; the canvas was as big as that one of Laurie's, on which the chalk outlines still lingered,—and there were but two figures in it. The maid in the low arched doorway, in her white kirtle, was dismissing her lover with an inexorable sweetness and sadness; the young man was resisting, and refusing to be dismissed, his dark face glowing with love, and trouble, and angry protest against fate. They were the representatives of two races, hostile, yet fated to mingle; and there was in the picture, moreover, a deeper issue,—that struggle of love and duty which it is sometimes best for the world should not be decided on duty's side. Laurie would stand and look at it, and wonder why he could not have done it as well. Sometimes a vision of the Edith of his imagination, with a still deeper force of expression in her face, would flit across this canvas; but he had discrimination enough to know that Suffolk, in his place, would have painted that Edith had all the world been against him. After all, it was his own fault, but that was no particular consolation; and he felt himself left outside, out of their calculations, almost out of their sympathy, at this particular crisis of fate, when everybody was too much excited about his own luck, and his neighbour's, to have leisure to think of the rest of the world. The moment for sending in to the Academy was like the eve of a great battle in Fitzroy Square and its environs; and Laurie, who was not even a volunteer to come in the *mêlée*, could not but find himself sometimes out of place among those excited groups, with their one subject. He was interested in their fate; but he was not himself putting his own to the touch—and he was a little low in consequence, and heartily wished the crisis over, and things going on again in their usual way. Let who would object, Laurie said to himself, with a kind of desperate resolution, he would have something to send next year.

It was while he was full of these melancholy thoughts that the padrona's little note came to him. He had been there the night before, and Miss Hadley had been present,—even in the studio, to which, in former times, she never dreamt of penetrating. To be sure, there was a kind of a reason for that now in the renovation that everything was undergoing; but still it was rather hard never to be able to say a word to one's friend, never to receive an expression of her opinion or of her kindness, without Miss Hadley's keen eyes upon one's face. And Laurie had grown almost angry at this perpetual intrusion. He was idling over one of his school studies when Mrs. Severn's note was brought to him. It was the briefest little note,—but at least Miss Hadley had not interfered with that.

'Come,' it said, 'and lunch with us at two, and meet the Riches. They have just sent me word they are coming to see my pictures. They are my great patrons, and they may be of use to you. I will tell them who you are,—a Grand Seigneur turned painter,—and they will be immensely interested. Don't laugh at them; they are such good souls.

'You were a little cross, do you know, the other day? and I cannot have you cross. We are all so busy there is no time for talk.

'M. S.'

This was the note, and there was not much in it. It was the padrona's soft heart which had made her add that last little coaxing, half-apologetic sentence, and perhaps it was foolish of her. But then, though it was certainly necessary that Laurie should be cured,—and that without mercy,—of any foolish notions that might have stolen into his foolish young head, still for one moment, once in a way, it was a comfort to be free of Miss Hadley; and she had said nothing that his mother might not have said. But perhaps Mrs.

Severn would not have been so sure of the perfect judiciousness of her words had she seen how Laurie lighted up under them, and expanded into content. It was eleven then, and his invitation was for two; but yet he decided it was best to send a note in return. It is a species of communication which is very attractive sometimes. Laurie jumped at it with an exhilaration for which he did not attempt to account. It was a different thing altogether from those other little notes conveying mamma's messages, which he still preserved somewhere; but not, it must be confessed, with such lively feeling as he once did. Quite a different matter! It was his friend who had written to him now,— only a dozen words, and yet herself was in them,—herself, always full of kind thought, of that gracious interest in him, wanting to help him on though he was so unsatisfactory, finding fault with him in that soft, caressing way, which was sweeter than praise. Laurie,—foolish fellow,—put away his work, and spent half-an-hour of the short time that was to elapse before he should see her in writing the following note. It could have been written in five minutes; but there was, it cannot be denied, a certain pleasure in lingering over it, and a certain skill was required to put a great deal of meaning into few words. He did not think he had succeeded, after all, when it was written. But here it is:—

'I will never be cross any more, padrona mia. I have been thinking you meant to cast me off. But you don't? I will go and meet the Riches or the Poors, or anybody else you like, and thank them for the chance. You I never could thank,—not half or quarter enough. So silence shall speak for me.

'Yr—— 'L. R.'

It is not to be supposed that Laurie wrote 'your' in plain letters. He made a hieroglyphic of it. It might have been only '&c.;' in short, it was as like that as anything else. He was beguiled into the use of the pronoun, he did not quite know how, as he hung over it with his pen in his hand like a pencil, anxious to add just a touch somewhere, as might have been done in the line of the lip or the droop of an eyelid, to express what he was feeling. It was of purpose and intention that he made it undecipherable. Perhaps she would find it out; and if not, still at least he had expressed himself, which was always something. He was not thinking of any result, or anything that might come of it, as Miss Hadley did. At the present stage such an idea would have been simple profanity. He did not think of it at all. He was her disciple, her servant, her subject. That she should reverse the position and be his, and subject to him, was an idea which had never entered Laurie's mind. It would indeed, as we have said, have appeared sheer profanity to him. Such delicacies of feeling do not come within the range of the Miss Hadleys of life. And so Laurie made his hieroglyphic, expressive of the deepest devotion, and felt his heart and his face expand with a delicious softness, and put on his hat, and himself gave the note to the maid-servant in the Square. It was but a few steps round the corner; and when he was out, he went a few steps farther and got himself a lily of the valley to put in his coat. It was still early, and the flower cost him as much as a meal; but when a young man's heart gives a sudden jump in his bosom, reasonably or unreasonably, it would be hard if he could not give utterance to his satisfaction with himself and the universe in general by so simple an expedient as a flower in his coat. And at the same time he ordered some pots of the same lilies to be sent to the Square, not for that day, but for to-morrow, on which Mrs. Severn was to exhibit her pictures to her friends before sending them to the Academy. This little matter occupied the morning until it was time to present himself at the Square. A very fine carriage stood before No. 375 when he reached the door, with a gorgeous coat-of-arms on the panel, and liveries and hammer-cloth, which looked like a duke's at least. The big footman stared superciliously at Laurie as he went up the steps. He was but 'a poor hartis' it was evident to that splendid apparition. The patron had arrived with all the pomp which ought to attend such a celestial visitor, and naturally the house from top to bottom bore evidence of a certain excitement. Forrester, in his best coat, opened the door to Laurie, his face beaming with cordiality and smiles. 'I can't say as he knows much, Mr. Renton,' said Forrester, 'but he's a stunning one to buy; and I wouldn't take no notice, sir, if I was you, of his little ways,—nor the lady's neither, sir,' said the old man. Laurie laughed and nodded in answer to this advice, without any distinct idea what Mr. Rich's little ways might be; and so walked into the great drawing-room, which it was strange to see by daylight, full of the grey spring atmosphere, out of which an east wind had taken all the colour. The white curtains hung over the long windows; the fire burned with a little cheerful noise; and the padrona, in her black dress, sat on a sofa beside a rich, rustling, luxurious woman, fifteen or twenty years older than herself. Mrs. Severn's figure had filled out into the gracious fulness of matronhood. She was not a sylph, like her child; but she looked something like a sylph beside the vast form on the sofa. And in front of her stood a little man, very plump and rosy, with a double-eyeglass in his hand. The padrona looked a little flushed and a little excited. Perhaps it is not in human nature to receive unmoved a visit from a patron.

'This is Mr. Renton,' she said, as Laurie came in. 'Mr. Laurence Renton, Mrs. Rich;' and, to Laurie's great surprise, the large lady got up from the sofa to shake hands with him, which was a great deal more than the padrona did. Mrs. Rich was very large and very wealthy, and looked as if she might be rather oppressive; but, nevertheless, she had been smiling very benignly on the padrona, and Laurie consequently saw some good in her face.

'Mr. Renton, I ought to know you, for we are almost neighbours in the country,' said Mrs. Rich. 'Don't you know Richmont? Ah, I daresay you have been a great deal from home, like so many young men. Mr. Rich, Mr. Renton has not seen Richmont. It is only six months since we took possession. Mr.

Rich bought it for the situation, and gave I am ashamed to say how much money for it; and then the house wanted everything done to it,—new rooms built, and I can't tell you all what. I believe your mamma does not visit anywhere, Mr. Renton. She is a great invalid, I hear; and of course, unless she was so kind as to signify a wish, I could not call first. But I am sure if you are at Renton when we are there, it will give us the greatest pleasure to see you at Richmont.'

'Thanks,' said Laurie, feeling rather aghast. He did not know what more to say till a half-comic, appealing glance reached him from the padrona's eyes. Then he bestirred himself. 'I have been a long time from home,' he said, 'and at present my mother goes nowhere; but I don't know,—pardon me,—where Richmont is. I am so stupid about localities,—I never know anything that is not close to my eye.'

'It was called Beecham once,' said the rich woman; 'but we are not the old family;—we are the new family, Mr. Renton; and Mr. Rich thinks it only right, when he has bought it, to give it his own name. We are not ashamed of being new people. I have just been talking to our friend here about painting one of the rooms for us,—in panels, you know. She is so clever. I never knew a woman so clever; but that is between you and me,' said the patroness, patting the painter patronisingly on the arm. 'She does not hear a word we are saying. I never would tell her she was anything out of the ordinary to her face.' Such were the astounding manners and customs of the new species of humanity to which Laurie had been unexpectedly presented. It took him half-an-hour at least to realise the unfamiliar being. No doubt there are patrons in England of the type known in old days, when one monarch leaned on his painter's shoulder, and another picked up his painting-brush. But these are chiefly patrons of the old masters, not of the new; and Mr. Rich and his wife were the specimens best known in Fitzroy Square. When they went in to luncheon the padrona looked more and more flushed, though Forrester was present to wait, looking as solemn as any family butler, and listening with a sore heart,— but no outward token,—to Mr. Rich's views about art. He had his views, too, as well as his wife, though he was not so immediately audible. It was when he had swallowed some wine that he found his tongue, and then Mrs. Rich was silenced by the more influential stream.

'Glad to make your acquaintance, Mr. Renton,' he said. 'We'd have been very glad if your mother had come to see us. It would have done her no harm, and it might have done Mrs. Rich a little good. We don't pretend to be above that sort of thing. But of course all this fuss about the will must have been hard upon you. I'm told you're one of the rising young men of the time. Stick to that. You may buy houses and lands, but you can't buy talent. I'll be very glad to go and see anything you may have to show. If our friend Mrs. Severn is to be trusted,—and I've always found her to be trusted, sir,—her eye is so true,—you've got something that will suit me very well; and I hope we shall know each other better before we part.'

'I did not mean that Mr. Renton had anything to show this year,' said the padrona. Laurie had never seen her so embarrassed. Was it that the people were overpowering?—or was it——? But there was no time to cogitate possibilities in the midst of this stream of talk.

'Mr. Renton must come and see us at Richmont?' said Mrs. Rich. 'He must come with you, some day, Mrs. Severn. I have got some of her sweet pictures hung in my morning room; and she has been so kind in her suggestions about the furniture. It is such a thing to have an artist's eye; and such pretty eyes too,' added the stout lady, in an audible aside to Laurie, who was seated next to her. 'Don't you think so? To me she is prettier than ever she was. She is like Alice's sister. She looks young,—and she is young,—and to think of all she has done!'

Laurie sat by her, and never said a word. He could not pay compliments to the padrona as a mere indifferent spectator might have done, entering into the fun of the situation. And Mrs. Severn sat at the head of the table, with a flush of embarrassment on her cheek. But perhaps even she was not so sensitive as Laurie; and they were patrons, and brought her commissions,— and they were bread! These are mean recommendations, no doubt, but they have a wonderful effect.

'What I like is a picture I can understand,' said Mr. Rich. 'What I say to a painter is;—"Tell your story. Choose what subject you like, old, or new, or middle-aged; but, whatever your incident is, stick to it, and tell it, without need of any description in a book." That's my principle, sir. And I like a good, warm wholesome colour; none of your cadaverous-looking things. There are plenty of sad things and nasty things in life without putting them in pictures. Like as I prefer a good ending in a story. I have some pretty pictures to show you, sir, when you come to see me. Crowquill painted that last series out of the "Vicar of Wakefield" for me. I could have got twice the price I gave for them from a gentleman I know in Manchester; but nothing but necessity would make me part with these pictures. When a thing's painted for you, it has a value it would not have had otherwise. And I have as fine a little Millais as you ever saw. I hope to have a picture from you in my collection before all is done.'

'You have not a Welby, I think,' said the padrona, who worked rather hard at her part of the conversation. 'You should make haste to secure that; for he paints very little now.'

'I don't care very much for Welby,' said Mr. Rich, indifferent to the awful countenance of Forrester behind his chair. 'He's a deal too classical for me.

I had not a classical education myself; and I am not ashamed to say I don't appreciate that sort of thing. Nature is what I like. I don't pretend to go in for the old masters. They're very fine, I daresay; but give me a nice modern picture with colours, sir, like what you see in life. I hope you are of the real school, Mr. Renton,—not to carry it to excess, you know. The thing for modern collections,—and I know a great many collectors of my way of thinking,—is modern life; the sort of thing one understands. How am I to know about your Greeks and your Romans? I like pretty English girls, and nice young fellows making love to them. Why shouldn't they make love to 'em, Mrs. Severn? I did it in my day. And as for your pictures, could anything be sweeter? It's the next step in life. We've all gone through that phase,' said Mr. Rich, waving his hands; 'and that's the sort of thing we want in our collections. I say this to you, Mr. Renton, as a young man beginning life.'

'Mr. Renton will prefer the pretty girls, of course,' said the patron's wife, with a good-humoured laugh. And Laurie sat by, not knowing what reply to make, while the padrona, with that flush on her face, sat at the head of the table, and let them talk. What was the use of arguing the question? The finest reasoning in the world does not convince people whose minds are incapable of receiving it. And they bought the pictures they commended, which is what better critics seldom do.

'There must be a variety of tastes,' Mrs. Severn said, with a meekness that was not natural to her. 'I am not so pleased with my tame little groups that you are so good-natured about. There are many things I would rather do if I could.'

Then Mr. Rich laughed, and told the story of Listen, whose dream it was that tragedy was his forte,—not a novel story certainly, but not inappropriate at the moment. 'I should like to see Welby's pictures all the same,' he said, cheerfully. 'We could not come to-morrow, so I should like to make a round to-day. I'm going to Crowquill, and Baxter, and some more,—as long as the light holds out;—and if you can tell me of any others——'

'There is Suffolk,' said Laurie, looking at the head of the table; and then he paused surprised. The padrona was but human. To let her own live patron go out of her hands to the studios of celebrated painters whom everybody knew was a thing inevitable, against which she could never dream of struggling; but to send him, in cold blood,—her own precious property,—to Suffolk,—a new name, a rising painter,—one of the men whom it would be a credit to patronise! Mrs. Severn had a struggle with herself. Generosity was easy where Laurie Renton was concerned; and she would have shared her purse with the Suffolks, with all the unthinking open-heartedness of her kind. But send him her patron! That was a trial. Laurie looked at her surprised. He knew her face so well that he saw the struggle in it, though without knowing what it meant; and he was startled by the pause she made before she answered him. A flood of thoughts rushed through the padrona's mind at that moment. She thought of herself and the children, and the need she had of patronage; and then, on the other hand, she thought of Suffolk's wife, with an unmanageable man, who would not paint popular subjects, with no power to help herself, with children too,—babies always coming,—and all sorts of troubles. It was not of the artist she thought, and his long unrewarded labours. She was only a woman, after all; and it was the woman who came to her mind, anxious and powerless, and overwhelmed with anxiety. All at once the face, obscured by some cloud which Laurie could not penetrate,—to his supreme annoyance,—cleared up with a sudden light, which he did not understand. 'Yes,' she said, 'I should like Mr. Rich to see that picture. It is not quite the kind of subject he likes; but we all think it one of the finest things; Mr. Renton will tell you about it. It was spoken very highly of the other day in the "Sword."'

'Ah; then it must be fine,' said Mrs. Rich. 'Perhaps Mr. Renton will take a seat in the carriage with us, and introduce us. I like to see everything I can see; and we have not much time for the light. And you will not forget, dear, that you are engaged to us for Easter week. It will be so nice to have you; and you shall plan out your pictures for the east room. She is going to do the fairy tales for us, Mr. Renton,—it will be charming. If the carriage is up, Mr. Rich, I am afraid we ought to go.'

The padrona called Laurie to her as he was about to follow them down-stairs. 'They have given me a beautiful commission,' she said, with a little excitement,—'a year's work! And I was so mean that I hesitated to send them to Suffolk after that. Try and make them buy the picture, Laurie. They will, if you are clever, and talk to them a little of Renton, and draw them on. I trust you to do it.' It was only for a moment at the drawing-room door. Was it the year's work, and the contest with herself about Suffolk's picture, which gave her that look of agitation and excitement? Or was it the time of year, the eve of the Academy, and all the crowd that would come to-morrow? Laurie could not give himself any answer as he rushed down-stairs to guide the Riches on their beneficent course; but his eyes shone, too, and his heart beat loud. As if he could have had anything to do with it,—a mere boy!

CHAPTER IV.

SUCCESS.

WHEN Laurie Renton drove from the padrona's door in Mr. Rich's carriage, opposite to that patron of art, it was his sense of the comicality of the situation which came uppermost. Art student, art critic, artist, he had been with a certain satisfaction in each office. But to be showman and salesman too was a new branch. These are the vicissitudes to which a man is subject who puts himself under the dominion of a woman, in the absolute and unconditional way which Laurie had done. But that was not how he regarded the matter. He was pleased to do it even for Suffolk's sake; though he could not but laugh within himself when he took his seat on the luxurious cushions, with the couple opposite to him who breathed wealth, and filled the very atmosphere with its exhalations. One of the exhalations was not so pleasant as could be wished; for Mrs. Rich's favourite perfume was of a character too distinct and decided for the narrow enclosure of a carriage; but the rustle of her silk, and the soft warmth of her velvet and her furs, and the wealthy look about her altogether,—wealthy and liberal and self-important and kindly,— was not without a certain human interest. She had been a pretty woman. Laurie, whose eyes were open to such particulars, was at once aware of that; and she was a good-looking woman of her age still. Her husband had less apparent character about him; but there was in both a consciousness of being able to give pleasure and scatter benefit around them, which was not unprepossessing. No doubt they were vulgar, perhaps purse-proud,— horribly ostentatiously rich. But they meant to benefit other people with their wealth, which was always something in their favour. Laurie glided with natural skill into the part allotted to him. He talked of Renton; of his mother's invalid condition, which made it impossible for her to call; and of his young brother Frank the Guardsman,—for he had not yet negotiated his exchange,—whose battalion was stationed at Royalborough, and who, he was sure, would be glad to make their acquaintance. And then he went on to Suffolk's story with the most natural sequence;—a man so full of talent, so laborious, so devoted to art, with such a pretty little wife!

'Ah, there we have you, Mr. Renton!' said jolly Mrs. Rich; 'but it is naughty to talk so of a married lady. You ought to have eyes only for the pretty girls.'

'A pretty young woman is a pretty young woman, whether she's married or single,' said her husband; 'but I don't like a man who goes on painting pictures that don't sell. What is the good of it? No man in business would think of such a thing. It's a sinful waste of capital as well as a waste of time. He ought to have changed his style. I'll tell him so. You do a many foolish things, Mr. Renton, you artists, for want of a plain common-sense man of business to give you a little advice.'

'That is very possible,' said Laurie, with candour; 'but even in business a man may go on with a speculation for a long time, though it is not immediately successful, if he is sure it will succeed in the end;—so long as he can afford to wait.'

'Ah, yes, that is the whole question,' said Mr. Rich,—'as long as he can afford to wait; but a man should think of his wife and children. If I had a little family dependent on me, and had to paint for a living, I'd make them comfortable, Mr. Renton, if I had to change my style every other day.'

'But that is not so easy as you think,' said Laurie; 'and the wife and children do not complain. Mrs. Suffolk is as proud of those boys in the Forum as she is of her own babies.'

'Are there boys in the picture?' said Mrs. Rich. 'Then I shall like it for one. And she must be a nice little woman; but you young men, you should not go paying attention to a married lady. It is not because it is wrong,—for I never was so strait-laced as some, and never objected to a bit of fun,—but it keeps you from marrying and settling, which is dreadful. You are all so selfish, you gentlemen. As long as you have a woman to go and tell your little tales to, and get her sympathy and so forth, and no danger of going any further, you are quite satisfied;—and the girls are left, and nobody pays any attention to them. That is what I don't approve of. We matrons have had our day, Mr. Renton, and we should be content with it. When I see married women dancing and going on, and young girls sitting without partners, I could beat them, though, perhaps, it is vulgar of me to say so. I like a young man when he falls in love honestly, as people did in my days, with a nice young girl.'

'We can't all afford to fall in love,' said Laurie, laughing, yet with a faint, distant recollection of the possibility he had himself given up. Curious it was how far off that looked now! But, like most sinners, he was utterly unconscious that there was any moral which he could apply to his own case in this little sermon. His mind glanced off to somebody else whom, perhaps, it might have touched. 'And as for Mrs. Suffolk,' he added, 'she does not think there is a man in the world who comes within a hundred miles of her Reginald; and, as I said, she is as proud of those boys in the Forum——'

'What's the Forum? Tell me the story; I like to know the story of every picture,' said Mr. Rich. And Laurie told, to ears which received it with all the interest of ignorance, that well-known tale. Mr. Rich thought he had read something about it in a book; and shook his head over an incident so remote in antiquity. 'I like English subjects,' said the patron. 'I don't care for your

Italian things. I never was in Italy myself, and how should I know if they are true or not? English pictures are the things for me.'

Then Mrs. Rich reminded the millionnaire that he had promised to take her to Italy next winter, and that it would be well in the meantime to make a little acquaintance with that country. And Laurie fell back on the 'Sword,' giving his companions the benefit of his own article, which, being a solitary effort, he had kept in his memory. It was a scene of genteel comedy, in which he was at once actor and audience,—and perhaps no other description of audience had such an exquisite sense of the points of the drama. He went through his part with a fluency which amazed himself, and chuckled and clapped his hands in secret with an infinite sense of his own humour. Mr. Rich's grand coachman was too fine to know the locality, and made a great many turns and rounds before he reached Suffolk's door, which left time for the little play to play itself out. It was curious to see the vast woman of wealth in her vast seal-skin cloak, in her rustling silken train, with plumes nodding on her bonnet, and lace streaming, get in at the narrow door. The house looked as if it could not possibly contain her. Laurie gave a comical glance to the upper window, with a momentary idea that he must see her head looking out there while still her train was on the steps at the door. And when she shook hands with the painter's little wife, who got up from her work to receive them in a nervous flutter of agitation, not knowing what to expect, it seemed to Laurie as if he had brought a good-humoured ogress into this little fairy palace.

'And a very pretty little woman she is,' the patroness said in a whisper, nodding to him aside. 'I like your taste, Mr. Renton.' Thus it will be seen that Laurie's hands were full.

'We did not expect anybody till to-morrow; and I don't know if Reginald is ready. If you would but go up and tell him, Mr. Renton?' Mrs. Suffolk said, appealing to him also in an aside.

Suffolk was not the least ready to receive visitors. It was an east wind, which had impaired his light and affected his temper. 'I've no time to go and change my coat,' he said, like a savage. 'What's the good? Laurie, you're the best fellow in the world; but Thursday is the last day, and you know what I've got to do. Look at that sky! By Jove! stop a man in the middle of a sky like that, and ask him to be civil to strangers! You might as well tell me to put this confounded east wind out of my eyes!'

'Only for ten minutes,' said Laurie, 'there's a good fellow! You are doing too much to that sky. Leave it for an hour, and you'll see what's wanting twice as well as you do now. And I do believe there's a chance of selling the Angles! Think of Mrs. Suffolk and the children. Surely they're worth half-an-hour and the trouble of changing your coat.'

Suffolk paused in his painting, and grew pale, and stared at his friend. 'Selling the Angles!' he said; and then he put down his brush, and turned away with an impatient exclamation. While Laurie stood looking anxiously on, the painter went to the nearest window and began to open the shutters, but stopped in the midst and turned back upon him. 'It's all rubbish,' he said; 'I don't believe in selling the Angles. Why do you come here and mock a fellow even in the midst of his work? I say, Laurie, tell me one thing,—who is it?— quick!'

'It's old Rich, the City man,—the padrona's friend. It was she who sent him,' said Laurie, breathless with suspense.

Then the painter broke down; he gave a sudden sob all at once. 'God bless that woman!' he said, and rushed at his shutters. As for Laurie, he made himself housemaid, studio-boy, with his usual facility. It was he who dragged out the spare easel to the best light, and took down the picture from the wall where it hung somewhat in the shade. He took the dust off it lovingly with his handkerchief, while Suffolk changed his coat. His hands were rather black, and there was a cobweb on his breast close to the lily in his button-hole when he went down-stairs; and it would be hard to say which was the fairer ornament. Then he turned himself into a groom of the chambers, and ushered the patron and patroness up-stairs, Mrs. Suffolk following. The little woman trembled all over, though she did her best to hide it; and Laurie's heart went jumping like a thing independent of him, in his breast. Suffolk was the most self-possessed of the three, but he purchased his composure by putting on a morose and forbidding aspect. Not that he meant to be morose; on the contrary, his brain was in a greater whirl than that of either of the others. If it might indeed come to pass,—if he too should really possess a patron, giving commissions, making life secure beforehand for his wife and the children! And then it occurred to him that this was the padrona's patron. The thought nearly overcame the painter. If she had taken her children's bread from her table and sent it to his, he would not have felt it so much. 'God bless that woman!' he said again in his heart. If the attempt failed or succeeded he was equally bound to her for his life. But he did not think of Laurie's good offices with the same effusion, though Laurie by this time had come forward equal to the emergency, and resumed the showman's part.

'When you are in Italy, Mrs. Rich,' said Laurie, 'I know what you will say to yourself some spring morning. You will say, "Now I feel Mr. Suffolk's picture!" Look at that golden air; you can see the motes dancing in it; and I can smell the orange-blossom out of the convent gardens. I have seen English children look like that,—like little roses,—with the dark Romans all round, admiring them.'

'Have you now, Mr. Renton?' cried Mrs. Rich; 'I should like to see that. Dear little angels! Though my own are all grown up, I adore little children. And you never saw such a skin and such hair as my Nelly had when she was a little thing. They are lovely, Mrs. Suffolk—I think they are quite lovely. Mr. Rich, don't you think that group is just like our Charlie and Alf? I mean what they used to look. And that woman with the white thing on her head,—that is a beauty! I am sure your husband must have painted you scores of times,' she went on, graciously laying her hand upon little Mrs. Suffolk's shoulders. 'Now come and show me this other one, and let the gentlemen talk. I hope Mr. Rich will buy that picture. I think he will buy it. And they tell me there was something very nice about it in the "Sword."'

'Yes,' said the painter's wife, all confused and breathless with anxiety, straining her ears to hear what the gentlemen were saying; 'and the "Looker-on" had an article too. They were all very complimentary; they said it was quite a work of genius——'

'But it has not begun to pay just yet,' said Mrs. Rich, with a little wave of her hand. There was a melting, liberal grandeur about her patroness. She looked like a conferrer of favours,—a rich, mellow, embodied Fortune. 'I think Mr. Rich will buy it,' she repeated, looking round upon her husband.

This was not a speech calculated to still Mrs. Suffolk's agitation. Could it be possible? Oh, if Reginald would only be civil! If he would but condescend to talk and show it off to the best advantage! But it was Laurie who was talking. It was he who was pointing out all its great qualities. And then there was a pause, awful as the pause,—not before a thunderstorm,—that is nothing,— a mere accident of nature,—awful almost as the pause you make when you have opened the letter which is to bring you news of life or death!

And then, once more, it was Laurie Renton's voice that broke the silence. If he had been pleading with a woman whom he loved, his tones could scarcely have been more insinuating. 'If I remember Beecham rightly,' he said, 'there was a space left for a picture just opposite the little organ in what used to be the music-room. Have you changed that? or perhaps you have placed some picture there?'

'That is just the thing,' said Mr. Rich; 'I knew there was a place. You have got an eye, Mr. Renton, and a memory too. Fancy, my dear,' he said, calling to his wife, 'he remembers the rooms at Richmont better than I do myself,— calls it Beecham though; but of course that is quite natural. Yes. And he is quite right too. I should not wonder if it was the exact size. The music-room is Nelly's particular room, Mr. Renton;—my daughter Nelly, the only one I have at home. I think that is just the sort of thing she would like. Girls are full of fancies. She would not have my last Crowquill, though it is a lovely specimen, and that one of Mrs. Severn's that she fancied was not big enough.

I should think this was just about the size. Mr. Suffolk, a word with you, sir,' said the patron, with all the confidence of a man whose cheque-book was in his pocket. Laurie stood with his back to them, measuring the picture with his handkerchief, and Mrs. Suffolk, before the new picture on the easel, stood trembling, trying to show it to the patron's wife. What a moment it was! Mr. Rich was very audible; but Suffolk, in his agitation, spoke low, and looked more nervous than ever. His wife thought, oh, if Reginald should be disagreeable!—oh, if the rich man should be affronted, driven away by his bad manners! And it was only manner all the time. She stood in a fever of suspense, not knowing what Mrs. Rich said, who chattered on, drowning even her husband's voice. She gave Laurie one look of appeal. Oh, if it were only ordained in Parliament, or by nature, that artists' wives and friends should do their business for them;—at least when they were men like Suffolk! If it had lasted long, Mrs. Suffolk must have fallen fainting at her patroness's feet.

But just when the strain had reached its highest point, Mrs. Rich fell silent by some chance, and took to examining one particular corner of the picture, and the voice of the millionnaire became distinctly audible. 'If that's all, I'll give you a cheque at once,' he said. 'I'd like to have the picture as soon as you can send it; for you see Nelly is from home, and I'd like to give her a surprise. Perhaps Mr. Renton and you would run down and see it hung? A day in the country would do you good after all your hard work. Have you pen and ink? What, not pen and ink in your place!—every man of business should be supplied with that. I couldn't put in my signature in paint, you know,' the man of wealth said, with his large laugh of ease and careless liberality. He joked over it as if it were sixpence! as if it was a thing that happened every day! while to two of the people who listened to him it was something like coming back from the dead.

Suffolk, with his voice choked, made some feeble response. He tried to laugh too; he tried to say it did not matter,—there was no hurry,—any time would do. A poor little piece of hypocrisy, at which his wife quailed, trembling lest he should be taken at his word.

'No, no; I like to settle such matters off-hand,' said the patron;—'there's Renton, like a sensible fellow, off for the ink. I like that young man; never saw him in my life till this morning; but he feels like an old friend, and his people are our neighbours in the country. You and he must make a run down by the one o'clock train,—I don't know a better train,—brings you down twenty-five miles in thirty minutes,—not bad, that. And I'll send over a trap for you. What day will you come? Thank you, Renton; that's practical; that's the sort of thing I like. I want you both to come down and have some luncheon, and see the picture hung. Let it be a day in the end of the week; a day in the country never harms any man. Settle it with my wife. My dear, come here and look at the picture. It's ours; or rather, it's Nelly's. Don't you think she'll like it? And I want to have them down to see it hung.'

Thus was this extraordinary piece of business accomplished, in a moment,—as it were in the twinkling of an eye. Neither Suffolk nor his wife knew what their visitors said and did, or where they were, or what had happened to them, till Mr. Rich suddenly recollected that there was no time to lose, and so many other studios to visit in daylight. It was all settled about that visit to Richmont, which Laurie, disagreeable though it was to him, had not the heart to refuse. And I suppose Suffolk talked and assented and behaved himself like any ordinary mortal, though he knew no more of what had passed than a man in a dream. Laurie put these blessed rich people into their carriage afterwards, and took as much care of the vast woman as if she had been the queen. 'I will ask your brother over to meet you, Mr. Renton,' she said, as she took leave of him; and Mr. Rich followed her, rubbing his hands. 'I have done a good morning's work,' said that happy man. 'Two hundred and fifty! I don't doubt I could sell it for six to-morrow,—that's what it is to go to the fountain-head.' Laurie himself felt a little giddy as the carriage drove away. And when he returned to the studio, he found that Mrs. Suffolk was crying, and her husband not much more steady. The painter had forgotten all about his sky. He had his cheque in his hand, and was looking, first at that, and then at his Angles. 'By Jove, Laurie, you have done it at last!' he said, bursting into a loud laugh, and crushing Laurie's hand as in a vice,—and then he went to the inner room, and put on his old painting-coat, which was a good excuse.

But whether it was Laurie who was to be commended this time, or the padrona, who,—let it be confessed,—with a moment's hesitation and reluctance, had sent the patron to her friend, was a doubtful matter. They had both a hand in it. It was 'our little business,' as Laurie said, pleasing himself, in his foolishness, with the thought of this partnership. And he went, of course, to the Square, not by roundabout ways, like the fine coachman, but as fast as his feet could carry him, to report how everything had happened. Duty and courtesy both demanded that not a moment should be lost till the report was made.

CHAPTER V.

A DISCOVERY.

WHEN Laurie reached No. 375 with his budget of news, the padrona was out! It was nothing very dreadful to be sure. She did go out sometimes, like everybody else; and in all likelihood no very long time would elapse before she returned. But, all the same, Laurie was intensely *contrarié*, and felt as if this were a special spite of fortune. She must have known he would come to make his report of what had happened at Suffolk's, and to inquire into the news she had given him as he left the house. A beautiful commission,—work for a year! That was what she had said. And then, without any regard for his curiosity, his interest in everything that concerned her, she had gone out! He went up to the studio to wait for her, passing the door of the dining-room very quietly that Miss Hadley might not hear him, and rush in with her usual officiousness to make one of the party. At this moment, after all his excitement, he did not feel equal to general talk with three or four people. It was the intimate conversation *à deux* for which Laurie longed. Never had he seen the studio in such preternatural good order before. The pictures that were going to the Academy were placed all ready for exhibition, each on its separate easel; a few touches were still wanting to one of them, but that it was evident the padrona had calculated upon doing with the morning light, before her visitors began to arrive. The Louis Quinze fauteuil was placed in front of the principal picture; a great Turkish curtain of many colours, one of poor Severn's acquisitions in the days when he was rich enough to buy things that pleased his eye, had been put up across the farther window, to be drawn as might be needful for the light. A great many sketches were placed about the room,—poor Severn's last drawing, unfinished, but always holding the chief place among his wife's treasures, hanging in the best light. And everything was cleared away that impaired the appearance of the studio, a proceeding which gave positive delight to the housemaid, and even filled the padrona's soul with a sense of comfort. 'If I could only keep it tidy like this!' Mrs. Severn had said, with a sigh. Whereas Laurie, with the untidiness natural to man, was disgusted with it, and hated the place in its unusual decorum. He walked about with his hands in his pockets, and stared blankly at everything. What did she mean by going away? What did she mean by putting herself, as it were, out of her studio, and filling it up with knickknacks that did not belong to it? As for poor Severn's last sketch, it was not a drawing for a woman to be proud of. She might have known that at least by this time. It might be valuable to her for the sake of association, of course,—anything, a table, or a chair, might be dear for association's sake,—but she must have known better than to prize it as a drawing. And then Laurie went and looked at the picture, which smiled sweetly at him out of its frame, full of sweet nature and expression, but undeniably wanting a few finishing touches still. How could she go out roaming about in that strange way, and leave the picture unfinished? Laurie in his heart was angry with his padrona. It was not like her to go out and stay out like this,—doing shopping perhaps!—which any woman without an ounce of brains could have done just as well;—which Miss Hadley might have been sent to do: getting her out of the way at the same time! Laurie in his impatience hunted up his friend's brushes, and mixed her colours, and went at the unfinished picture himself to fill up those tedious moments. There was a pleasure, too, in thinking he would have a hand in it; not that there was anything of the least importance to do;—a touch of light upon the floor, a bit of perspective which was not quite complete. When he had put in a few lines caressingly, with a half sense that it was her hand, or her dress, or something belonging to her that he was touching, another fit of impatience came upon him. Where could she have gone? What could she be doing? It was of no use waiting here, making himself angry in her absence. He might as well go and see old Welby, and leave her to the surprise of finding that some one had been doing her work while she was out. Of course if she came in, Miss Hadley would be with her, or Alice, or somebody. Laurie accordingly put down the brushes again, restoring the room to something of its ordinary aspect, and took up his hat and went down-stairs. 'She will think of the lubber-fiend,' said Laurie to himself; 'and I wonder if she will put me a bowl of cream for my hire.' Would the bowl of cream answer the purpose? or was there any other hire of which Laurie thought? There came a little gleam over his face, and the shadow of a smile; but I do not think it was in anticipation of anything in particular, only a certain pleasant sentiment, half tenderness, half amusement. Laurie was the kind of man whose eye softens and whose lip smiles under any circumstances at the thought of a reward from a woman. It was as he went down-stairs that he noticed for the first time the film of cobweb on his coat beside the flower,—and he left it there, though he was very dainty in point of personal appearance. Perhaps he thought it was a mark of the work he had been doing, which the padrona would smile to see; or, perhaps, that her hand was the hand which should brush it off.

With these ideas in his mind he went down-stairs, possessed by a kind of sweet love-in-idleness; not the passion of a young man for a girl; a tenderness made up of many things,—of that soft reverence just touched with pity, which a man of generous temper has for a woman in such a position; and yet pity is not the word,—or else it was a kind of pity in which there was all the softness and none of the superiority which usually mingles with that sentiment; and of admiration for the brave creature who had gradually grown the central figure in his landscape; and of a longing to help her; and of pride in the regard she gave him and the sympathy between them. There was perfect sympathy between them, though he had never, Laurie thought, seen any woman worthy to stand by her side. This was part of his delusion, for there were women as good, and with far greater gifts than the padrona, to be met with in the world. But still it was not wonderful if the young man was proud of her friendship. Friendship,—that was the word; with no result to come, no thickening of the plot towards a climax; but only a delicious accompaniment to life, an interchange of every thought and sentiment, a soft but strong support in every chance that might befall a man. This was all that was in Laurie's mind. It was something more akin to worship than the passion which appropriates can ever be. It had not occurred to him to seize, to take possession of, to secure her as his own; the idea itself would have been a profanity; only to be nearer to her than any one else, to be her subject and yet her counsellor; an indescribable perfect relationship such as exists only in imagination. Laurie himself had never gone any deeper. The padrona's life and condition were to him as settled and everlasting as the skies, the ordinary constitution of the world. And all would go on as it was going on. And at the present moment he would not have exchanged that visionary tie for anything actual in life.

Mr. Welby was standing before his picture when Laurie went in, looking at it with that intense inspection of the cultivated eye, which no uneducated critic can give. He held out his hand to his visitor, but did not change his attitude. Welby, R.A., had his anxieties about the Academy's Exhibition as well as another. True, his picture was sure of a place on 'the line,' and every advantage a benign Hanging Committee could give it; but there were other dangers before the face of the Academician from which the younger men were safe. Mr. Welby knew that if there was a faltering line in his canvas, or one neglected detail, even the critics who were his friends would say he was growing old. 'It would ill become us, who are indebted to Mr. Welby for so many noble pictures, to be eager to mark the indications of approaching decadence; but, alas! no man can remain of primitive strength for ever,' would be the philosophical comment of the 'Looker-on.' And the 'Sword' would be still sharper in its judgment. Such words as these were echoing in the old painter's ear as he looked at his picture. He was aware he was old, and life had no such charm to him that he should cling to it unduly,—but such criticisms were hard to bear. He was going over the picture himself, criticising its every detail, and he held up his hand with an unspoken warning to Laurie, who understood, as he had a faculty of doing, and waited behind till the inspection was over.

'I think that will do,' said Mr. Welby at last, with a long and deeply-drawn sigh. 'Come here, Renton, and give me your opinion.' Laurie was full of the natural instinct of admiring and believing in the work of the old man,—who was leader and patriarch, as it were, of his own special party;—and, besides, it was a fine picture, and he thought it so, though very different no doubt from Suffolk's 'Saxon Maiden,' or from the lovely children in the padrona's pictures upstairs. Art, to be the everlasting thing it is, is as yet as much bound by fashion as any silly woman. The fashion of the day had changed; but yet old Welby's picture was a fine picture still.

'I don't want those fellows to be picking holes in my coat,' said the R.A., 'though of course they will do it all the same.'

'I don't see what holes there are to pick,' said Laurie, strong in his *esprit de corps*, and ready to swear to the excellence of his master in contradiction of all the critics in the world. 'We have just sold Suffolk's picture,' he added suddenly, glad to deliver himself of the wonderful news, which had been burning holes, as it were, for want of utterance, in his heart.

'Sold Suffolk's picture!' the Academician said with a start. It was the most wonderful piece of news that had been heard in the artists' quarter for many a year. For no man had gone so consistently in the face of popular opinion as Suffolk, or held so obstinately by his own style. Laurie, nothing loth, told the whole story, with excitement and a natural satisfaction; and how it was old Rich, the City man, who was well known to be the padrona's special property. And as he told it he looked down upon the bit of cobweb, by this time gone to the merest speck,—the sign in that particular matter, of his close partnership with the padrona,—which was still on his coat.

'So she sent him her own patron?' said Mr. Welby; 'that was good of her, Renton,—that was very good of her. To be sure, he had just given her a commission. I suppose you heard of that. A private patron is a great institution, my dear fellow,—there is more satisfaction in it than in dealers. He has given her a commission to fill one room with pictures. There are to be twelve of them I think, and the subjects from the fairy tales. She'll do it very well. She has wonderful invention, you know, in her way, and Cinderella and little Red Riding Hood, and all the rest will just suit her; and there is a year's living secured at once. I am sorry for that woman, Renton. I am more sorry for her than I can tell,' cried the R.A., with unquestionable emotion in his voice.

'Sorry for—the padrona?' cried Laurie, half laughing, half angry. He would have liked to have knocked down the man who presumed,—and yet to be sorry for that hopeful, dauntless woman, so full of life, and strength, and energy, seemed too good a joke.

'Yes, sorry for her,' said Mr. Welby, severely, 'though you don't know what I mean, of course. She is at her best now, and I suppose she is making a good deal of money; but look at her principles, sir. Her principles are,—you need not contradict me, I know her better than you do,—never to shut her heart nor her purse against anybody she can help. What kind of an idea is that, I ask you, for this world? Of course, she can't lay by a penny; and when the fellows in the newspapers begin to say of her as they say already of me——'

'But you!' cried Laurie, 'you——' and then he stopped, not knowing how to end his sentence.

'I am old, that is what you were going to say,' said Mr. Welby. 'I am two-and-twenty years older than she is,—just two-and-twenty years. It's almost as long as you have been in the world, my dear fellow, and you think it's centuries; but two-and-twenty years pass very quickly after thirty-five. And she'll age sooner than I did,—never having been, you know, so thoroughly trained a painter. Her quick eye will fail her, and her fine touch, and she will not have knowledge and experience to fall back upon; and the public will tire of those pretty pictures. Her genius will pall, and then her courage will fail, though she has pluck at present for anything. Do you think I've never seen such things happen? If she has ten years more of success it will be all she can hope for; and the boys will scarcely be doing for themselves by that time; and she will have to reduce her living, which will go sadly against the grain, and struggle with all sorts of anxieties. When I look at that woman, sir, my heart bleeds. It's all very pleasant just now,—plenty of work and plenty of strength, and a light heart, and her friends round her, and her children; and she feels she is up to her work,—knows she is up to her work. But when they come to say of her what they are beginning to say of me——'

Laurie raised his hand with a speechless protest and denial of the possibility, but the words he would have spoken died in his throat. What could he say against this prophet of evil?—only that every pulse in him and every nerve thrilled fiercely at the suggestion;—and that was no answer, heaven knows.

'Even if she did keep on long enough to get the boys launched in the world,' said Mr. Welby, who seemed, Laurie thought, to take a certain pleasure in the torture he was inflicting,—'what is to become of her afterwards, unless she were to die off-hand, which is not likely? People don't die at the convenient moment. Most likely she'll linger for years, poor, and old, and unable to work, on some pittance or other,—lucky if she has that. It's hard upon such a woman, Renton. I tell you, when I look at that fine creature and think what's before her, it makes my heart bleed.'

'But, good heavens! why should you imagine such things?' cried Laurie, when he could speak. 'Of course we may all go mad, or get ruined, or perish miserably,—one as well as another;—but to forebode such a fate for her——'

'I said nothing about getting ruined or going mad,' said Mr. Welby, pettishly. 'I said Mrs. Severn would outlive her market,—ay, and outlive her powers,—

and that my heart ached for her, poor thing! I declare to you, Laurie, my heart so aches for her, that if I thought she could make up her mind to it, I would marry her to-morrow,—though it would break in upon all my habits,' said the R.A., sinking his voice, 'in a most annoying way.'

'Marry—her—to-morrow!' cried Laurie, and he made a step towards the old painter with a savage impulse which he could scarcely restrain. He was wild with sudden passion. 'Marry her!' It was hard to tell what kept him from raising the hand which he had clenched in spite of himself. But he did not, though it was a courageous thing of old Welby to keep facing the young fellow with that sudden transport of fury in his eye.

'Yes,' he said, calmly. 'I am getting old, and I have saved a little money, and I have no near relations. If I thought she could make up her mind to it, I would ask her to marry me to-morrow. I have thought of it often. For her sake, that is what I would do.'

Laurie made no answer; he walked away from the old man to the very end of the studio, and stood there staring at the Angelichino which stood against the wall. His blood seemed to be boiling in all his veins, and his heart throbbing as if it would burst. Why should he be angry? Why should he object to old Welby for his desire to shield the padrona from even a possible evil? But Laurie's mind was in too great a ferment to permit him to think articulately. He did not understand what was the meaning of the sudden tumult within him,—the sharp shock which his nature seemed to have sustained. To get away and be alone was the immediate necessity upon him. If he could have gone through the wall, or leaped out of the window, probably he would have done it. But that being impossible, he composed himself as well as he could, and returned to where old Welby stood calmly, taking no notice of him, looking once more at his picture. At the sight of the old man's tranquillity Laurie felt ashamed of himself.

'I suppose my nerves are more easily affected than most people's,' he said, with an attempt at a laugh. 'I can't think of all those dreadful things happening,—to—the padrona,—and take it calmly. Good-night! I must go now.'

'If such a thing as I said should ever happen,' said Welby, shaking hands with him,—'I may as well warn you,—I'd have no more padronas. How poor Severn put up with it is more than I can say.'

This parting speech sent Laurie forth in a renewed tempest of rage and indignation. He had meant to return up-stairs after his visit to old Welby, but that was now impossible. He had let himself out, and closed the door sharply behind him, before old Forrester could make his appearance. Daylight by this time was beginning to fail, and the lamps were being lit along the street, twinkling across the Square through the smoky trees, which were swelling with the fulness of spring. The look of the outside world as he came thus suddenly into it,—the tall, glimmering houses,—the lamps like candies in the pale, waning daylight,—the trees all bristling with half-opened leaves, and the sky, leaden yet light, with its remoteness, and colourless serenity, looking down upon all, never went out of Laurie's mind. He forgot all his displeasure at her absence, all his wondering where she was. He did not even look if she might be coming, or remember that he might meet her suddenly face to face so near her own door. His mind was too full of her idea to remember herself, if we may say so. He went round and round the Square without any particular sense of where he was going, and then took the first street, any street,—what did it matter?—and got out into a crowded thoroughfare, where lights were gleaming, and men hurrying, and every sound and stir of life. It was a long time before he could even make out his own thoughts, what they were. All was dimness and chaos and commotion, like the scene around at first; lights gleaming, cries coming out of the obscurity,—a tumult he could not comprehend. Then by degrees the clouds rolled off, each to its own corner; the foreground cleared, the central figure reappeared. What was it? Laurie stood still for a moment, and looked himself, as it were, in the face, aghast. He had not so much as suspected it till now. She had been his friend; nothing so tender, nothing so near, had ever been in his life; yet he had not dreamed what the truth was until old Welby, with his detestable suggestion, had thrust it thus unveiled in his face.

And Laurie stood aghast. It may injure him in some people's eyes, yet I cannot but avow that when the young man found that he loved a woman much older than himself,—a woman with children, and a separate, independent past, with twice his experience, and,—metaphorically at least,—twice his age,—he was appalled by the discovery. He had known her another man's wife; he had himself been as a child beside her in the first days of their acquaintance. There was less difference in point of age between himself and her daughter than between himself and her; and yet he loved her. No, it was not friendship. Friendship would not have resented hotly and wildly, with a half-murderous passion, old Welby's suggestion. Friendship would not have moved any man's heart into such a mad commotion. He loved her. That it never had occurred to himself to change the relationship between them, or seek a closer one, was nothing. Another man had but to talk of marrying her, and lo! the whole world was lit into conflagration. There was a sweetness in the discovery too. His heart warmed and glowed in that fire; words which he but half understood went whispering through the air about him,—'There is none like her; none.' No girl, no young heroine of romance, could be such a creature as was this woman, tried, and proved, and developed, with all the sweetness in her still, and yet all the strength of life. If he had been proud of her regard, proud of her sympathy, how much more proud would he be of her love! If that were possible! Could it be possible? Going on in this distracted range of thoughts, the fact gleamed upon Laurie that no girl could make such sacrifice of pride and natural position in loving him as this woman should,—if she would; and was it likely? It would be as vain to attempt to follow him in the maze of passion that possessed him, as in the streets he wound his way through, while the night darkened round him, and the lights shone brighter. A storm of thunder and lightning might have been going on, and he would never have known it. Such a thing had befallen as he had never dreamt of. The soft love which he had put aside with a pang of tender regret as a thing impossible,—too sweet for him and too costly,—had come back at unawares, and come in and taken possession, no longer soft and easy to be vanquished, but twined in with every thread of life. It was so easy to come away from Kensington Gore,—from the world he had lived in for years,—from the pensive-pleasant hopes of his youth; but to leave this place, which had not an attraction but one, would be tearing up his life by the roots. This was the fact, though he had not known it. Wonder, and terror, and delight, and a vague overwhelming dismay, filled Laurie's mind as he found himself standing thus after the earthquake, with the solid ground rent under his very feet. There were flowers growing still, so sweet that he was intoxicated with their breath; but yet there had been an earthquake, and the sober soil was torn with that convulsion. He walked and walked, charged with those thoughts, till he got to the very skirts of far-reaching London, and came to himself in a gloomy, suburban road. It was the rain falling in his face out of the almost invisible skies that roused him first, and then he had to grope his way back to a thoroughfare and get a cab, and go home. When he reached his room and looked at himself in the little glass over the mantel-piece he saw a pale apparition, with gleaming eyes and a visionary smile; appalled, shaken to the very depths of his being, and yet with a subtle happiness at his heart. He was happier, and more bewildered and utterly astray in all his reckonings, than he had ever been in his life.

CHAPTER VI.

LAURIE'S FATE.

NEXT day was the day of the private exhibition made in the artists' houses of their pictures before they were sent off to the Academy; not a day in which a man could make his appearance with any passionate or sentimental errand in the studio of a painter. All day long a stream of carriages were flocking about Fitzroy Square, and driving into the adjacent street, where carriages were not frequent visitors. There was a suppressed excitement about the district generally. It was, as we have said, like the eve of a battle, and every new spectator who appeared to judge of the pretensions of the combatants increased the commotion. Perhaps at another moment Laurie would have felt a certain oppression in a day which was so exciting for all his friends and so indifferent to himself; but now he had a shield against any such sentiment. He got up that morning with something of the lassitude of a man exhausted by great exertions. The sun was shining, which had been a rarity of late, and the consternation of the previous night had somehow died out of his mind. To-day he should see her, that was certain. To-day the sweetness of the presence of the woman whom he loved would smooth away all perversity of circumstances, and make rough places seem straight. He had a longing to see her, to make sure that she at least was the same, notwithstanding the wonderful change that had taken place in himself, or rather the wonderful unsuspected revelation he had had of his own sentiments. Somehow, with such a sympathy as there was between them, she must have divined, must have been affected by the extraordinary convulsion he had passed through. The daily impulse to seek her, and lay bare his thoughts to her, which had become a second nature to him, was mingled now with the curiosity a young man might have felt to see the person to whom he had been betrothed in his cradle, but had never seen. In a manner, Laurie had never seen this lady of his affections. When he parted with her yesterday she had been his friend; now she was his love,—the first and only woman in the world to him. It was impossible that she could be the same, look the same, in the face of this amazing change. He hurried to get one glimpse of her while the morning lasted,—to make acquaintance with her,—to familiarise himself with her looks and her ways.

But when Laurie reached the Square he found, alas! that he was not the only one who had been moved to visit the padrona in the early sunshine. Miss Hadley was there putting the finishing touches to the room; and so was Mrs. Suffolk, leaning back in the Louis Quinze chair, laughing and crying and chattering to the children in the picture as if they had been real babies. 'Oh, you darlings!' the little woman was saying, 'I wonder how many people will go on their knees to you when you are out in the world. But though you are little angels, you are not so nice as your mother. You are sweet, but not so sweet as our padrona.' This was the chatter Laurie heard as he went in. And it gave him a shock which it would be impossible to describe, when the padrona herself turned round upon him, palette in hand, smiling and placid and gracious, the very same woman from whom he had parted yesterday. All the heat and agitation of suppressed passion might be in his eyes, but in hers there was only the brightness of every day,—the composure of her usual, ordinary looks. Nay, as if to emphasize more and more the perfect unity, so far as she was concerned, of to-day and yesterday, she turned to him with the very words which, when he left that room last, before heaven and earth had changed for him, he had fancied her using. 'Here comes the lob of spirits,' said the padrona, 'and his bowl of cream has not been placed for him as it ought to have been. Here is Robin Goodfellow, who does his friends' work, and never asks even to be praised for it. Where were you that you never came near us all the night?'

'Where was I?' said Laurie. He was too much agitated to tune himself immediately to the key of his present companions. Fortunately Miss Hadley was busy arranging his lilies of the valley, and Mrs. Suffolk, who had sprung up to take him by both his hands, was not sharp-sighted. He looked over the little woman's shoulder with dilated eyes, which looked to the padrona as if he had been up all night, or in some trouble. 'I will tell you another time where I was,' Laurie said, with a voice full of tender meaning. The padrona gazed at him with wonder unfeigned. 'The boy has got into some scrape,' she said to herself. And then both the women plunged without drawing breath into the story of the Angles and Mr. Rich, and Suffolk's sudden and unhopedfor success.

'We had given up thinking of it even,' Mrs. Suffolk cried. 'I did hope if the Saxon Maiden got a good place at the Academy——but I never even hoped for the Angles. Call him the lubber-fiend! when he rushed up to poor Reginald yesterday, and made him put on his good coat, and did everything for him, he was more like our guardian angel.'

What was it all about? Laurie had to stop and ask himself, glancing at them in a kind of consternation. Suffolk's picture! why that was months and months ago! What did they mean by bringing that up again? And before he had recovered himself, the visitors began to arrive. He stood by her a little, watching, as in a dream, while the padrona shook hands with her friends, and explained her pictures to them, and received their plaudits. Yesterday he would have been proud of their universal admiration; but to-day it made him sick to see her receive such vulgar homage. He would have liked to take her hand publicly before them all, and draw it within his arm, and lead her away from such a scene. 'Do you think your praise is anything to her?' he felt himself saying; and then he took his hat abruptly and disappeared. So far, at least, the revelation to himself of the nature of his own feelings had not increased his happiness. And I cannot tell what old Welby meant by lifting the curtain so rudely from the poor young fellow's dream; whether it was done in spite or kindness, or whether it was entirely unintentional,—a simple expression of his sentiments without any reference to Laurie,—is what I cannot tell.

The next day was again a day of exhibition, and the day after that was the one on which Laurie had engaged to go down with Suffolk to Richmont. He had been very reluctant to go at the time, and it may be supposed how much more reluctant he was now. It was his own country,—the very journey in the railway would bring a hundred recollections before him. His mother and his home would be within reach; but how could he go near that peaceful place with this agitation in his heart? Two days before he could have done it, and spoken of the padrona with that tender fervour which knew no need of concealing itself. Now,—his mother would find him out in a moment, and so would Mary Westbury. Indeed, it was wonderful to him that Suffolk did not find him out. So that it would be Saturday before he could actually see her with any chance of knowing her mind.

I will not enter into the visit to Richmont, which belongs to another portion of this history and had nothing to do, so to speak, with Laurie's life. He got it over, and he got over those three days, but from Wednesday to Saturday he never entered the house at which he had hitherto been a daily visitor. He could not go now while she was surrounded with people, and talk ordinary talk to her as if she was anybody else. When he saw her, he must see her alone; and accordingly Laurie denied himself, and passed by her door, and saw others admitted, and watched the light come into the windows of the great drawing-room, and shadows appear on the blinds. This curious experience he went through as well as the rest, and gradually came to forget what was unusual in the story of his love; though not even now, after three days' brooding over it, could he see how it was to be, or how she was to answer what he would have to say.

It was on Saturday morning that at last he made his way to the Square. It was a holiday, thank heaven, and the children were out in the Park with their maid, and Alice was at her music when he went in. To-day, at least, there could be no Miss Hadley. To-day there was no excuse for the presence of strangers. Somehow the sound of Alice's piano struck him with an unpleasant sensation as he went up the stairs almost stealthily, fearing that a third person might start out from behind some door at the sound of his step, to mar the interview he sought. Alice was no common musician, even at her early age; and yet was her daughter. It may be understood how this consciousness, and the sound of the music the girl was playing, came in like one of the discords in his strange story. Had Alice been a child like her little sister, the effect would have been much lessened; but to love a woman whose daughter sat playing Mozart and Beethoven! The thought which passed through Laurie's mind was not articulate, but yet the sound jarred upon him. Softly he went past the door. If his love-tale had been for Alice there would have been no incongruity in it. He went past the room where the young girl in her meditations sat alone, and knocked softly at the door of the other, in which her mother was pursuing her occupation. The padrona was not painting on that particular afternoon. She was standing by the table, with a portfolio of drawings open before her, searching for something. She called him to come in, and looked up with a bright look of pleasure when she saw who it was.

'You have come at last,' she said, holding out her hand to him. 'What has been wrong? I thought you had forsaken us;' and looked at him full in the face with candid, unembarrassed eyes.

'Nothing has been wrong,' said Laurie, holding her hand fast. His heart began to beat, but what could a man say in cold blood with a pair of frank, steady eyes looking at him, restraining him with their friendliness? The padrona withdrew her hand without even any appearance of wonder at his clinging clasp. She was glad to see him. She had wanted to see him; and new events had come in, effacing from her mind for the moment her temporary alarm on his account; and she could understand that he was glad to come back, though his absence had lasted only three days.

'I was looking over some old sketches,' she said. 'I told you of the commission Mr. Rich had given me; I was looking for a drawing my dear Harry made some years ago,—you may have seen it,—for Cinderella. It would be a pleasure to me to go upon that; but I can't find it in all those great portfolios,' she said, with a sigh. Why she should have brought poor Severn in at that special moment it would have been hard to say; perhaps it was chance alone; perhaps there was in her some unconscious warning of nature as to what was coming. Laurie withdrew a step or two with sudden discomfiture. He hated poor Severn for the moment as he had never hated any man before.

'You will do it much better yourself,' he said, and his tone was such that the padrona turned and looked at him with wonder in her eyes.

'How strangely you speak!' she said; 'and now I look at you, how strangely you look, Laurie! What is the matter? I have scarcely seen you since you were so good to the Suffolks. Something has happened. I heard from them last night that you had been in the country. Is it anything about home?'

'No,' said Laurie, in a kind of despair, 'it is nothing about home.'

'Perhaps it is something you cannot tell me,' said the padrona, 'and in that case never mind my questions; you may be sure of my sympathy anyhow, even without explanation. If you are vexed, I am sorry; you know that.'

'How should I know it?' said Laurie. 'Yes, perhaps if I did not tell you,—if I left it to your imagination,—you are so kind to everybody,—you would be kind to me. If I did not tell you,—that might be my safeguard!' For by this time it had begun to appear to him that madness itself could not be more mad than his dream.

'It is strange to hear you speak so to me,' said Mrs. Severn. 'I never thought of being kind to you, as I am kind to everybody. What is it, Laurie,—tell me?' And she laid her hand softly on his arm.

Then the young man's composure and his boldness both abandoned him. He took her hand and kissed it wildly. 'Perhaps it would be best to go and leave you,' he cried, 'never to come near you more!' And then he left her, and paced up and down the room, trying to master the strange tumult of his thoughts. Nothing in the world could have disarmed him as her kindness did, and sympathy. But as he turned away, the padrona came to herself, or rather came to a recollection of the warning she had received. In a moment she saw how it was; and, as was natural, in a moment her anxiety to know what ailed him suddenly came to an end. Mr. Rich's commission, which was a great event to Mrs. Severn, had startled her out of thought of Laurie. His little hieroglyph at the end of his note had gone almost unnoticed in the excitement of the moment, and every hour had been occupied since then. But now it all rushed back upon her, and the error she had been guilty of in asking any questions. If she had not made this discovery, most likely her sympathetic, kind unconsciousness would have staved off what was coming. But the moment she found it out, a thrill of tremulous knowledge came into her voice.

'Well, never mind,' she said, hastily; 'you must not think that I want to pry into your secrets. Come, I am not working now; let us go to Alice and hear what she is about. You are pre-occupied,' said the padrona, closing her portfolio and talking against time, 'and I am *désœuvrée*. Let us go and listen to the child. Come, I will lead the way.'

'Not yet,' said Laurie. As soon as she knew the truth she lost her power, and he recovered a portion at least of his courage. He came and took her hand and brought her back. 'Perhaps I may never ask it again,' he said, 'but you must listen to me now.'

'Of course I will listen,' said Mrs. Severn, much alarmed; 'but just as well beside the child as anywhere else. If you have anything to tell me, she will be too much engaged with her music to hear. Come,—I was going to her when you came in.'

'But now you will stay with me,' said Laurie, leading her back. She was so much afraid of betraying any signs of trouble, that this time she did not even withdraw her hand. She sat down in the great chair, growing pale, but preserving with a great effort her composure, at least in appearance.

'This looks very solemn,' she said, with an attempt at a laugh. 'What dreadful tale of misdemeanours has your mother-confessor to hear? Have you been robbing an orchard, or running away with a lady? I will put the Suffolks' story against it, whatever it may be, and grant you absolution. You never did an hour's work that will give you more pleasure than that. I suspect they had been badly off, much more than they permitted any one to know.'

'Do you think I care for Suffolk,' said Laurie, 'or anybody else? Padrona! you know what I am going to say before I speak. You have found it out as well as I. Don't you know for months back,—since ever I came here,—there has been but one person in the world for me,—but one! Whatever I have done, it has been to please you;—whatever I have given up, it has been for your sake. Night and day I have been thinking of you,—contriving to get a word from you or a smile. And I tried to make myself believe I could be content with what you give to your friends;—but that delusion is over. Padrona mia, what will you do with me?' he cried, kneeling down by the arm of her chair.

It never occurred to him that he was kneeling, nor did he intend to kneel. It was but the most practicable way of getting close to her, and seeing into her face. There was something of the pleading look of a child in Laurie's eyes. He did not make any passionate claim on her, nor appeal; he only put his fate into her hands, with a humility more like the diffidence of age than the equality of love.

Then there was a pause. The padrona was too much overwhelmed, too agitated, to speak. She said—'For heaven's sake, Laurie, rise, and do not break my heart!' and took away her hand which he was still holding; but that was no answer,—rather the reverse.

'Break your heart!' he said. 'I would heal every wound it ever had, if I had the power. I don't seem to care for anything else in the world. Give me a right to stand by you, to take care of you. Padrona mia, you cannot always do all things, as you are doing, for yourself. Let me be the man to guard you, to labour for you. I don't know what I am saying, and you don't answer me one word,—not one word!'

'To labour for her, to take care of her!' Such words to her who was far better able to protect and care for another than he was. But that was not the thought that entered her mind. Her eyes filled with tears. To see this young man at her feet pleading with such passionate folly, woke all the tenderness in her heart. She was fond of him at all times. She put her hand caressingly on his head; her voice softened and broke as she spoke to him.

'Laurie, I am old enough to be your mother,' she said.

'It is not true!' he cried, with sudden fierceness; 'and if it were, what matter? All the happiness I desire in life is in your hands.'

And then the woman, quite melted and overcome, was so weak as to cry, leaving him to think for the moment that he had won his wild suit. This love was so strange to her, so new, so old, such a sudden dash of the sweetness of youth into her sober cup! She was roused by the words that he began to pour into her ears, and with a little cry of pain drew back from her lover,— her lover! What a word for such as she to speak! She put him back with her outstretched hands.

'Laurie,' she said, 'are we mad, both you and I? Do you know what you are doing? For some moments you have made me as foolish as yourself. But I am ashamed. Do you know who I am? Harry Severn's wife,—Alice Severn's mother! Yes,—that, and nothing else, so long as this life lasts! Can a woman make herself into two people? Laurie, let all this be as if it had never been.'

'It can never be as if it had not been!' he cried. 'For a punctilio, for a form, for your pride,—you would cast aside a man's love and life for that! Padrona! that is no answer. The past has nothing to do between us. To-day is to-day.'

Mrs. Severn turned upon him, and took his hand in hers. 'Laurie,' she said, 'let me speak.' Her eyes were full of tears; her face lighted up with a tremulous smile. 'To-day is to-day, as you say. I am very fond of you. I will say I love you, if you like. Patience, and hear me to an end. If you go away, I shall miss you every hour; but if my child's finger were to ache I should forget your existence, Laurie. A single hair on their heads is more to me than all the world beside. Do you understand? My poor Harry is past, if you will. God forgive me for saying so!—but to-day is so full there is no room in it for any other. Laurie, I want my friend. I want nothing else;—nothing else that any man can give.'

The young man stumbled up to his feet with the strongest passion he had ever known in his life maddening him, as it seemed. His heart was wounded, and so was his pride, bitterly,—beyond reach of healing. It was he who drew away from her the hand she had retained in hers, with kindness which felt to him like an insult.

'Mrs. Severn, I have made an ass of myself!' he said. 'Don't think of me any more,—it is not worth your while. As for your friend——'

He went to the table and took up his hat, and made as though he would go away. He was half blind, and did not see where he was going,—the room and the house swimming round him in his agitation. His last word had been said in a tone of contempt,—contempt to her, after all this passion! The padrona had not moved; she sat looking after him with her eyes full of tears and her hands clasped. Was it all to end and be over like this,—like a bad dream? But poor Laurie had not hardness enough in him to make such a conclusion. He faltered on his way to the door; he turned round, only half conscious of what he was doing, to look once more at the woman who had become the life of his life. And she, on her part, made a half-conscious movement of her hands towards him. He went back to her, and threw himself again at her feet. I don't suppose anything was said,—at least, anything that either recollected. They kissed each other with that strange refinement of anguish which belongs to those movements of human affection which are beyond the simplicity of nature. The two beings met and clung together for a moment, and parted. He was speeding along the streets, half wild, wrapt in a mist of excitement and misery, not caring,—as he thought,—what became of him, before the steady hand of the clock had moved two minutes farther on. And she, in the great chair where her visitors used to sit and criticise her work, lay back, trembling, with her face hidden in her hands.

Alice, meanwhile, had played through Beethoven's Moonlight Sonata, the pure, young soul carried away by it into a celestial dream; nothing articulate in her mind,—soft breathings of blessedness present, of joy to come, making an atmosphere around her,—a sacred creature, without a single discord in her, or jar of pain or trouble. And old Welby in his studio in the leisure of the moment,—his pictures gone to the Academy, and his year's work completed,—mounted, classified, and made a catalogue of his Titians, with the truest satisfaction and content, thinking no more of what he had said three days before to Laurie Renton than of last year's snow. The old painter and the young girl pursued their serene occupations under the same roof while this scene was going on, and knew no more than that the door had opened and closed abruptly, when poor Laurie, with all his wounds fresh and bleeding, rushed out into the outer world.

CHAPTER VII.

A FULL STOP.

THE padrona was not a woman given to little ailments,—headaches, or the other visionary sufferings which are conventional names for those aches of the heart or temper to which we are all liable; but yet on the evening of this day she found herself unable for once to face her little world. It was not so much that her eyes were red, for eyes that have had to weep the bitterest of tears, and which have watched and toiled through most of life's serious experiences, soon recover their outward serenity; but her heart was sore. It has been said so often, that most people by this time must be sick of hearing it, that love is the grand occupation of a woman's life; and that, while in man it is subordinate to a hundred other matters, in her existence it is the chief interest. Whether this is or is not the case with the great majority of women, is a question which must be decided according to the experience of the observer; but we doubt much whether in any case it applies to women over thirty,—and it certainly did not apply to the padrona. There were many interests in her life; and love, as ordinarily so called, had no more to do with it than if she had been a stockbroker. Nothing more annoying, more out of place and harmony with her existence, could have happened than this curious interpolation of misplaced passion. Being a woman, her heart had melted over the foolish boy. She was fond of him, as she had avowed. His soft, devoted, tender ways,—the deference and subdued enthusiasm which women love,—had made his society a very pleasant feature in her life, and perhaps she had not seen as she ought to have done the dangers that might attend it. And now this sudden awakening all at once,—the force and reality of his feelings,—the doubt lest she had been to blame,—the compunctions over his pain, and even her sorrow at the loss of him, which was not the least poignant part of it all,—overwhelmed her. She went to her room as soon as the little ones had gone to bed. These little ones should of themselves have been a safeguard to her. A certain shame came over her when she looked at her own daughter, who was almost old enough to be herself the chief figure in some episode of the universal drama, and remembered what words had been said, what wild ovations made to Alice's mother. The padrona's friends were aghast when they were told that she was not well enough to receive them. Miss Hadley, who had come round to the Square with a mixture of jealousy and alarm on finding out that no sign of life had that day been seen at Laurie's windows, was driven almost out of her senses with curiosity to know what it could have been that had given the padrona a headache. 'Gone to bed with a headache!' Miss Hadley did not believe it. She was angry not to be admitted,—not to judge with her own eyes what it was. But Alice, who suspected nothing, watched her mother's rest like a young lioness. 'I cannot let you go up; she will be better to-morrow,' said Alice; and Miss Hadley could not for shame ask the child, as she longed to do it, if this mysterious headache had come on after a visit from Laurie. 'She has been working too hard,' people who were more charitable concluded without question, and congratulated themselves that the pictures had been sent in, and that now, if ever, a painter might draw breath for a moment. But the padrona had not gone to bed. She heard them come and go away as she sat up in her room; and she heard Jane Hadley's voice, and trembled lest that enterprising woman should seek her out even in her retirement. She could not have borne any keen eye upon her that night. Alice was different, to whom her mother was as far lifted above such vanities or such suspicions as if she had been a saint in heaven. 'I think it would kill Alice!' the mother said to herself with a shudder. And I believe she would rather have died herself than betray to her woman-child what had happened;—although nothing had happened, except that a foolish young man had mistaken himself and her, and put love in the place of friendship. But her thoughts were very soft towards poor Laurie,— poor, foolish fellow!—to throw away all his love and fresh heart and feelings upon a woman old enough to be his mother! Anybody else might have laughed at him for it, or despised him; but Mrs. Severn did not despise him. It went to her heart to think of that gift being thrown at her feet. And she was fond of the boy,—poor Laurie!—and if all the world scorned him for his mad, boyish fancy, at all events it was not her place to scorn.

At the same time, after the edge of her compunction and regret and soft yearning over the poor boy that loved her had become a little blunted, the padrona had reason enough to be put out and vexed by the disturbing influence of this unlucky event. Love,—vulgarly so called,—was, as we have said, as much out of her way as if she had been an elderly stockbroker. Love,—of another kind,—was, it is true, her whole life and strength; but yet no man, however steeled by the world, could have been less disposed to any sentimental play of emotion than was this woman. Before Laurie came that morning her mind had been full of a hundred fancies, all pleasant of their kind. They were not thoughts of the highest elevation, perhaps. One of them was the rude, material reflection that she had her work secured and clear before her for a year certain; her living secured; no doubt about the sale of a picture; no sharp reminder of the precariousness of her profession to keep her uneasy;—but her work safe and sure for twelve months. And then it was pleasant work, and such as her soul loved. She had been commended by her visitors,—some of whom were people whose praise was worth having,—as she had never been before. Things were going well with her. The children were well, and developing their characteristics every day. She could look the world in the face and know that she was doing her best for them. When all at once,—in a moment,—the bitter-sweet of this boy's love was thrown into the crystal fountain, and the surface that had been so clear, reflecting the heavens, was in a moment troubled and turbid. With a certain impatient pang she said to herself, as so many have said, that there was always something to lessen one's satisfaction, always some twist in the web of life to obscure its colours at its best. And poor foolish Laurie, who had thrown away the best he had for nothing! Poor boy! how her heart ached for him! how it hurt her to think of his pain! and there was little, very little comfort in the thought that he was lost to her. His friendly talk, his ready heart-service, his difficulties and errors, and even his weakness, which it had been so pleasant to minister to, to reprove, and exhort, and accept,—that was all over now. A gap and dreary void was suddenly made in her closest surroundings,—a gap which was hard on him and hard on her, and yet inevitable,—to be made at all hazards. The padrona was very much downcast about the business altogether, and shed a few tears over it in her solitude. Nothing could have prevented, nothing could mend it,—except, perhaps, Time; and Time is a slow healer, whom it is hard to trust when one's wound is of to-day.

If such was the effect this incident had on the padrona, it may be imagined what sort of a tempest it was which swept through Laurie's mind and spirit when he left her. He disappeared under the bitter waves. Not only was there no sign of life in his windows, but, so far as he was himself conscious, there was no sign left in life to represent what he had done with that distracted, incoherent day. The chances are that he did most of the ordinary things he was in the habit of doing,—was seen at his club, and talked to his friends somewhat in his usual strain. Indeed, I have heard a *mot* attributed to Laurie, which could have been spoken but on that special evening, if it was spoken at all. I do not suppose he made any exhibition of himself to the outer world; but I can only take up the tale at the moment when, worn out and weary, he got back to his room in Charlotte Street, and came to the surface, as it were, and looked himself in the face once more. The agitation of the past three days had told upon him. He had been shaken by the strange sweet shock of his discovery that he loved her; and now upon that came the other discovery, involved in the first, that he had spent his strength for naught, and wasted all his wealth of emotion on a dream. Of course he had known all along it must be a dream; so he said to himself. He had poured out his heart as a libation in her honour. What more had he ever hoped it could be? And now he was empty and drained of both strength and joy. His pain was even mingled with shame,—that shame of the sensitive mind when it discovers that its hopes have been beyond what ought to be hoped for. His cheeks burned when he remembered that he had dreamed it was possible for this woman, so much higher placed than himself in the dignity of life, so far before him in the road, to turn and stoop from her natural position, and love him in her turn. He would have dragged her down, taken her from her secure eminence, placed her in a false position, exposed her to the jeers and laughter of the world,—

all for the satisfaction of his selfish craving! He would have gone in the face of nature, ignored all the sobering and maturing processes which had made her what she was, and drawn her back to that rudimentary place in the world which her own daughter was ready to fill. Was not this what he would have done had he had his will? A hot flush of shame came over Laurie's face in his solitude. He felt humiliated at the thought of his own vanity, his own folly. When she had held out her hands to him, when she had given him that kiss of everlasting dismissal, nature had asserted itself. Youth is sweet; it has the best of everything; it is the cream of existence; but yet when the grave soul of maturity drops back to youth, and gives up its own place, and ignores all its painful advantages, is there not a certain shame in it? Had the padrona been able to make that sudden descent,—could she have done what on his knees he would have prayed her to do,—then she would no longer have been herself. This consciousness, unexpressed, flashed across his mind in heat and shame, aggravating all his sufferings. That it could not be was bad enough; but to be compelled to allow that it was best that it should not be,—to feel that success for him would have been humiliation and downfall for her,— was not that the hardest of all?

It would be vain to follow Laurie through that long, distracted monologue, confused 'In memoriam' of the past, with jars and broken tones of the future stealing into it, through which every soul struggles, after one of those shocks and convulsions which are the landmarks of life. To be stopped every moment while forming forlorn plans of practicable life by mocking gleams of what might have been, by bitter-sweet recollections of what has been,— does not everybody know how it feels? Laurie's life was snapped in two, or so, at least, it seemed to him. What was he to do with it? Where was he to fasten the torn end of the thread? Could he stay here and turn his back upon the past, and work, and see her at intervals with eyes calmed out of all his old passion? But when he came to think of it, it had been for her he had come here. At the first, perhaps, when he had dreamed of that gigantic Edith and of fame, had he been permitted to go on, he might have found for himself a certain existence belonging to this place which could have been carried on in it after the other ties were broken. But he had not been allowed to go on; and Charlotte Street had become to him only a kind of lodge to the Square, a place where he could retire to sleep and muse in the intervals of the real life which was passed in her service or presence. He exaggerated, poor fellow! as was natural. It seemed to him at this moment as if in all his exertions, even for Suffolk, who was his friend, it had been her work he was doing. One thing at least was certain,—it would never have been done without her. She was mixed up with every action, every thought, even fancy, that had ever come into his mind. He had done nothing but at her bidding, or by her means, or with her co-operation. His work had languished for months past. If he had pretended to study, it was to please her. And how could life go on here, when it had but one motive, and that motive was taken away from it? There are moments in a man's life when everything that is painful surges up around him at once, rising, one billow after another, over his devoted head. That very morning, moved by some premonition of fate, he had been collecting his papers together, and putting his affairs in order; and though so vulgar a fact had made little impression on him in his state of excitement, still Laurie had been aware that his accounts were not in his favour, and that it might be necessary one day to look them full in the face, and put order in his life. He had gone on all the same, without pausing to think, in his mad love. That was perfectly true, though he was the same Laurie Renton who, six months ago, had put away the girl's little notes whom he had begun to think might have been his wife. He had given up that hope then without a moment's doubt or thought of resistance; and yet now, in a still worse position, he had rushed on blindly to make confession of his love and throw himself at another woman's feet. I cannot account for the inconsistency.

But now,—whatever shock he may sustain, howsoever his hopes may perish, a man must go on living all the same. His life may be torn up by the roots; he may be thrown, like a transplanted seedling, into any corner; but yet the quivering tendrils must catch at the earth again, and existence go on, however broken. Laurie was a man easily turned from his ambitions, as has been seen; a man not too much given to thought, easily satisfied, of a facile temper,— and with more power to work for others than for himself; but still he had to live. Something had to be done to reconcile natural difficulties, something decided upon for the future tenor of existence. Nor was he even the sort of man who could come to an abrupt stop, and stand upon it. His thoughts were discursive, and rushed forward. Even in the bitterest chords of that knell of the past there was the impatient whisper of the future. I think there can be no doubt, on the whole, that what would have been best for him would have been that government office, to which he would have been tied by the blind hand of routine, and which would still have left him leisure for his amateur tendencies. Had he been so fortunate as to possess such a prop of actual occupation, Laurie would probably have removed from Charlotte Street,—to which, indeed, he never need have come,—and gone on steadily with his work, composing his quivering nerves and healing his wounds. He would have gone on doing kindnesses to his neighbours, pleasing himself with little pensive sketches, reading more than usual perhaps; subdued, like a man who had gone through a bad illness; and by degrees he would have come back, calmed and healed, and able to take up his old friendship. But that was impossible now. A change of some kind or other he must have been compelled to make, even had there been no personal cause for change. He must work; he must spare; he must recall himself to a sense of the probation on which he had entered six months before with a light heart. And the natural thing to do was at the same time the wisest thing. Rightly or wrongly, the artist, whoever he may be, trusts in Italy as the country of renovation, the fountain of strength. Laurie scarcely hesitated as to his alternative. He could stay no longer where he was; his experiment had failed, his position had become untenable. The readiest suggestion of all was that one in which there still lay a certain consolation,—he would go to Rome.

He resolved upon this step before he went to bed, and on the next morning he began to pack up. Miss Hadley, from the other side, watched his open windows with a curiosity much quickened by her sister's surmises and doubts, and saw, to her amazement, the great canvas moved from its position in the corner,—a step which she found it difficult to understand. 'I suppose he is going to take to his painting again,' she said to Jane, when she came home. Jane shook her head, with dubious looks. The truth was she did not understand it. The most strange of all possible orders had proceeded that morning from Mrs. Severn's studio. It was that she was extremely busy, and that no one was to be admitted. No one! Miss Jane Hadley had her doubts that, though this was the audible command, an exception had been made in Laurie's favour, and that so unusual a step was taken by the padrona in order to secure to herself, without interruption, the society of her lover. Though Miss Hadley loved her friend truly in her way, and had a respect for her, and even believed in her, this was the evil thought which had crossed her mind; and consequently she was disposed to scoff at her sister's suggestions. But there were soon other facts to report of a still more bewildering character. A van came to Laurie's door, and carried off the big canvas; and a workman in a paper cap became visible to the elder sister's curious eyes in the centre of Laurie's room, packing in a vast packing-case the young man's belongings. 'He is going away!' Miss Hadley said, with dismay, when her sister came home. She could have cried as she said it. He was as good as a play to the invalid who never stirred out of her parlour. Laurie, with his kindly ways, had made himself a place in her heart. He had taken off his hat as he came out every day to the shadow of her cap between the curtains; he had waved his hand to her from his balcony; he had never found fault with her investigations; and when he bought the flowers for his window he had sent her some pots of the earliest spring blossoms to cheer her. She, too, had grown fond of Laurie. 'He is going away!' she said, with the corners of her mouth drooping. 'And the very best thing he could do,' said Miss Jane decidedly; upon which, though she was a very model of decorum, old Miss Hadley felt for the minute as if she would have liked to fling her tea-cup at her sister's head.

It did not take long to make Laurie's preparations for this sudden change. He pushed them on with a certain feverish haste, glad to occupy himself, and eager to put himself at a distance from the house he could no longer go to as a privileged and perpetual guest. Somehow Charlotte Street, though it had two ends like other streets, seemed to converge from both upon the Square. It suggested the Square every time he looked out upon it; indeed, all roads led to that door which was shut upon him, which he knew must be shut. But he had not gone back to hear of the extraordinary barricade raised by the padrona against the world in general. Laurie had nobody to consult,—nothing to detain him now. He did not even see one of the 'set' for more than a week, during which all his preparations were made. The day on which by chance he met Suffolk in the street was ten days later, when everything was settled. Suffolk stopped eagerly, and turned with him, and took his arm.

'What has become of you?' he said; 'and what did you mean by sending me that canvas? After all, I wish you had gone on with it. We waited, thinking you were coming to explain; and I have called twice, but you were always out; and you look like a ghost,—what does it mean?'

'It don't mean anything,' said Laurie, with as gay a look as he could muster, 'but that I'm off to Rome to-morrow; where, you'll allow, a man cannot carry canvases with him measuring ten feet by six. I meant to have come to bid you good-bye to-night.'

'Off to Rome!' cried Suffolk, amazed, 'without a word of warning? Why, nobody knows of it, eh? not the padrona, nor any of us? What do you mean, stealing a march upon your friends like this?'

'My friends won't mind it much,' said Laurie. 'No; I didn't mean that. I should like you to miss me. I rather grudge going, indeed, till I know how they've hung the Saxon Maiden——'

'Oh, confound the Saxon Maiden!' said Suffolk; 'it is you I want to know about, running off like this without a word. It is not anything that has happened, Laurie?'

'What could happen?' said Laurie, with a forced smile. 'The fact is I am doing nothing here. You all set upon me, you know, about that picture; and I must do something. It is no use ignoring the fact. I am going in for our old work in the Via Felice. And I shall be in time for the Holy Week,—it is so late this year;' he said, with a half laugh, at his own vain attempt at deception,—quite vain, as he could see, in Suffolk's eyes.

'But you don't care for the Holy Week,' said the painter. 'I don't understand you, Laurie. What does the padrona say?'

'The padrona approves,' said Laurie. He got out the words without faltering, but he could not bear any more allusion to her. 'Paint something on my poor canvas. I have got fond of it,' he said. 'I'd like to see something on it worth looking at.'

'I won't touch it!' cried Suffolk. 'By George, I won't! I'll beat Helen if she rubs out a line, whisking out and in. Laurie, think better of it. I don't know the set at the Felice now; they are not equal to our old set. Stay, there's a good fellow, and paint at home.'

'I can't,' said Laurie; 'I must not. I will not. And the worst is, you must take me at my word, and not ask why.'

'I will never say another syllable on the subject,' said Suffolk, humbly, and they walked half a mile, arm in arm, without uttering a word. This was the first notice Laurie's friends had of his new resolution. When he had parted from Suffolk, he went straight, without pause or hesitation, to Mrs. Severn's door. It was Forrester who opened it to him; and Forrester, being a privileged person, paused to look at Laurie as soon as he had closed the door.

'You've been ill, sir,' said Forrester; 'the whites is all green, and the flesh tints yellow in your face, Mr. Renton. Master was asking about you just yesterday. Don't you say a word, sir. I can see as you've been ill.'

'I can't answer for my complexion,' said Laurie; 'but I'm not ill now, Forrester. I am going away, and I've been awfully busy. I want to see Mrs. Severn. I won't disturb your master to-day.'

'Master's out, sir,' said the man, 'unfortunately; he's at that blessed gallery, a hanging or a deciding on the poor gentlemen's pictures. And a nice temper he do come home in, to be sure! And Mrs. Severn's—— engaged, sir,' said Forrester, making a stand in front of the stair.

'Engaged!' said Laurie, aghast.

'Them's the words, Mr. Renton,' said the old man. 'She's a designing them twelve pictures, as far as I can hear. She's busy, and can't see nobody. It's more than a week since them orders was give. And folks is astonished. It ain't her way. But I can't say but what I approve, Mr. Renton,' said Forrester, stoutly; 'designing of a series is hard work. They've all to hang together, and there's harmony to be studied as well as composition. And she ain't going to repeat herself if she can help it and, on the whole, I approve——'

'That will do,' said Laurie, putting him aside; 'I will make my own way; and I will tell Mrs. Severn you did your duty, and stopped me. This could not include me.'

'But, Mr. Renton!' cried Forrester, making a step after him.

'That is enough,—quite enough,'—said Laurie. 'It could not include me.'

But his heart beat heavily as he went up the familiar stair. She had shut out all the world that she might make sure of shutting him out,—'Though she might have known I would not molest her!' poor Laurie said to himself, with a swelling heart. It was unkind of the padrona. Had he not been going away it would have wounded him deeply. He went up heavily, not with the half-stealthy eagerness of his last visit. It would not have troubled him had he encountered a dozen Miss Hadleys. 'I must see Mrs. Severn alone;' was what he would have said without flinching had he met her; but, as it happened, there was no one at all apprehensive or curious now. The order had been given, and the stream of callers had stopped, and there was an end of it. He went up without any haste, his foot sounding dully,—he thought,—through all the silent house. She would hear him coming, and she would know.

'Come in,' said the padrona.

She was standing at her easel, drawing, with a little sketch before her, putting in the outlines of her future picture. Somehow she looked lonely, deserted, melancholy; as if the stream of life that had flowed so warmly about her had met with some interruption. In fact, she had felt the withdrawal of that daily current more than she could have told; and she had missed Laurie; and her mind had been full of wondering. Where was the poor boy? What was he doing? How was he bearing it? This was the thought that was uppermost in her mind as she put in the Sleeping Beauty. Somehow the picture was appropriate. Life seemed to have ebbed from her too, though it was her own doing. She did not feel quite sure sometimes that it was not a dream; and lo, all in a moment, without any warning, he appeared standing at the door!

The chalk dropped out of the padrona's fingers. She trembled in spite of herself. It took her such an effort to master herself, and receive him with the tranquillity which was indispensable, that for some moments she did not say a word. Then she recovered herself, and let the chalk lie where she had dropped it, and made a step or two forward to meet him. 'I am glad you have come,' she said, holding out her hand. And it was quite true, notwithstanding that she had given orders to exclude the world for the sole purpose of excluding him, if he should come.

And thus they met, shaking hands with each other in the same room, under circumstances quite unchanged, except——

'I am going away,' said Laurie. 'I would not have come,—you know I would not have annoyed you. You need not have told the servants to keep everybody out. You might have trusted me.'

'You know I do trust you, with all my heart,' she said, 'and that is why I tell you I am glad you are come; I am very glad;' and then she sat down feeling somewhat breathless and giddy, and pointed him to a chair. He sat down, too, not knowing very well what he was about; and again there was a pause.

'I am going away,' he said, abruptly. 'Looking over everything, I found it would be better on the whole to go away——'

The padrona bowed her head, feeling her guilt;—it was her fault;—how could she say she was sorry, or appeal against his decision as any other friend would have done? It was she who was the cause.

CHAPTER VIII.

YOUNG FRANK.

I HAVE already mentioned that Frank Renton, being up in town on the business of negotiating the change he desired into a regiment of the line, was taken one evening by his brother Laurie to No. 375, Fitzroy Square.

It was a thing very lightly done, as so many things are that affect our lives. 'Come with me and see the padrona,' Laurie had said, as the evening darkened, before they went out to dinner. 'You've heard me talk of her. She has such charming children.' This was the first thing it came into his head to say; for being foolish he could not launch into praise of herself. And Frank had gone very carelessly, looking with open eyes of amused wonder at all the artists' houses, and at the dinginess of the Square. Alice was playing when they went in, and Frank, sitting down in the shade before the lamp was lighted, and observing, still with a half-amused surprise, how familiar his brother was in the house, was softly penetrated by those unknown strains coming from he could not tell where, and made by he knew not whom. The door of the great drawing-room was open, and there came from it the usual gleam of red firelight, the usual ghostly appearance behind of the curtained windows. When he had listened for a long time in silence, not feeling himself quite able to join in the conversation which was going on, Frank at last took heart to ask who was the musician. The lamp was brought into the room at this moment, and the padrona turned to him, with a smile as soft and tender as the music, just dawning about her lips. 'It is my child,' she answered, in that full tone of love and pride which comes only out of the heart of a woman who has a daughter. There was such softness in the tone, such love and profound complacency and content, that it touched the young soldier. Somehow it occurred to him for the moment that there must be some painful defect about the creature whose name came thus from her mother's lips— blind, perhaps, or sick, or somehow not just an ordinary child. Then with a curious impulse, which she could not have explained, the padrona lifted her voice and called 'Alice!' Frank turned to the open door as the music stopped, with unusual curiosity, expecting some pale vision, with signs of decay in its countenance, or sightless eyes at the least; when all at once there looked out upon him, 'Alice with her curls,' like a rose between the falling folds of the vague, dim-coloured curtains, with eyes like stars, half dazzled, confused with the sudden light, and those sweet tints for which, as I have said, the beholder was grateful to her. He looked and looked, and the young man's eyes were touched as by Ithuriel's spear. No man had yet seen in her what, all at once, Frank Renton saw. She was to him no child, but a woman. He got up off his chair stumbling, confused. And Laurie was sitting calmly there talking to the mother with this fairy princess coming to them! It seemed incredible. And, in fact, Laurie scarcely looked at Alice even as he shook hands with her. He gave her a kind, half-paternal smile, and went on talking, which was to Frank such a mystery as no explanation could clear away. Then she sat down and took her work with the quiet of a child, totally unaware of young Frank's reverential admiration. Fortunately he knew a little about music. 'Was that so-and-so that you were playing?' he said, when he had sat for some minutes looking at her work and listening to Laurie's interminable talk with the padrona. The young soldier had a certain contempt for them as they sat and chattered—talking nonsense about any stupid subject that came into their heads, when they might have been talking to Alice, or listening to her music. 'You must practise a great deal,' then said the young man, in the safe obscurity into which his silence had thrown him—for, though the padrona had received him very graciously as Laurie's brother, what was she to find that could be said to a speechless young Guardsman who probably had not an idea in his head? Frank, however, had several ideas; but he was discomposed, as most people are when brought suddenly into the company of familiar friends who know all each other's ways of thinking and habits of mind. He could not strike into the full stream of their conversation, and it was natural that he should draw towards Alice, who was also left out of it. 'You must practise a great deal or you could not play so well,' he repeated, taking a little courage. And nobody paid any great heed to the two sitting apart, as it were, in the shade.

'I am very fond of music,' said Alice; 'I like it better than anything;' and then there was a long pause, and the conversation on the other side of the table thrust itself into prominence again, and became offensively audible. There was talk chiefly about pictures of which Frank did not know very much, and about people of whom he knew nothing—not the kind of people talked of in society whom he would have known. Laurie had always had strange friends; but how odd it was to find him in the midst of a new world like this, and a world so entirely apart and separate from the known hemisphere! But yet Frank did not find it disagreeable to sit silent against the wall now that Alice was at the table with her work. After ten minutes more he made another attempt at conversation. 'Have you heard Madame Schumann play that?' he said; and Alice glanced up at him and softly shook her curls.

'I have not heard much music,' she said. 'We never go out. It bores mamma going out in the evening. I shall when I am older, perhaps; but not now.'

'But if you never go out in the evening, what do you do with yourself?' said Frank, with some consternation. Upon which Alice startled him completely by answering, in the softest matter-of-course voice, 'We have mostly people with us at home.'

Here Frank came to a dead standstill. He glanced round upon the room, which, though pleasant, and cheerful, and homelike, bore no appearance of being adapted for such perpetual hospitality. 'We have mostly people with us at home.' Did they give dinners or dances, or what did they give in this curious, grey-green, picture-hung, half-lighted place? As if in answer to this question Mary at that moment came in with the tea, carrying a vast tray before her, with heaps of cups and saucers, substantial bread and butter, steaming urn, and all the paraphernalia of that modern meal. The young Guardsman looked on bewildered to see Alice rise, in the same calm, matter-of-course way, and rinse the teapot and make the tea. Was it the tea-party of humble life which he was in for? Would the guests come in presently and take their seats round the table and munch their bread and butter? And what if there might be muffins, perhaps, or buttered toast? Frank would have been amused had not Alice been there in the midst of it. He would have concluded that his brother had brought him to make acquaintance with the habits of the aborigines in these dingy regions out of the world. But then how came this creature there? He was relieved when he saw little Edith clamber up to her high chair, and became aware that it was only to be a family party after all. Frank was not sufficiently philanthropical, being a Guardsman, to interest himself much in the children and the bread and butter; but by degrees Alice surmounted all the obstacles of her surroundings, and began to cast a lovely haze upon the whole scene. He did not say much; he sat, if the truth must be told, in rather an embarrassed, sheepish way in his chair against the wall, with very little of the assurance natural to his profession. But then it must be taken into account that this was an undiscovered country,—such an America, as Columbus discovered, full of strange new beings, new customs,—a foreign world to Frank. He was out of his depth. When the padrona now and then turned to address him, with a vain attempt to make him comfortable, he felt himself drawl and yaw-haw as does the ordinary young swell of romance. And it was evident to him that his brother's friend gave him up as quite impracticable. Little Edith, however, was less fastidious. She got down out of her high chair and placed it close to the stranger, and took him under her little wing.

'Sit next to me,' said Edith, 'and you shall have some cake. Are you Laurie's little brother? You are bigger than he is. Didn't he say it was his little brother, Alice? But I always say Harry is my little brother, and he is a great deal,—such a great deal,—about six feet taller than me.'

'And older too,' said Harry. 'I am eight and you are six. You're not six till your birthday, and Alice is sixteen, and me and Frank——'

'Nurse says girls are quite different,' said little Edie. 'You are only boys, you two. Are you Mr. Renton, as well as Laurie, Mr. Laurie's brother?—how funny it would be to call you that!—or have you another name all to yourself?'

'I am Frank,' said the Guardsman, laughing; and then the boys drew near him, and Alice looked up smiling from her tea-making, and a certain acquaintance sprang up. To know that Alice was sixteen on the one side,— and to know that this young fellow, who gazed and addressed her in a tone so different from Laurie's tone, for instance, was Frank, seemed somehow to give each of them a certain hold on the other. Frank put down his hat, and drew his chair to the table; and by-and-by they were all sitting round it, drinking tea and talking.

'Laurie's brother is not so stupid as I thought he was,' the padrona said afterwards, as she made her *resumé* of the whole proceedings; and with that slight remark Mrs. Severn dismissed the matter from her thoughts. Laurie himself was trouble enough, the foolish fellow; but that any further complication should arise through Laurie's brother was a thing which never entered into her mind.

When the two brothers left the house there was silence between them for some time. Indeed, little was said till they had got as far as Harley Street. Then, all at once, Laurie spoke.

'You were out of your element in the Square,' he said, with a little forced laugh. 'You don't understand the kind of thing; but I can tell you it is no small matter to me to have such a house to go to.' This was uttered abruptly, and was not at all what he meant to say. To seem to apologise for the padrona and her house was as far as possible from his intention, and yet it sounded like an apology in his brother's ears.

'I daresay,' said Frank; and then he too added hastily, with a shade of embarrassment,—'She is quite lovely, I think.'

'No;—do you though?' cried Laurie, with a mixture of amaze, and delight, and indignation. 'I never saw you look at her even, all the time we were there.'

'And she plays wonderfully,' said Frank. 'Music goes to one's heart, you know, coming like that, out of the dark, one can't tell how. I thought she must be blind, or consumptive, or something; and then to see a face like a little rose!'

'Oh, you mean Alice,' said Laurie, drawing a long breath of relief, and amusement, and kindly contempt. Alice was a very nice little thing; but how it should occur to any one to put her in the first place! To be sure, the boy was only twenty. Laurie, who was twenty-four, felt the difference strongly.

'Who else could I mean?' said Frank, calmly;—'there was no other girl there. But, Laurie, really you ought to mind what you are about. We may have come down in the world, you know, and seen better days, and all that; but we need not fall quite out of the habits of gentlemen all the same.'

'Am I falling out of the habits, &c.?' said Laurie, laughing. 'I am only a poor painter, my dear fellow. I am not a swell and a Guardsman like you.'

'I shan't be a Guardsman a minute longer than I can help it, and you know that,' said Frank, with a little indignation; 'but I hope I shall never see a girl like that come into a room without treating her with proper respect.'

'Proper respect!' cried Laurie, much mystified; and then he laughed. 'Alice is only a child,' he said. 'I have known her since she was that height. She thinks me a kind of old uncle, or godfather, or something. Yes, of course, she plays charmingly,—but she is only a child all the same.'

'A child! she is sixteen,' said Frank; 'and lovely, I think. I don't know the family, of course; they are your friends; but a young lady like Miss Severn is generally considered entitled to a little ceremony. I don't want to be didactic,' said the Guardsman, 'but——'

This remonstrance furnished Laurie with laughter for the rest of the evening; but Frank did not see the joke. Of course the young lady was nothing to him. This he explained fully. But it vexed him to think that his brother was falling into the free and easy habits which, he supposed, were current among the people who lived in those dingy streets, where every house boasted a long, central window, and the very atmosphere was redolent of paint;—beings who lived all their lives in shooting-coats and wide-awakes,—wild, untrimmed, hairy men, not fit to come into a lady's society at any time. People on that level might be utterly indifferent and irreverent, and treat a woman as they treated their comrades; but that Laurie should fall into such ways vexed Frank. This was the chief subject of his thoughts as he bowled down through the darkness in the twelve o'clock train to Royalborough, where his battalion was quartered. It was another of the results of his father's unfortunate will. Frank had been, as Mr. Renton foresaw, the one who felt it least. His nominal allowance had always been just what it now was, and his mother was as ready now as ever to supply him with those odd five-pound notes which drop in so pleasantly to a youthful pocket. It made no more difference than his father's death must have made under any circumstances. There was no longer a bright and pleasant house to take his friends to, but that had nothing to do with the will, and was at the present moment a necessity of nature. And then he had his profession, and liked it, and might hope for advancement in it. And in the meantime he had made up his mind to go to India, a proceeding which had its pleasant as well as unpleasant aspects. He had sold his pet horse, to be sure, which cost him a pang; but still a man may get over that. And he was noway banished from the society he had been used to, or from the kind of life. Nothing was changed with him to speak of, but everything was changed with Laurie; and as for Ben, he had disappeared under the waters altogether,—disgusted, or indignant, or furious with fate. Frank's heart was heavy as he went back in the dreary 'last train,' dropping people at all the stations,—coming every now and then to a jarring, tedious stoppage in the blackness of the night. It is not a cheerful mode of locomotion when a man is alone, and has thoughts which are the reverse of agreeable. Laurie's intimacy in the painter's house, the accustomed, familiar way in which he sat down amongst all those children and took his tea, the homely table, the talk in which his brother was so absorbed as to forget everything,—even common politeness,—how fatal was all this! Had he gone there, indeed, kindly as a chance visitor,—as any potentate from Belgravia might look in now and then, it might have been well; but to become an *habitué* of such a house, to give up for it,—as he seemed to be doing,—all the charms of society, could that be well? 'Why should it be so?' Frank asked himself. No doubt Lady Grandmaison would have invited Laurie all the same,—as, indeed, she had invited himself, Frank,—notwithstanding the temporary cloud under which they all were living. No doubt the Barnards and the Courtenays would have been just as kind as ever. He might have kept up all his friends, Frank concluded to himself, with the premature prudence of a young man of society; why shouldn't he? Nothing but the absence of a coat or a pair of gloves could have absolutely shut out Laurie Renton from society; and his coat, Frank felt, was quite presentable, and had even a flower in it, the extravagant wretch; and yet his world had become Fitzroy Square!

Frank Renton dwelt so much on this thought that the apparition of Alice Severn went out of his head,—and yet not, perhaps, quite out of his head. He had not been such a fool, he would have said, as to fall in love with a girl whom he had only seen once,—a girl belonging to the objectionable locality in which Laurie had lost himself; yet the little picture she made as she stood for a moment answering her mother's call in the doorway, with the dim curtains falling round her like a frame, and herself so bright in colouring, so sweet in all her rose-tints, lasted in his mind as such impressions seldom did. Perhaps it was the quite unexpected character of the appearance that made him dwell upon it. In a ball-room, or at a picnic, or, in short, at any party, or in a country-house where there are a number of people assembled, a man knows he is likely to meet some pretty girl or other, and is prepared for the vision; but when you are making a humdrum call, in a house quite out of the world, on people quite unacquainted with anybody you know,—in short, very respectable people, but moving in a different sphere,—and are, all at once, confronted by a creature like a rose, playing Beethoven in the dark, standing looking at you from the doorway with dazzling, lovely, half-seeing eyes,—of course you had not been looking for anything of the kind, and it makes a certain impression on you. Frank was not in any way addicted to art. He did not understand it much, nor care for it. Now and then something struck him as being 'a pretty picture;' but it might be one of Laurie's drawings, or it might be a Raffael, and the difference was not very evident to the Guardsman. Perhaps it was the first time that he had of his own accord, or rather involuntarily, in spite of himself, by impulsion of nature, hung up as it were a picture of his own making on the walls of his mind. 'By Jove, if Laurie were to paint something like that,' he said to himself, altogether unaware in his simplicity that neither Laurie nor any of his fellows could have done justice to the evening darkness, and the soft lamplight, and the dark, undefined curtains draping themselves about the bright young face. Frank made it for himself, which was much more satisfactory, and left it there, hanging in his private closet of recollections, though, so far as he was aware, he thought but little of Alice Severn, and was much too sensible a fellow to fall in love at first sight.

Besides, he was busy, and had no time just then for nonsense of any kind. It was not quite so easy to manage the exchange he wanted as he had believed it would be; and Mrs. Renton, though she interfered so little in her son's proceedings, did what she could to put a stop to this movement on his part. 'I never even hear from Ben,' she said, pathetically. 'I do not know where he has gone or what has become of him; and Laurie, though he writes punctually, has not been to see me for ever so long; what shall I do if you go too?'

'But, mother, I must go,' Frank would say; 'I can't get on where I am now. No, mamma,—thanks; I ought not to take it. What my father meant was that we should go and seek our fortune. And beside, if Ben and Laurie don't have money from you, I ought not to have it. That is as clear as daylight.'

'If Ben and Laurie were here they would have everything I could give them,' said Mrs. Renton; 'they ought to know that; but you are the only one of my boys that stands by me, Frank. Put it in your pocket, dear, and never mind. Ah! if your poor dear papa could but have seen the harm it has done!' and she cried, poor soul, longing for her other children, though she had not energy enough to seek them out; 'but we must not blame your dear papa,' she added, hastily, drying her eyes.

'No,' said Frank. 'But it has done harm. Laurie was not like himself last time I saw him. He has got among a queer sort of people,—artists and that sort of thing. I don't feel quite easy about him, to tell the truth.'

'Among low people, do you mean?' cried his mother, with the tears ready to flow from her eyes.

'N—no; not exactly low people,' said Frank; and somehow a hot flush of colour covered his own face. All at once that picture rose up before him, and Alice out of the doorway looked at him with reproachful eyes. 'I heard that favourite thing of yours so beautifully played the other day,' he added, hastily; and then he hummed a few bars to identify the melody; 'charmingly played. I don't think any one could have done it better.'

'Mary plays it very nicely,' said his mother, who was easily led away from one subject to another.

'Oh, Mary!' said Frank. 'Yes, she does very well, of course; but this was almost genius, you know. She played it as if she were making it up herself. Quite a young girl, fifteen or so,' Frank went on; 'and sitting in a dark room, so she must have played from memory. I wish you could have heard her.'

'Was it any one I know?' said Mrs. Renton.

'It was somebody Laurie knows,' said Frank shortly. 'I suppose he'll stick there for ever and ever, and never do anything. I wish he were not such a lazy beggar. In one way he is the cleverest of us all.'

'My poor Laurie! so you all say,' said the mother; 'but this I know,—Laurie is never lazy when he can serve other people, Frank; and he is not so clever as Ben is,' she added. 'Your dear papa always said so. Ben was the clever one, he always said. I would not mind about cleverness if I but knew where he was and what he was doing. That breaks my heart.'

'Oh, he will turn up,' said Frank, whose heart was not in any danger of breaking. And he put his mother's gift in his pocket, though not without compunction. 'It seems like stealing a march upon them,' he said to himself as he went away. This was just about a month before the time when Ben suddenly appeared at Renton Manor to bid them all good-bye, and when Laurie was near the climax of his little drama. Frank, whom no necessity had urged on, was but beginning to make his arrangements for setting out in the world, when they voluntarily or involuntarily had completed theirs, and were about to take their plunge. As he went down the walk to the river, under the budded trees, his own idea was that he was the only one of the three who would really go off, as his father wished, to seek his fortune. Ben had hidden himself somewhere in a fit of disgust, but would repent and become reasonable, and return to Renton to manage his mother's affairs, which needed some one to look after them. After all, Renton was his mother's for the time being, and it was the natural home of her eldest son; and as for Laurie, he would stick fast where he was, and would not have pluck enough to make any change. So that it was utterly out of the question that he, Frank, should relinquish his plans and prospects in order that one of his mother's children might be near her. Mrs. Renton, indeed, was not a woman to exercise such an influence on her sons. They were fond of her; but either they were not fond enough to make a sacrifice for her, or she was not the kind of woman to require it. She kept in the background, wailing softly, but was not energetic enough to demand a response from any one. Frank marched down to his boat, which lay waiting for him, with a feeling that if he was not the clever one, he was at least the energetic one, of the family, and probably would be the only one to make his fortune. The first step, to be sure, was a little slow and troublesome, but, once in India, everything became possible. He resolved within himself that he would scorn delight and live laborious days, as soon as he had got himself made into a real soldier instead of an ornamental Guardsman. He would go in for his profession with all his heart. No doubt it was a resolve which might call for a good deal of self-denial, but for that young Frank was prepared. Parties, and pleasure, and music, and even love affairs, were things he meant to be out of his way. As for falling into a lower sphere contentedly, as Laurie seemed to have done, Frank hoped that such a descent was impossible to him. He pulled down the stream to Cookesley, though it was cold; for the river was at once the best and most expeditious way of passing between the manor and Royalborough. Frank pulled down the stream, and felt his heart glow and tingle as he thought of all he was going to do. He had some 'pluck' he admitted to himself, if not so much cleverness as Laurie or Ben. So it will be seen he had quite forgotten that momentary peep at Alice Severn, and the equally temporary impression which her young beauty had made upon his imagination or his heart.

CHAPTER IX.

NELLY RICH.

IT was not very long after this that Frank Renton was accosted by one of his friends in the regiment with what seemed to him a very odd sort of request. 'Look here, Frank,' said young Edgbaston, who was a son,—it is unnecessary to add,—of Lord Brummagem, and a very popular, good-natured young fellow, 'I've promised to produce you at the Riches', where I am going to lunch. Don't struggle, my boy. They are going to have your brother Laurie, and you must come.'

'My brother Laurie!' cried Frank in amazement. 'And who are the Riches; and what do they want me for? I never heard of the people that I know of. I suppose it is one of your jokes?'

'It's very witty to be sure,' said Edgbaston, 'but it is not one of my jokes. Papa Rich is something in the City. He was a cheesemonger once upon a time, I believe; but that's all left behind long ago. Alf Rich, of the Buffs, is one of his sons. You know Alf. He gives capital dinners and eke luncheons. And they're all intensely jolly, from the pater down to little Nelly. Come along. I promised to bring you. And you'll meet your brother, if that's any inducement. Old Rich told me he was to be there.'

'Laurie to be there! I don't understand it,' said Frank.

'Old Rich buys pictures to no end,' said Edgbaston; 'perhaps that's why your brother's going; or perhaps he's after little Nelly. And not a bad speculation either, I can tell you. She's a nice little girl;—and heaps, cartloads, mountains of tin. If Laurie don't go in for that style of thing, I'd recommend it to your own consideration.'

'If it's so desirable, why do you let it go among your friends in this liberal way?' said Frank. 'It's not in Laurie's line, I fear,' he added with a sigh. To tell the truth, the conditions and prospects of his elder brothers lay much on Frank's mind. He felt easy about himself; but he disapproved of the others, especially Laurie, whom everybody had disapproved of from his cradle,—and felt that he was in a bad way.

'Then come along, and try your luck, my boy,' said his friend. And the consequence was that by noon Frank and half-a-dozen more were flying over the green, balmy, awakening country on Edgbaston's drag. They were all in high spirits, with that delightful sense of fulfilling every duty that can be looked for from a Guardsman which is the soul of pleasure. And Frank Renton, puritanical as he had been in respect to his brother Laurie and Alice

Severn, was soon chatting about 'little Nell,' whom he had never seen, as familiarly as any of them. So that it is evident stern principle alone was not involved in his displeasure with his brother. The young men were not at all contemptuous of the good things to be had at Richmont; but the family who were to receive them there did not count for much. Old Rich spent his money freely to give them pleasure, and got laughed at for his pains; Mamma Rich, or Rich *mère*, as they call her, was not much more respectfully treated; and as for Nelly Rich, her name was bandied about from mouth to mouth with the most unscrupulous ease. 'If I were you, So-and-so, I'd certainly go in for little Nell,' one and another of those lively youths would say from time to time. She had 'heaps of tin'—that was her grand characteristic,—and was evidently ready to drop into anybody's arms who should do her the honour to hold them out to her. But the talk was a matter of course, not meaning half that it seemed to mean. And half at least of her critics were dumb before Nelly, and had an unfeigned dread of her keen little bright eyes and sharp speeches. Richmont itself was a big house in a big park, conveying to the ordinary spectator no sense of present incongruity with its past. The old part of the mansion was in the east wing, and not visible from the front, and all that could be seen by the party in the drag was the vast white modern façade, very fresh and clean as yet, with great plate-glass windows, and a wide hospitable door, opening into a hall with scagliola pillars. At this door old Rich stood, waving his hand in sign of welcome. The flower-beds on the lawn were already full of every bright thing which could be had at the season, and the whole place was alit and alive with wealth, and warmth, and movement. 'To think that a fine old place like this should drop into the greasy hands of an old cheesemonger!' said one of the men as they drove through the leafy avenue. But they were all quite willing to be the cheesemonger's guests, and to drink his wine, and enjoy the good things his greasy gold had provided.

'Glad to see you all,' shouted Mr. Rich; 'delighted we've got such a fine day; almost good enough for croquet, it appears to me. Good morning, my lord. Oh, any friend of yours! Ah-ha, Mr. Frank Renton,' stretching forth his hand with a cordiality which took Frank by surprise, 'now I call this kind. Had everything been as it ought to be, of course we'd have met before now,— country neighbours, you know. Your brother has just come by the last train with a friend of his, a wonderful clever fellow from town. He's too much of a swell himself ever to paint much, eh? but he's hand and glove with all of them. Come along up-stairs, and I'll take you to him. Lord Edgbaston, you know your way to the drawing-room. Mrs. Rich will be delighted to see you; and I trust to you not to let my Nelly leave the room till I send for her. I mean to give the child a little surprise,' added the millionnaire, rubbing his fat hands. 'Come along, Mr. Renton.' Frank followed in a state of partial stupefaction. What reason there could be for this old fellow's cordiality; why he should leave a live lord to find his own way up-stairs and conduct him,

Frank Renton, instead; why Laurie should be here; what he had to do with the surprise Mr. Rich was going to give his child;—all these were mysteries to Frank. He seemed to have gone into an enchanted house. Had Mr. Rich taken him aside and offered him his daughter's hand and fortune on the spot, his surprise would scarcely have been increased. Was this what it meant? Or if it was not this, what did it mean?

The Rentons and the Beauchamps had been friends in the old days, and Frank knew the house through which he was being guided almost as well, perhaps, as the owner of it did, who walked before him, looking not half so imposing as his own butler. Frank, who had a good deal of prudence for so young a man, thought it would be better on the whole to say nothing about this; but when his host preceded him through passage after passage, and up one short flight of stairs after another, surprise got the better of him.

'We must be going to the music-room, I suppose,' he said; 'this is the way;' for the new master paused uncertain between two turns.

'That's about it,' said Mr. Rich; 'droll though, to see a stranger know one's house better than one does oneself. I suppose you were a deal here in the time of the old people? Very nice people according to all I hear. But, you know, I didn't turn them out. Bought the place at a fair price, as anybody else might have done. It was their doing, not mine. Ah! it's a sad thing to outrun the constable, Mr. Frank. It should be a lesson to you as a young man.'

'I am just going off to India,' said Frank, determined, at least, to let his new acquaintance know that little was to be made of him in the way of society, 'and I shall not have much chance.'

'To India, eh?' said Mr. Rich, with an unchanged tone. Clearly after all, he did not mean to offer the young Guardsman on the spot his daughter and her fortune. 'India's a fine thing at your age. My eldest boy went off a dozen years ago, when we were not quite so well off as we are now; and he's coming home this summer, please God. If you had been at home we might have had no end of jolly meetings; but your mother goes out nowhere, I hear.'

'Not now,' said Frank; 'my mother is a great invalid.' And there was something in his tone which betrayed a certain offence,—What right had this man to speak of his mother? And this tone conveyed itself at once to the other's lively ear.

'Ah, well! she has a right to please herself,' said Mr. Rich. 'Here we are at last. Halloo, gentlemen, I hope it fits. I wouldn't have it too large or too small for a hundred pounds.'

'Never fear, it will fit beautifully,—I knew it would,' cried Laurie's voice from behind a great picture, which was being hoisted into its place. After having been rather splendid and haughty about his mother to this commonplace individual, who had no right to hope for her acquaintance, it must be admitted that it gave Frank a pang to find his brother as busy as a workman, and quite at his ease in his occupation, putting up Mr. Rich's pictures. Here was something worse even than Laurie's slovenly ways and contented relapse into lower life. When a man has a brother in the Guards he owes it, if not to himself, at least to his relations, to remember that he is a gentleman. And to play the fool in such a house as this was worse than anything, with all those fellows below to tell each other how sadly Frank Renton's brother, 'the artist fellow,' had fallen back in the world.

'I did not know my brother was in the habit of carrying home his work,' he said, with a certain savage irony. But Laurie did not hear this speech, and Mr. Rich, who did hear it, took no notice. There was nothing for it but to stand and stare at the daub as it was raised to its place. In the middle of the floor, in front of it, stood a bearded stranger, whom Frank did not know, nor care to know. He was watching the progress of the picture with anxious interest. Was it Laurie's picture? Whether it were or not, Laurie condescending to make a carpenter of himself for the moment was a sight which shocked his brother much. He strode away to the end window, and gazed out to show his indifference, with a soft whistle of impatience, which would have made itself into words anything but soft had circumstances permitted. But nobody remarked either his impatience or his anger. The room was long and not very broad, and the panel in which the picture was being placed was immediately opposite the gilded pipes of a chamber organ, which was let into the wall. To be sure, if it had been a picture of chorister boys instead of little barbarians it would have been more harmonious with the place; but Suffolk's Angles shone out of the dark wall like positive sunshine. There were three broad mullioned windows in one end of the room, and at the other a great east window full of heraldic designs in painted glass,—the arms of the Beauchamps and their connexions. Under this blaze of colour, on either side, the panels were carved, running into little pinnacles and canopy work of a semi-ecclesiastical kind. It had been, indeed, a chapel in the early ages, when the Beauchamps were Catholic. A few high-backed, heavy, oak chairs were all the furniture in it now, except quite at the west end of the room, near where the picture was being placed, where a grand piano stood under one window, and a small easel in the other. This picturesque place, in which priests in glittering vestments, and knights in steel, and ladies in flowing robes, would have been the natural actors, was now the music-room in Richmont, occupied chiefly by the ex-cheesemonger's daughter,—an out-of-the-way place in which she could pursue her occupations as she pleased. Reflections, not exactly to this effect, but of a somewhat similar meaning, were in Frank's mind as he turned with disgust from his unconscious brother. The poor Beauchamps!—who had the best blood in England in their veins, and were now vegetating at all sorts of wretched Continental baths and watering-places. To be sure, old Beauchamp was a blackleg, and his wife no better than she should be,—and the music-room, when Frank knew it, had been a lumber-room and play-room, dear to the children, though nobody thought anything about its picturesqueness. Still, those were the Beauchamps, and these Riches,—and what a falling off was there! Frank was full of these thoughts, and in a very discontented mind generally, not condescending to look at the picture with which all the rest were absorbed, when Laurie emerged from behind the frame, and, to his amazement, saw that it was his brother who interrupted the light in the middle window. It was a kind of bay window, projecting just a little out beyond the line of the others, and in it there stood a low chair covered with old brocade, and a small table with a vase of fresh spring flowers. Frank had not noticed these little accessories, but Laurie, having the eye of an artist, took them in at a glance. Somehow Frank's attitude, standing between the low chair and the little table, suggested ideas to Laurie's mind of a different kind from those which moved his brother. This was the favourite haunt of the millionnaire's daughter. The chair was hers, and the flowers, and the book which lay on the ledge of the window; and Royalborough was close at hand, not too far for a young soldier to ride over any day. Could Frank be Nelly Rich's property too?

'Frank!' cried Laurie, 'you here! Who could have dreamt of seeing you?'

'I have more reason to say so,' said Frank. 'We are quartered close by; but what can you be doing carpentering in a house like this? Perhaps that's the branch of art you have taken to at last,' the Guardsman continued with a sneer. As for Laurie, he had been good-natured from his cradle, and laughed at this little ebullition.

'Not quite,' he said. 'Come and look at the picture. Of course, I know you don't know anything about it; but so long as you have eyes you may look, at least. What games we used to have up here! Is the goddess worthy of the shrine now?' he added, glancing up with a little curiosity into the young soldier's face.

'I don't know what you mean by shrines and goddesses,' said Frank, still angry; 'but I do think, for the sake of your friends, if not for your own, you ought to mind what you're about, and not be so very complaisant in the house of a cad like this.'

'Hush!' said Laurie, 'don't call names, my big brother. What have I been doing, I wonder, to come under your great displeasure? Dust on my coat, is it?' and Laurie suddenly bethought himself of the cobwebs which he had hoped the padrona might have brushed off for him; and stopped short, the foolish fellow, and smiled and sighed.

'Dust!' cried Frank, indignantly. 'I wonder you did not take it off to do your work the better. It would have been the right thing to do.'

'And so it would,' said Laurie; 'I will recollect another time. But come along, old fellow, and look at the picture, and don't make yourself so disagreeable. Old Rich has sent for his daughter, and we can't go on squaring before a lady. Stand here, and look at it well.'

'Is it yours?' said the reluctant Frank. And Laurie laughed and shook his head.

'He asks if it is mine,' he said; 'there's a Guardsman's idea of the possibilities, Suffolk! You might as well have asked if that Madonna was mine.'

'Well, and what if I had?' said Frank, stoutly, in his ignorance—and went and stared with a determination to see nothing. The three figures were standing thus grouped,—Frank looking at the picture, and Suffolk, who had taken no part in the conversation, looking with mild surprise at the natural curiosity called a Guardsman of which he knew little more than the other did about the Angles,—when Mr. Rich came back triumphant with his daughter. They made a curious centre to the room, from which, by this time, the workmen who had been placing the picture had disappeared, leaving them alone. Frank, the very impersonation of scepticism and critical ignorance, stood with his face turned upward to the Angles, and defiance and disdain in the very attitude of his feet resentfully planted on the polished oaken floor. Suffolk, turning round and round in his fingers the rule which one of the workmen had left behind him, stood half a step behind, looking at Frank, with the faintest of smiles on his face, and that curious faculty of seeing, which never deserts a true painter, somehow making itself visible in his eyes. He was not studying the figure which thus defiantly posed before him, and yet there was an amusing consciousness of the pose, and of all expressed by it, in his look. Frank was so unaware of this, and Laurie, as he recognised it, became so divided between sympathy with his brother and amusement with his friend, that the three faces made a very curious group; and so Nelly Rich thought as she came into the room, not knowing why it was that her father had brought her here. She was followed by the entire party, Mrs. Rich leading the way, and leaning her substantial weight on Edgbaston's arm. She had but a minute to notice the group, but it made an impression on her; and curiously enough,—or, perhaps not curiously,—Nelly's sympathies fixed upon Frank in the moment she had to identify him. The others were laughing at him, and he was young and single-handed, and,—so handsome. Nelly Rich piqued herself upon being intellectual and fond of art; and yet it was neither the painter nor the amateur that caught her eyes; it was the ignorant, unintellectual, handsome young Guardsman, which no doubt was quite natural in a way.

She gave a cry of wonder and delight when she saw the picture; but the kind father, to whom that cry was music, had made a mistake by bringing the party with him. After the first outburst Nelly retreated and was silent. She was not the kind of Nelly Rich whom either Frank or Laurie Renton had expected to see. Anything more unlike the portly, comely mother who came in after her, sweeping her gorgeous skirts all over the brown oak floor, could not be conceived. Nelly was very small; she had the figure and the foot of a fairy; and how her dark, clear, olive complexion,—her hair so dark as to be almost black,—her brilliant dark-brown eyes,—could have been derived from the two ruddy, roundabout people beside her, was a puzzle to everybody. She might have been a fairy changeling, but that her small figure was perfect in form, and instinct with life, health, and activity. She was as plainly dressed as her mother was gorgeous, with a black gown and knots of crimson ribbons, like a Spaniard, which, indeed, was the most becoming dress she could have chosen. And she was not a timid maiden generally, taking shelter from the crowd; but a creature quite able to express herself and defend herself. Nevertheless she stepped aside as her mother entered on Edgbaston's arm, and said not a word more about the picture. The party invaded the music-room, filling it with noise and movement. The scene was changed. It was no longer a retired, half-solemn place, full of associations of the past, and one soft, pleasant suggestion of the present conveyed by the fresh flowers, the instruments, the little easel, and the book, which harmonised everything; but a show place, with vulgar sightseers and a vulgar showman,—vulgar, though the visitors came of blood to which no objection could be taken. They gazed at the painted window, and at the carved oak, and at the pictures, alike with suppressed yawns, and referred stealthily to their watches, wondering when luncheon would be announced. Suffolk, who was the only stranger whom no one knew, stood aside, and looked on with a certain indignation. His picture, newly placed, newly arrived,—a picture which Academicians had condescended to praise, and the 'Sword' had noticed favourably,—should have been, no one could doubt, the chief thing to be noticed; but what the newcomers did was to cast a careless glance at it, and say, 'Ah! oh! pretty thing, to be sure,' and turn their backs with that unspeakable calm of indifference which galls the artist mind beyond endurance. 'Like old Woodland's style, ain't it?' said Edgbaston, with his glass in his eye. If there was one man or painter whom Suffolk regarded with especial contempt it was old Woodland! The painter turned to the window stung and smarting all over, and tried to look out; and then one of the young men found a sketch upon Nelly's little easel, and went into ecstasies over it. They all crowded, a mass of tall heads, to look at it with an interest which no one had dreamt of showing in the Angles. 'Parcel of empty-headed coxcombs!' Suffolk said to himself; and then certain reflections overtook him as to the kind of people who were likely to see his work where it was now placed. Was not the

Guardsman the very highest possible class of visitor who could come to Richmont; and was this all for which he had spent his brains and his strength? He had turned, and was looking with the most curious wonder and contempt upon the group round Nelly's easel. Could he help being contemptuous? The sketch was an unobtrusive little performance, pretending nothing, and not meaning much. And it was for such eyes as these that he had painted his picture! He was thinking so with a certain bitterness, when Nelly herself, with a little rush, penetrated the group, and, seizing upon the harmless drawing they were gazing at, thrust it before their eyes into a portfolio.

'It is not worth a glance,' she cried; 'it's a bit of waste paper. Oh, for heaven's sake, don't stare, and make me ashamed of myself before Mr. Suffolk! It was the picture you came to see.'

'I came because you were coming,' said one of the young men.

'Oh, never mind the picture. Come and show us what you have here,' said another, laying his hand on the portfolio. This was how they talked, with Suffolk looking on. As for Nelly, her cheeks grew crimson. She was not, as we have said, a timid maiden; and she was given to speaking her mind, as even these gentlemen knew.

'Yes,' she said, with her eyes sparkling; 'to be sure, you know best. You shall have the portfolio to look at—art brought down to the meanest capacity. I might have known that would be the most suitable for you; and, Mr. Suffolk, come and tell me about it,' she said softly, turning to the painter. She held out her hand, that he might offer her his arm, and led him, in spite of himself, opposite to the poor picture which had been so scorned. 'I want to clear them all away, those stupid men,' said Nelly, confidentially. 'I hate young men; they are all so idiotic. Mr. Suffolk, when I look at this I could cry, out of envy and spite. How is it you can do it?—And I work and work and can't do anything. I would give my head if I could paint only that little bit of a tree; and I suppose you never gave it a thought?' she said, turning the brilliant brown eyes upon him. 'Tell me about it, please; for it will be my chief friend, and live with me all day long.'

'What am I to tell you, Miss Rich?' said the painter, taken by surprise, and yet standing on his dignity still.

And then Nelly gazed at the Angles for at least a minute in silence, holding his arm. 'It does not matter,' she said, at last, with a long-drawn breath of satisfaction,—'I shall learn it all from their faces. You must know, I live in this room, and they will never ask me what they are to tell me. I shall find out all their story in little bits. That one is quite happy to have so much change and variety, and to feel himself in Rome,—you painted him when you were happy, Mr. Suffolk; and that one is thinking of home,—something had happened to you then. I shall find it all out by degrees. Those men don't find themselves so happy as they thought they would be over the portfolio,' she broke off suddenly, with a little laugh; 'but please to remember I have got eyes, and there are other people besides Guardsmen who come here sometimes. Mamma, I hear the bell for luncheon; please take all those men away.'

'You must not be shocked with Nelly, Mr. Suffolk,' said Mrs. Rich. 'I have told her all about your charming little wife, so she knows she need not be afraid to speak to you; and that's her way, making up all that nonsense about the pictures she likes. I think it looks perfectly charming, now that it is in its place. Nelly, this is Mr. Renton, whom I told you of. He is such a friend of Mrs. Severn's; and this is Mr. Frank Renton; neighbours of ours, you know, when they are at home, and cousins to that nice Miss Westbury you made acquaintance with the other day,—such a nice, lady-like girl. But I hear the bell. I am sure you must all be quite hungry after your long drive.'

'Yes, come along,' said Mr. Rich; 'come along, and let us have something to eat. Nothing like art for giving one an appetite. I am as hungry as a hunter. All with getting up Suffolk's lovely picture! Gem of my collection, I call it, though I have half-a-dozen Crowquills down-stairs, which I'll show you after lunch. Come along, gentlemen. As for Nelly, you know, and the painter, they'll follow. Ladies and men of genius don't want to eat like us common mortals. Come along, come along,' said the millionnaire, his voice dying off in the passage. The two Rentons, who had just been presented to Nelly, stood by her, waiting till she led the way; and Nelly, for her part, had no inclination to lead the way. She had got rid of 'those stupid men,' and she was rather in the humour for a little talk.

'Now they're gone one can breathe,' she said, with complimentary confidentialness. 'We need not go down just yet. Please, Mr. Renton, tell me about the Severns. You are grand people, and I don't suppose Miss Westbury would like it if I quoted her as an acquaintance; but I may ask about the Severns. Do you know them too?'

'I have only seen them once,' said Frank; 'but I don't think you do Mary Westbury justice. I am sure she would be charmed——'

'Tell me about the Severns, please,' said Nelly, with a little wave of her hand.

Then there was a pause, which nobody could have explained. Laurie, it is true, knew very well why it was that he, excited and confused as he was, should feel himself unable to speak of the padrona; but why could not Frank answer so simple a question? In the meanwhile Frank, on his side, saw suddenly before him, as in a vision, that picture of Alice standing in the doorway, with all the shadows round her, and felt his lips sealed, and could not speak.

'If these gentlemen will not tell me anything,' said Nelly, 'Mr. Suffolk, speak. I'm sure you know them too.'

'I have only seen them once,' repeated Frank, hastily. 'Miss Severn plays like—St. Cecilia. I have not heard anything like her playing for a hundred years.'

'Well,' said Nelly, shrugging her shoulders, 'here is one fact elicited by dint of inquiry. Miss Severn—that is, I suppose, Alice, who was a little darling when I saw her last—plays. I don't care so much for playing as I ought to do. And I wanted to hear of the padrona and all the little ones. Couldn't you tell me anything more, Mr. Renton? Yes, I call her the padrona too. Mr. Severn used to give me a lesson sometimes—not for money, but for love. It may seem strange to you,' said Nelly, demurely, 'but he was fond of me. And I am fond of her, and all of them. And Alice plays! I suppose that is all one could ever get out of a man. If any one asks you about me, Mr. Frank Renton, I know exactly what you will say: "Miss Rich—draws." It is nice to be so concise, but oh, tell me about my pretty padrona, please!' cried Nelly, clasping her hands together, and turning appealing eyes to Laurie. It was almost more than Laurie's composure could bear, for it was just at the moment after he had made his discovery, and was waiting to know what was to be done with him; and his heart was, so to speak, in his mouth.

'She is as pretty as ever,' said Laurie, in that strange tone of suppressed emotion which makes itself almost more distinctly apparent than the plainest confession of feeling; 'and I don't think I could tell you how good she is. Suffolk knows her. We cannot trust ourselves to speak of the padrona,' said Laurie, nervously, 'we people who live about the Square.'

And then Suffolk said something to the same purport in words, but in so different a tone as to throw the thrill in Laurie's voice into fuller relief. And Nelly looked at him full in the face, not disguising the little gleams of discernment, half surprise, half mischief, in her eyes. This was the only sign about her of inferior breeding. She had not sufficient delicacy to conceal the enlightenment his tone had given her. She looked at him so that he felt he was discovered, and his face flamed with the sudden consciousness; and then she turned to Frank, who was the particular mouse with which at the moment Nelly felt disposed to play.

'This room must have been made on purpose for Miss Severn, who plays,' she said. 'I should think anybody who was musical would be in paradise here. There is the organ and the piano, and in that closet there are harps, and sackbuts, and dulcimers, and all kinds of music. I shall ask Alice Severn to come to see me, and Mr. Frank Renton shall come too, and hear her—play.'

'I ask no better,' said Frank, responding to the challenge as became a Guardsman. And Nelly took them down-stairs, leaving the two graver, pre-occupied men to follow, and making Frank her partner by some subtle sleight of hand. He was very much at home at Richmont before the day was over. Even Laurie remarked the rising flirtation, and laughed to himself in the midst of his own excitement at the possibility of his brother's fortune coming in so easy a way. And his friends congratulated him on his success, and pledged him in bumpers when they got home. 'I tell you, my boy, she has cartloads of tin,' said Edgbaston. 'Better that than going out to India.' And as for Frank, he did not deny to himself that on the whole, notwithstanding Laurie's undignified aspect, and Mr. Rich's soap-boiling, or cheesemongering—which was it?—he had spent a very pleasant day.

CHAPTER X.

BROTHERLY ADVICE.

NEXT day, however, Frank Renton was full of many thoughts.

I doubt whether it is in my power to give any clear impression of the reflections naturally produced in a young man's mind by the first suggestion of marrying money. In ordinary cases, marriage is not the object set before the youth—the purpose contemplated from the beginning of an acquaintance. He is attracted by some stranger, whose name he never heard before, perhaps, and of whose existence, previous to the eventful hour which brought them together, he had no knowledge. Chance or inclination brings them together. Then the germ warms, quickens, bursts into flower. Love comes spontaneous, unsought, perhaps almost unwelcome, and marriage becomes but a necessary accident in its course. But to approach that idea of marriage in cold blood, and without any soft compulsion of feeling, is a very different matter. It is a thing which women are called upon to do every day; but it is not so inevitable among men. It had been brought before Frank in what seemed a very distinct way. True, Nelly Rich was a little flirt, almost confessedly avenging herself on the world for her father's uncomfortable position, and the spurns her family endured, by doing as much harm as she could among the men who ate Mr. Rich's dinners and laughed at him. She had no mercy upon them, and more than one, within the knowledge even of the battalion at Royalborough, who had supposed themselves sure of Nelly and her fortune, had been ignominiously turned off when the crisis came. This very fact naturally made Frank think the more of the impression, which all his comrades informed him he had produced. Fifty thousand pounds down, and some further share in all probability when the father and mother died, not to speak of Nelly herself—pretty, and bright, and amusing, and clever as she was! The idea, as was natural, awoke many reflections in the young soldier's mind. I have said that he had not suffered by his father's death; but yet had he meant to remain in his present position at home, no doubt Frank would have shared in the disadvantages which his brothers had felt so keenly; and to have it in his power at twenty to secure his own comfort for life without any particular trouble was a dazzling prospect. It is not to be supposed by this that Frank had developed at so early an age the mercenary instincts of a fortune-hunter. On the contrary, the good things which the gods seemed thus to have placed within his reach, gave him a shock rather than a thrill of satisfaction. He had no wish to marry,—to plunge into serious life at his age, and give up the wayward ways of youth. The idea would never have entered his mind had he been left to himself. But when a young man sees such a golden apple nodding at him from an accessible bough, and thinks he has but to put forth his hand and secure to himself at one stroke all the advantages of wealth, the sensation is a startling one. He went about thoughtful for two days, turning it over and over in his mind. It is true he did not think very much about Nelly. She was very nice, very jolly, and a man need not fear to have a dull companion for life whom duty called upon to marry Mr. Rich's daughter; but the truth was that she did not count for very much in the matter. Frank was honest with himself, and affected no delusion on that subject; but then he had heard of people marrying money all his life without any particular reprobation. Many men had done it, as he knew, who got on very well with their wives, and made admirable husbands. Indeed, as Frank reflected to himself, with the mild cynicism which was inseparable from the kind of education he had gone through, marriage was one of the things in which there must be many mixed motives. Love, of course, was all very well to romance about; but love could not be, never was, the only thing taken into account, except indeed by fools. If it was mere love you married for, of course you did it in the style of King Cophetua, and scorned the consequences. But few men went so far as that. There were questions of income and settlements, and how people were to live, which came in along with the purest affection, and brought marriage,—necessarily,—into the same category with all other human affairs. Edgbaston, for instance, as everybody knew, had been desperately in love with Fanny Trent, who married old Oatley, the brewer, after all. Edgbaston himself, in a melting moment, had told the story to Frank. 'I've got nothing but mortgages to look forward to,' the young lord said, 'and of course I knew that was how it must end. I had only a shabby old coronet to offer her, and Oatley was a bag of money. Poor Fanny! I don't think she liked it any more than I did; but what can a fellow do when circumstances are dead against him?' That was how it happened in ordinary life. Even when a man was as fond of a woman as he could be, still he must take other matters into account,—how they were to live, what provision was to be made for the future, and a hundred other details about connexions and position and the like. Therefore, whatever your feelings might be, Frank argued with himself, marriage was always a matter of mixed motives; and to reject a rich alliance which had nothing particularly disagreeable in it, or indeed to put aside the thought of it, as if marriage was not one of the things to be calculated about and carefully considered in all its bearings, was simple folly. He had never thought so deeply on any subject, his profession and general circumstances being rather against any very lively exercise of his mental faculties. This question of Nelly Rich cost him two days' painful deliberation. To have her and to suspend his negotiations about India and the marching regiment, and to strike out a shorter path instead to wealth, and ease, and comfort—or not to have her! It even interfered with his sleep, though he was so young and healthy. It was not a matter on which he could consult any one, and this increased the difficulty tenfold. Even as to Edgbaston, though he was so good a fellow, Frank had sufficient delicacy to feel that if he should hereafter marry a woman about whom he had thus consulted his friend, he could never allow that friend to enter the house in which his wife should be supreme. If she ever became his wife it would be indispensable that no living creature should know how he had once questioned and doubted. Frank might be susceptible to worldly motives, as most people are; but he was full of honourable feeling all the same. He might marry money, but no one should ever be able so much as to hint to the woman who brought it that it was not her he loved best. He would do all a man could to love her if he did marry her; and he would breathe his secret to no one. And thus he turned his difficulty over and over in his mind, and denied himself the comfort of friendly counsel on the subject, which indeed was as high an evidence of the young man's honourable feeling as could well be desired.

But his reasonings with himself were far from being successful. His arguments, like those of philosophy, were irrefutable, but produced no conviction. The more clearly he saw that it was expedient for him to seize so unusual an opportunity, and secure his own prospects for life, the more unwilling did he feel to take the first necessary steps. India suddenly acquired an attraction for Frank which it never had before. Tiger-hunts, warlike expeditions,—all the pomp and circumstance of Eastern life,—suddenly gleamed up in his imagination as contrasted with the tame amusements and monotonous life at home. Yes, home had been very pleasant before any other visions came. Hunting, and fishing, and boating, and going to balls, are very agreeable modes of filling up a young man's time, and leave him little leisure to think what is the good of it all. But if by any chance that question should penetrate through the maze of pleasures, it either has to be answered or it leaves an unpleasant echo among sounds otherwise most agreeable. Frank had made a virtue of necessity after his father's death, and had compelled himself to ask and to find an answer to this demand. After all there was no good except amusement in it. He was a lovely spectacle,—he was modestly aware,—on state occasions in his grand uniform; but these occasions were but few, and there would still be heaps of men left to hunt the foxes and fish the rivers of England after he was gone. A man who remained and grew old and yet was never anything more than a beautiful Guardsman, was not an imposing being. And the money he might marry was not enough to give him occupation and a solemn status in the country. Had it been fifty thousand a-year indeed, that would have been as good as a profession; for of course it would have involved estates to manage, and a hundred things to do; but fifty thousand down, though it would make him extremely comfortable, would leave him as ornamental and useless as ever. And India was all novel, and fresh, and full of excitement;—troops to lead, mutinies to quell for anything he knew, principalities to conquer perhaps,—shawls, diamonds, tigers, everything new. Frank had a hard time of it with all these thoughts. And once or twice there did actually spring up before him, quite uncalled-for, among his serious reflections, the shadowy apparition of that doorway with its curtains, and the young face looking through. That had nothing to do with it, you may well say,—less than nothing; but yet it had a sort of confusing effect on the young man's intellect, and added a perplexity the more. The way in which he finally extricated himself from the maze, and saw daylight at last, is one which, I suppose, few people would divine, and which could have occurred only to a younger brother in conscious possession of many qualities, both intuitive and the result of experience, which Providence had denied to the rest of his family. He wrote a letter to his brother Laurie; and this is what the young Machiavel said;—

'MY DEAR LAURIE,—

'You will be surprised I don't doubt when you see what I am writing to you about. Perhaps you will think it is not the part of the younger to advise the elder; but if we don't hang together, and do the best we can for each other, what are we, under our present circumstances, to do? I am not quite as old as you are, but perhaps I have been thrown more into the world. You have always taken to artists, and those kind of people, you know, who are out of the tide, and have queer notions; beside being,—no offence intended,—of a diffeent sphere from us. You think, on the other hand, that we are an empty-headed set, and perhaps you are not far wrong; but a fellow picks up a great many wrinkles even among men that are stupid enough to look at,—don't you see?—when they've got some knowledge of the world.

'The fact is I am beating about the bush a little, because I don't very well know how to begin what I've got to say. It is just this. You must have noticed the other day when you were at Richmont how favourable everybody was to you and to me. Of course, one does not care for the opinion of an old beggar like Rich. But his wife isn't at all so bad, and the girl, on the whole, is very nice. I assure you frankly I do think so. She's a clever little thing, and decidedly pretty and amusing too, and fond of pictures, and that sort of thing, so that there would be a sympathy between you. To say it out plump, my opinion is that she is the very sort of girl you ought to marry. It is not everybody that would suit you. You want some one that has money, and yet doesn't stand upon her money; and that would not be conventional or stuck-up, but take your friends along with yourself, and make up her mind to it. Now Nelly Rich has no right to be stuck-up; and yet she's nice, and looks nice, and we Rentons are well enough known to marry anybody we please. As for the father, I don't think you need mind about him. He is very liberal and hospitable, and ready to throw his money about in buckets-full, and that always tells. People may snigger at him, but they'll go to his house all the same. And you may marry a girl, you know, without marrying her father too.

The mother is not at all so bad. She's motherly, and that sort of thing. And Nelly has fifty thousand pounds. I can't tell you how much I have been thinking of it since that day. The fellows here have all advised me to go in for it myself, but I'm rather too young to marry; and besides I think it would suit you far better than me. I have my profession, and I can do very well for a few years on my allowance, especially in India, where there is double pay. But you,—forgive me, my dear Laurie,—have always been a fellow to talk, you know, and to do things for other people. I don't think you're the man to make your way in the world, and I can't help feeling that to have a nice wife who would take an interest in your pursuits, and a nice steady income that would keep you out of anxiety, would be the very thing for you. I have made every inquiry, and as far as I can make out, Nelly Rich is not what you would call a flirt. She is fond of a little fun, and I like her for that; and when a man is cheeky, they say she leads him on till he makes a fool of himself; but no sensible fellow would object to a girl for having a little spirit. She is very good-tempered, and no end of fun; and very clever at drawing, and everything of that kind. She doesn't go in for music, but neither do you; and she's the sort of girl that would travel with you, and work with you, and make an ass of herself about pictures, and old churches, and rubbish, just as much as you would. I think, on my word, Laurie, it's the very thing for you.

'Anyhow, old fellow, you won't take it amiss my having put it into your head? It would be a most sensible thing to do; and I feel sure a man might get quite fond of Nelly Rich, were he to try. I suppose it is because the Manor is so near that they are so friendly to us. As soon as mamma is well enough I'll make her call. She'll do it at once when she knows what depends on it. And if you play your cards at all well, you are as sure of success as anything can be. And then you would not need to give up any of your friends. She was as pleased with that painter-fellow the other day as if he had been a prince. And you remember how she talked about the people in Fitzroy Square. The more I think of it, the more it seems providential for you. My dear fellow, go in and win. I should have recommended her to Ben, had Ben been within knowledge. But she will suit you much better than she would have suited him. And it will be a real comfort to think that one of us is saved from the wreck, whether the others sink or swim.

'Yrs. affec.,
'F. RENTON.'

This was Frank's grand device for utilising Nelly's fortune, and yet preserving his own freedom. Laurie only received the letter when he was in the midst of his preparations for going to Italy, and he threw it aside with a painful smile. But our Guardsman knew nothing about his brother's preoccupied mind, and, satisfied that he had done the best for everybody, laid aside the subject, and went upon his way as usual. He was rather anxious for Laurie's answer, it is true; but then there are often irregularities in family correspondence, and Laurie might think it best to leave it until they met. As it happened Frank did not even visit his mother for the next ten days; and Mary Westbury, who was his home correspondent, was so full of the news of an unexpected visit from Ben, that she quite omitted to mention Laurie's intimation, which came immediately after, of his intended departure. So that Frank had actually no information about his brother when he went on the following Saturday to dine at Richmont.

CHAPTER XI.

THE MUSIC-ROOM.

FRANK was alone on his second expedition to Richmont, which was a satisfaction to him. He was full of his scheme, and anxious to see how the land lay, and what Laurie's prospects might be should he make up his mind to 'go in' for the fifty thousand pounds. And he was quite willing to divert himself in the society of his future sister-in-law. The invitation had a family aspect altogether, he thought; and, instead of returning to his quarters, he had made his arrangements to go home for the Sunday, and rouse his mother to such steps as were practicable for securing Laurie's advantage. Frank left Royalborough with all the lively zest of a matchmaker, pleased with himself and his own generosity, and rather elated on his brother's account. Fifty thousand pounds!—two thousand five hundred a-year, and always the prospect of something coming at the end of the seven years' probation! For a man who had no expensive tastes, and whose whole soul was wrapped up in pictures, it was a fortune! He could dabble in paint as much as he liked, and his wife could help him; and they could travel about as much as they liked, and go to all the pretty places that took their fancy. There was no one to whom he could have said as much in actual words; but the feeling in his mind was, that if anybody had ever originated a better plan he'd like to hear of it. Ben had turned up, as Mary Westbury's letter told him; and no doubt Ben would make his way in the world. And as for himself, Frank thought that there was no particular fear; but Laurie was the feeble one of the family, the one most likely to do little, to spend his strength for naught, or waste his own life for the advantage of others. And nothing could be so good for him as to be thus put on a comfortable shelf out of harm's way at the very beginning of his career. He was fond of Laurie, as most people were; and it pleased him as much in his brotherliness as in his vanity to take Laurie thus in hand and be the one to provide for him. This time it was to dinner he was going at Richmont, and he had written to the Manor to beg his mother to send over the dog-cart for him and his portmanteau. The millionnaire's house was beginning to be lit up in all its windows when he drove along the avenue: the lights in it sparkled like fairy lamps in the blue, spring twilight; and when he entered the great hall he was informed that nobody had come down-stairs yet, and that the dinner had been made an hour later in consequence of some one else who was to arrive by the train.

'The young ladies is in the music-room, sir,' the butler said respectfully, being himself a native of Berks, and feeling that the advent of a Renton was an honour to the house; 'and I was to tell you as tea is served in the drawing-room.'

'Oh, I'll join the young ladies,' said Frank, lightly, thinking of Nelly only, his sister-in-law that was to be. No doubt some one must be with her, but that did not matter. Indeed, on the whole, it was so much the better, for it would not be becoming to flirt, except in the very mildest way, with a girl who was going to be your brother's wife. He ran up-stairs, telling the man he knew the way, and thus making a daring leap into intimacy such as he would never have dreamed of had he taken time to think. But his own plan had taken possession of him. Of course she was going to be his sister-in-law, and it would be absurd to stand upon ceremony. Thus Frank, being unused to the excitement of so much thinking, was carried away by it, and took his own imaginations for granted. As he ran up-stairs, however, his ear was caught by the sound of the organ, a sound which had not been heard in Beecham so long as he had known the house, and to which Richmont, according to Nelly's description, was as little accustomed. The music seemed to fill the place, swelling through the stairs and passages, which were full of the darkness and stillness of the approaching night. Frank stood still to listen, and then went on with a surprised face, and with a new thrill in his heart. It was surely the same sonata he had heard softly breathing out of the dark drawing-room that night he visited Fitzroy Square. Who could be playing? Could there be two girls in the world who had the same power, the same feeling for music, the same subtle sentiment, and expressive strength? But then how did he know at all that it was a girl who was playing? It might be some old music-master, one of the sort of people whom Nelly loved. All the same, it had the effect of subduing his steps, and making his approach much less confident and unembarrassed. He lingered,—he thought of going back,—he felt himself a coxcomb and presumptuous animal. And yet he went on, led partly by the force of the impulse which was still upon him, and partly allured by the dulcet and harmonious sound to which he was so susceptible. He knocked at the door, but his summons was unheard in the midst of the music. Then he opened it softly, and went in. There was no light in the room except the pale twilight, which marked out every line of the windows, and the glimmering of the painted glass at the end by which he entered. He seemed to step out of the real world altogether into an enchanted place when he crossed that darkling threshold. The gilded organ-pipes caught a certain faint reflection, and under that dim shimmer sat a shadow, which was playing; while in the centre window, in the bay, looking out, as it seemed, into the night, another shadow, light and small as a fairy, stood listening or musing. The opposite wall of the room, and the picture which was so bright in the daylight, had retreated altogether into the gloom; and the painted window hung as if suspended in the air; and all the solid wall in which it was set, and the dark oak carving under it, had receded into obscurity. Frank stood with his hand on the door, and held his breath. He felt at once like a fool and like an intruder, not knowing who they were whose privacy he was invading, and having no right whatever to be there even had he been sure it was Nelly who stood in the window. He had burst into her particular privacy unannounced the second time he had been in the house! But Frank was bewitched, and stood still, blotting himself out as small as possible against the door.

But either the door had creaked or her quick ear had caught some sound of movement, for Nelly Rich turned round suddenly. She was not so absorbed in the music as the player was, or as Frank would have been had he been listening in a legitimate and proper way. Her mind was divided between that and a great many other thoughts, and gave but a partial attention to the sounds which filled the room. When she saw that another shadow had intruded into her retirement, Nelly gave a little cry, and flitted like a ghost towards the door.

'Who is there?' she cried with a sharpness which struck in just at a pianissimo passage, and startled the player as well as the intruder. The music ceased with a kind of long-drawn wail, and the musician too gave a little scream. Frank would have been thankful if the old oak floor had suddenly opened and swallowed him up.

'A thousand pardons,' he cried; 'it is I, Miss Rich; Frank Renton. I don't know how to explain my intrusion. Pray forgive me. I was told I should find you here,—and then the music; I have not a word to say for myself. Pardon?— that is all.'

'Was it papa who told you you would find me here?' said Nelly. 'It is just like him. But, Mr. Renton, I am not papa, and I admit nobody but my friends to this room,—especially in the dark,' she added, with a quiver of coming laughter, which reassured Frank. He sank down upon his knee, as she stood with her arms extended, metaphorically thrusting him away.

'What can I say for myself?' said Frank. 'I am a wretched sinner, not worthy to be admitted as a friend. Let me come in as a captive, like one of your Angles; or as a beggar, or—— Don't be too hard upon me. The evil is done. The mortal has crossed the threshold of fairyland. Let him stay.'

'Alice, advise me,' cried Nelly, turning to the silent figure at the piano. 'Shall we let him stay?'

So it was Alice! Something had told him so the instant he recognised that sonata. Now he turned his head towards her in the gloom, breathless, awaiting her answer. Alice, however, made no reply. She only returned to her organ, and took up her pianissimo passage. I cannot tell how she intimated her pleasure to the slave on the other side of the wall who 'blew;' but, anyhow, she took it up where she had left off, and the soft, delicious sounds, the very voice of the darkness and stillness, whispered over the two darkling, undiscernible figures,—one standing, one kneeling, in the gloom. A certain soft thrill of consciousness, half comic, half sentimental, moved Nelly. No doubt it had been partly in jest that Frank had put himself on his knees; but might it not be partly in earnest, too? Frank, for his part, had forgotten Nelly's very existence. It seemed natural to him to listen thus to such a strain. He was not intellectual, and could have heard the finest poetry in the world unmoved. All his pretty sentiments about fairyland, etcetera, were also the most superficial words; but the music seized upon, mastered him, put a soul into the young soldier. He turned half towards the instrument, kneeling, and unconscious that he was kneeling. To him it was poetry, art, passion, imagination, all in one. And Alice went on playing softly as in a dream; and the remaining rays of half light gradually extinguished themselves, till even the two shadows at the door became scarcely discernible, and the organ-pipes faded into obscurity. It was a curious situation altogether, but only Nelly was aware of it. To her the fact was very evident that a handsome young Guardsman, still kneeling on one knee, as to his sovereign, was before her; that twilight was settling down into night; that Mr. Frank Renton was a stranger: and that it was time to dress. Something prevented her from speaking, and cutting short the music; but her impatient mind having got over the first charm, began to grow weary, and long for a change. She could not make out how it was that the musician went on, unfatigued with all those lingering notes. 'That's the same thing over again,' Nelly said to herself, not being so fond of music as she ought to have been, as may easily be perceived. She glided back to the window, at last; and Frank, roused by her motion, rose from his reverential attitude. He knew that Alice could not stop till the movement had come to an end; and was not impatient, but absorbed in the lovely harmony. But after a while the thought stole into even his mind that it would be best to get as much into the light as possible, and he followed Nelly to the window. There was a glimmering of the park visible outside, and, what was more to the purpose, a great expanse of blue sky and stars. And in the room there was the painted window, hanging in the air like a picture worked in jewels, suspended without visible support; and the music—and the two girls;—even a poet could not have objected to all the accessories of the scene.

'Thanks, Alice, it is lovely,' cried Nelly; 'but all the same for the moment, my dear, I am glad it is done; for this is growing very ghostly. Mr. Renton, I think I can see that you have come in, though you never got permission. Go before us, please, and let us know if there are lights in the passages: and if you are good, and do everything you are told, we will forgive you for coming in. Alice, give me your hand. They are both intoxicated with the music, these two, cried Nelly, as if to herself; 'and I don't believe they have any eyes to see that window hanging there all by itself. Come along, you people, who can hear and can't see:—let us get into the light.'

'But I can see, too,' said Alice, softly, coming to Nelly's side.

'Ah, you are a painter's daughter,' said Nelly: 'but you would need to be a cat to see anything now. Thanks, Mr. Renton. Now wait a moment till our eyes are used to the light.'

'Coming down to the common world again,' said Frank, 'is hard. No one can feel it more than I do. Take care of that step,—even painters themselves cannot always see.'

'I wish the common world were not down so many stairs,' said Nelly; and then they emerged into the light. They were still in their morning dresses; and Frank's eyes, once more out of the darkness fell upon the fresh, girlish face, the mass of shining hair,—all those tints of rose and lily which belonged to Alice Severn and her sixteen years. There was a great deal more expression in Nelly's little brown, sparkling countenance. She had lived a year or two longer in reality, a hundred years or so longer in experience. Alice's face lay like an inland lake moved from above, from without, by soft, kissing breezes, by beams of sunshine, but not by any movements from within. There were no volcanoes underneath, nor quicksands, nor sunken rocks. She was very young, and ignorant as a child. That want of definite expression which was a trouble to some of her friends, to Frank was a beauty. She looked like a saint, or an angel, to his eyes. In his worldly-mindedness and curious calculations of what he called practical matters, this face disturbed him, experienced man of the world as he was. What would she think of his scheme for Laurie? The first effect of her presence had been to drive Laurie and all his schemes out of his mind. And now the very contrast of her innocence brought them all back with a rush. It was not this visionary creature concerning whom the plot was laid;—but Nelly, little sprite, who stood by her, a being manifestly of this world.

'I wish Laurie had been here,' cried Frank, abruptly, remembering his *rôle*. 'He is the only one of our family who has an eye. He would have raved about your window, Miss Rich.'

'That would have been kind of him,' said Nelly, with a slight touch of disdain. 'It was Mr. Laurence Renton you were speaking of, Alice. Did you say he had gone away?'

'Gone away!' cried Frank, with a start, which endangered his footing on the stair.

'To Italy,' said Alice. 'We were all so sorry. He went yesterday morning, and the night before he came to bid mamma good-bye. They say it was quite suddenly that he had made up his mind.'

'To Italy!' repeated Frank, in tones of absolute consternation. He stopped on the stair as he went down, to apostrophise mentally both heaven and earth. Gone! notwithstanding all the plans that were making for him. Frank stopped short, so much affected by the news that he forgot even the odd appearance that he made, standing on the stair. 'Then how is it to be done,—and who is to do it?' was the question that immediately suggested itself to his mind. Nelly Rich stood and looked up at him through the rails of the stair with bright eyes, full of mischief, contemplating his puzzled countenance. Who was to do it? By this time it seemed a matter of conscience to Frank that some Renton should appropriate Nelly and her fifty thousand pounds. And Ben was going to America, and Laurie had disappeared into the South. His face expressed the liveliest perplexity and self-interrogation. Who was to do it? Laurie being gone, and Nelly's fortune still unsecured, was it not necessary that he himself, casting all weaker ideas aside, should go in himself for the fifty thousand pounds!

CHAPTER XII.

A PRISONER.

FRANK found it very difficult to make out, both at that and a subsequent period, how it was that no dog-cart came for him from the Manor on that Saturday night. To be sure, the circumstance was easily enough explained as a matter of fact, and meant simply this, neither more nor less,—that his letter, intimating his intention to spend the Sunday with his mother, and giving instructions when he was to be sent for, reached Mrs. Renton only on Sunday at noon. But what Providence meant by permitting such a thing to happen, was of course a totally different matter. The mistake fitted in wonderfully, as mistakes so often do, with the course of events. Richmont might not be so refined as the Manor, but it certainly was, at the present moment, much more amusing. And though of course Frank, like a good son, had been quite willing to give up the Sunday to his mother, yet he was aware of the fact beforehand that the Sunday would be dull. Mrs. Renton had lived a semi-invalid life so long that it was rather a pleasure to her, now she was alone, to relapse into full and unmitigated invalidism. She had so many draughts to take, and precautions to bear in mind, that her whole time was filled up, and that not so unpleasantly as might have been supposed. She had her favourite maid, who never permitted her to forget anything; and when there was no draught to be taken, was always hovering in the background with cups of tea or arrowroot to sustain her mistress's strength. Mrs. Renton was very fond of her boys, but still, her own circumstances being of such a character, she was not entirely dependent upon them for her happiness. To be sure, if any one had so much as mentioned happiness to her, she would have wept, poor soul, and declared positively that no such thing was possible to her, thus left alone in the vacant house, her husband dead, and her sons absent. But, nevertheless, the draughts, and the care, and the tea, and the arrowroot, occupied her time, and gave that gentle support of routine which is so invaluable to a languid life. But it may be supposed that her room was not the most lively place in the world to a young man; and Frank, in the drawing-room at Richmont, with Mrs. Rich making all sorts of comical speeches, and Nelly quite disposed to flirt, and Alice ready to play, did not feel any sensation of despair when he was informed that no dog-cart had come, and that it was now too late to expect it. 'All the better luck for us,' said Mr. Rich. 'Nothing for making acquaintance like a Sunday in the country. There is your room ready, and we're delighted to have you. By Monday you will know how you like us, and we shall have found out how much we like you.'

'We know that already,' said Mrs. Rich, who was fond of little inuendos; 'and I am sure I don't know how far it is safe to keep a handsome young

Guardsman in the house along with two girls. For my part, I don't answer for the consequences. I can't be sure how I shall stand it myself,' she added, with a laugh, which was a little vulgar, no doubt, but mellow, and not unpleasant to hear. Nelly looked up at her mother as if she could have pinched her; but as for papa Rich, this kind of humour was in his way, and he laughed too.

'I'll risk it,' he said, 'especially as the Guardsman has other fish to fry, my dear, and isn't likely to interfere with you. What's the matter, little Nell? You need not knit your brows at me. I hope I may express myself as I like in my own house, and no offence to any one. Mr. Frank, here, understands what I mean; and I am very glad he is going to stop with us, whatever you may be, you little flirt. And where has Alice Severn gone to? I want to speak to her. Don't you think you could play us some nice, old-fashioned tunes, my dear? I don't understand your grand music. That's why I like your mamma's pictures, you know. 'Igh art goes a step beyond me; but give me a pretty woman and a bunch of nice children, and I know what that means. And it is just the same in music;—"Sally in our Alley," and two or three more,—I like them better than your sonatas; but I suppose you think me an ignorant old wretch for that?'

'No, indeed,' said Alice; 'I will play whatever you please.'

'Then come with me,' said the patron of art, giving Alice his fat arm. Alf of the Buffs, who had arrived by the train, and on whose account dinner had been postponed, was the only other member of the party, and he had stretched himself at full length on the sofa with all the appearance of being asleep. The other people had gone away early; and Frank had Mrs. Rich and Nelly, in the intimacy of the domestic circle, all to himself. Old Rich took Alice quite to the other end of the great drawing-room, to the piano, which stood there, and the conversation went on with a distracting accompaniment of tunes and the clapping of hands, with which Alice's audience hailed each air in succession. Frank's attention in particular was sadly distracted,—he could neither listen nor stop listening; and yet the talk had taken a turn which, on the whole, was rather interesting.

'How will your mamma bear your going away?' said Mrs. Rich. 'Her youngest;—I can feel for her. My eldest are married, and out in the world; and I know it's best for themselves, and I don't mind. But Alf and Nelly are my babies, just as you are your mother's, Mr. Frank. What should I do, if any one came to carry my little girl off to the end of the world? And it will be harder still on your poor, dear mamma.'

'But I can't help it,' said Frank. 'You know,—I suppose everybody knows,— the peculiarity in our circumstances. I can't go on as I am doing. India's the place when a man has no money. I don't know what would become of me if I were to stay at home.'

'Well,—you might marry an heiress, you know,' said Mrs. Rich.

'Mamma,' said Alf, from the sofa,—not asleep, though he looked like it,—'if you have any heiresses in your pocket remember your own flesh and blood first of all; don't turn them over to Renton;—he can manage for himself.'

'Oh, yes; I don't doubt he can manage beautifully for himself,' said Mrs. Rich, nodding her head; 'but still he may be the better for a little advice. An heiress is the very thing for you, Mr, Frank. As for Alf, of course,—though I say it that shouldn't,—he'll be very well off, and a catch for any one; as you would have been, but for that fancy of your poor papa's; Mr. Rich's opinion has always been that his brain must have been touched. But that is the thing for you,—as clear as daylight. Marry a girl with money, and settle down at home; and don't go and break your mother's heart. You take my advice, and tell her it was I who gave it, and she'll order her carriage directly, and come over to Richmont and hug me,—though she would not so much as call, you know, only for me.'

'Indeed you do her an injustice,' said Frank; 'she is a great invalid,—she never goes anywhere now.'

'Then her carriage goes to the Rectory, which is not half a mile off; but never mind,' said Mrs. Rich. 'I am sure I don't mind. Give us a little time, and well make our way. Yes; that's what you've got to do. Marry a girl with money. I'm sure you'd make her a good husband all the same.'

I hope, if I were a husband at all, I should be a good one,' said Frank, laughing; 'but I don't think I should like to marry money. A little could do no harm, of course,—just enough to keep her comfortable, and as she had been used to be.' As he said this, Frank, without knowing it, looked direct at Nelly; and, to his consternation, caught her eye, and saw her grow suddenly crimson; an example which, man of the world as he was, he immediately followed. Then, to make things worse, he came to an alarmed, embarrassed pause. 'The man who ought to marry money is my brother Laurie,' he said hastily, and then stopped. What had he done? Was it the fifty thousand pounds he was thinking of?—or what was it? This was only the second time he had been in her company, and yet he had committed both himself and Nelly,—or, at least, in the consternation of the moment, so he thought.

'It must be pleasant for the heiress to be discussed so calmly,' said Nelly all at once. 'Of course, any woman is ready to marry any man who presents himself. That's the conclusion, isn't it? But some girls are of a different way of thinking. Why should Mr. Laurence Renton marry money, I should like to know? I think he is very nice,—a great deal nicer than——most men,' said

Nelly, with emphasis. Her cheek was more crimson than ever, and the defiance was an exquisite compliment which went to Frank's heart. Yes,—it was droll, but it did really seem to him that if he was disposed he might have that fifty thousand pounds. With that he could have his horse and a great many luxuries besides; and Nelly was very pretty, sitting there, opposite to him, with that blush on her cheek, and soft indignation in her eyes.

'Laurie is the best fellow that ever lived,' he cried, recovering himself with an effort; 'but he does things for other people with a much better grace than for himself. He has always been like that. Lazy Laurence everybody calls him. He will never make his own way. I don't know what he has gone to do in Italy. But, all the same, there never was such a good fellow. He is the kind of fellow,' said Frank, with a little effusion, 'that something out of the way should happen to. He ought to find a beautiful princess in a wood, and fall in love with her, and save her from the giant; and then find out after all that she was the daughter of the king of the gold-mines, and had her pockets full of diamonds. That is the fate I should like for Laurie. Somehow he seems to deserve it; and it never would occur to him to plan anything for himself.'

'Now I like that,' cried Mrs. Rich; 'I like you for being so proud of your brother. There are heaps of heiresses, you know, in Italy—at least so one reads in books; ladies travelling alone, that a young man could make himself very useful to, and then in common gratitude—— Why it is quite like a fairy tale. And when will your brother go? and what will he do in Italy? Mr. Rich has promised to take us there next winter. I have wanted to go all my life, Mr. Frank. It has been my dream. How strange it would be if we should meet him! But, alas! we have no heiresses,' said Mrs. Rich, casting a glance at Nelly, who, for her part, gave her mother a quick, indignant look.

'We shall go like a caravanserai,' said Nelly, 'with servants, and companions, and all sorts of dead-weights. Papa says he means to take that Count with him who is sick, and heaps of people. What I should like to do would be to go all by myself, and live out of the English quarter, and see all the pictures, and never say a word to anybody. Fancy going to Rome and somebody saying to you, " Isn't it lovely?" as if it were a scene in a pantomime! I do so hate all that. I hate the books about parties to the Colosseum and rides in the Campagna. I want to go to Rome, and live and work. I wish I were your brother. I wish I could go wherever I pleased, and run about everywhere alone.'

'I wish you could go with Laurie,' said Frank, and for the moment it was said with absolute simplicity, without a thought of his scheme; 'that is precisely what he will do; and he knows everything,—where to go, and what to see.' Then he caught the odd, inquiring glance Nelly shot at him, and grew confused, he could scarcely tell why. 'Of course, that is nonsense,' he said, with a laugh. 'But it must be the pleasantest of all when two people, just two, can ramble all about the world alone.'

Then there was another pause. What did he mean? He asked himself the question, and could not answer it. Was it that he himself would like to be one of the two, with a bright, little, vivacious, enthusiastic creature by his side to make everything interesting? Or was it Laurie who should take that place? Frank was so bewildered that he did not know; and Nelly, sitting opposite to him, was so softened by this curious talk, and looked so much a sweeter version of herself, as with her face crimsoned and her eyes lit up, she sent a glance at him now and then, half stealthy, half candid, that the heart began to beat in the Guardsman's bosom. Not that he cared much for Rome, or for rambling about the world in general. The pictures would bore him. The rides in the Campagna and the parties to the Colosseum would be best for Frank; and as for running about among all the old holes and corners as Laurie did, would not India be a thousand times better, with promotion, and fighting, and tigers, and general novelty? Clearly Providence had made a mistake about that dog-cart. It was Laurie who should have been stranded at Richmont, and left to concert an Italian tour with Nelly Rich. How perfectly they would have suited each other! But all the time Frank's heart felt soft to the bright, sparkling creature, who was actually waiting, expecting the next words which he should speak.

'It is very stupid on my part to talk like this,' he said, with a little forced laugh. 'I shall be crossing the Desert most likely when you are on your way, or creeping about Bombay or Calcutta, or some other wretched place. But I must tell Laurie to look out for you, Mrs, Rich. He is sure to be of use,' he added, hastily. And then Frank's temples throbbed and grew crimson, and his heart gave a jump. Was it that Nelly sighed, and gave her head a little, scarcely perceptible shake, like one who has relinquished some pleasant thought? It was intensely flattering, and Frank could not but feel the compliment. What a dear little thing she was! How warm-hearted and how discriminating in her judgment! Frank felt disposed to kiss her hand, or even her cheek, out of pure gratitude. But still he was not disposed to give up India and his own way, and wander over the world with her, even had she possessed twice fifty thousand pounds.

And there was still the music going on at the other end of the room, and Mr. Rich clapping his hands at the conclusion of each melody. It was very different certainly from the programme up-stairs in the dark in the music-room; but yet there was a charm in the quaint old airs which Alice went on playing one after another, over and over again, without a sign of weariness. A distant, visionary, unconscious creature, still unawakened to any sense of personal life, rapt in the strains of her own music—half child, half angel—as calmly indifferent to him and every man as though they had all been like old

Rich! Somehow this was the image which most captivated the young man's perverse fancy. He turned his chair round and listened when the talk had come to this point. And Nelly did not wonder. It seemed as if all had been said that could be said thus. And Mrs. Rich began to applaud loudly. And then the Saturday came to an end. It was only the second time he had been in this house. That was the extraordinarily ludicrous part of it! In such a house men grow quickly intimate.

CHAPTER XIII.

SUNDAY.

PEOPLE are apt to talk of Sunday in the country as a pleasant thing, and yet there are few things which require a more delicate combination of circumstances to make it bearable. Far be it from me to say a word against the English Sunday which is good for man and beast, and only a little heavy upon the idle portion of the world, who have no particular occasion for rest. Sunday at home, with one's own occupations and pleasures about one, is precisely what one chooses to make it,—an oasis in the desert, a peaceful break upon the frets of life, or a weariness and a nuisance, according to the inclinations of the individual. But your Sunday is taken out of your hands when you visit your friends. Frank Renton was nothing more than an ordinary young man, neither less nor more devout than the average; and felt the weekly holiday often enough lie heavy on his hands. But he, like everybody else, floated upon the surface of the Sunday at Richmont,—a waif and stray, without any will of his own, to be made what his entertainers pleased. Sunday usually comprises morning church, which is one's duty, and a blessed relief from one's friends; and then lunch, which is a happy interlude of life; and then a dreadful afternoon to be got through somehow; enforced aimless walks, if it is fine; aimless compulsory talk, in any case; if it rains, confusion and despair till dinner comes,—a heavenly interval of occupation! After that, if there is anything at all genial in the nature of your interlocutors, the evening may be got through, with the assistance of sacred music; but, oh, the joy, the relief, the satisfaction, when ten o'clock comes, and one is justified in lighting one's candle and going to bed! Two girls in the house to walk with, and talk to, naturally modified this frightful programme to the young man. They all walked to church in the morning,—for Mr. Rich was old-fashioned,—and after luncheon looked at each other to know what was to be done. There was the flower-garden to visit, and the stables, and Mr. Rich's favourite walk round the grounds. Frank, being a stranger, went through the whole of these varied operations. He visited the flower-garden with Mrs. Rich, and the stables with Alf, and made the round of the little park with the father and son together, and had all the views pointed out to him. 'But you know all this ground as well as we do,' the millionnaire said, though not until after he had cheerfully pointed out everything that was to be seen, and all the points of vision. 'Ten thousand times better,' Frank groaned to himself; but he was too civil to speak out. It was a lovely day, in the end of April; heaps of primroses were clustering in the woods, and the flower-beds were gay with the first flush of spring; the lilacs and laburnums were beginning to bloom; the orchards were all white, and the air full of perfume.

On such a day, as Mr. Rich justly said, it was a pleasure merely to be out-of-doors. But Frank, who had abundant opportunity of being out-of-doors, was indifferent to the pleasure. He had not anything particular to say to Alf, and Alf had nothing particular to say to him. So that Mr. Rich had it all his own way, and did the chief part of the talking, and enjoyed himself. He went through the walks, a little in advance of the two young men, with his hands folded under the tails of his coat. His step was brisk, though theirs was sufficiently languid. 'This was a sad desert when I came here,' he would say, turning round, and bringing them to a stop for a moment, 'I had cartloads of rubbish cleared away from this bank,—scrubby bushes, all choked and miserable, without air to breathe or space to grow in. I had 'em all cleared away, sir. And over there, there had been a little landslip, as you see, which I stopped just in time. The whole slope would have fallen with those pretty birches, but for what we had done. You can see how it's all bound and shored up. They told me I never could manage it; that a City man knew nothing about such things. But just look at it now, and tell me if anything could be more steady. It would defy an avalanche, that bank would.' And Mr. Rich stopped and patted the slope with his fat hands.

'It seems beautifully done,' said Frank, and Alf gave a little grunt, as who should say, The old fellow knows what he is about.

'I flatter myself you won't see better work anywhere,' said the millionnaire. 'We City men know a thing or two, Mr. Frank. We may not be so fine as you soldiers, but we have an eye for practical matters. I was not much to brag of in the way of prosperity when I first came to this neighbourhood. We took a little house down here, my wife and I, for change in the summer; and I set my eye on this place. I said to myself, 'If I thrive I'll settle there, if money will buy it.' And there's nothing money will not buy. Here I am, you see, and my children after me. What would the Beauchamps have thought if they had known that the very name of their place was to be changed, and it was to be called after the Riches, people nobody ever heard of? But a great many people have heard of me now.'

'Immense numbers, I am sure, sir,' said Frank, throwing away his cigar. He had the natural civility of his family, and could not turn an absolutely deaf ear, sick as he was of the monologue. Even Alf took his cigar out of his mouth, and looked at it curiously, as if it perhaps could clear up the situation. 'All the same; I don't see that we are anything remarkable,' said Alf; which was almost as great a puzzle to his father as a similar accident was to Balaam.

'Oh dear, no, not all remarkable,' said Mr. Rich, after he had stared wildly at his son; and he gave a glance at Frank, and a little nod, to signify his appreciation of his boy. 'I don't suppose you soldiers have much need for brains,' he added, with benevolent jocularity. 'But to return to the subject. I don't know if you have observed how much I have done to the house, Mr. Frank. That music-room Nelly is so fond of was the merest wreck and ruin. Lumber in it,—actually lumber!—old pictures turned against the wall that were not worth sixpence, and trunks full of old papers, and everything that is most dreary. I had Runnymede, the architect, down, who knows all about that style of thing. I said, "Name your own price, and take your time, and come and dine with me whenever you are in the county." These were all the conditions I made, and in six months, sir, I had everything restored; and as pretty a little domestic chapel,—the best judges tell me,—as exists in England. All money, sir,—money and a little taste. You may think I have too high an opinion of what money can do; but I don't think one can have too high an idea. It can do anything. It's the greatest power known. You may have the best intentions in the world, but you can't carry them out without money. You can't serve your friends without money; for influence means money, you know, however incorruptible we are now-a-days. When I stand and look round me, and see all the changes that have been made, I feel that nothing but money could have done it. We did not have all this by birth, as the Beauchamps had. You should see my cattle at the farm. The Beauchamps never could afford to keep up that home-farm. I feel sorry for them; but it was clearly the best thing they could do to go away. They were keeping the sunshine off the land, and preventing it from thriving. You must have money, Mr. Renton, before you can do anything. It would be a great deal better for you young men if you recognised that at the first start.'

'I don't see what good it would do us,' said Frank. 'We can't invent money. Of course I know it would be very nice to have it,—but wishing is not having;' and with that he turned his eye towards the music-room, the windows of which were open. He was wishing to be there, there could be no doubt; but I don't think there was any calculation in his head, or at that moment the smallest recollection of the fifty thousand pounds.

'That is true,' said Mr. Rich; 'but when it comes in your way you should know better than to put it aside, as I have known some foolish young fellows do. There is your brother, for instance. Knowing who he was, and being neighbours, and so forth, why I'd have bought anything of his own as fast as look at it,—anything! As for merit, I should never have asked if it was good or bad. But, no! Instead of taking me to his own studio, where he must have had something to show,—must have had, don't you see, or what is the good of a studio at all?—he took me to Suffolk's and I bought that picture instead. That is what I call running in the face of Providence. Serve your friends next to yourself, if you like,—I don't object to that; but to serve them before yourself is going counter to every right feeling. Friendship is all very well, but you can command even friendship if you have money enough. You prefer to think of disinterestedness and all that sort of thing, you young fellows; but the only man that can really be disinterested is a rich man. Therefore be as rich as you can,—that has been my motto all my life.'

Frank laughed, though he did not much like the lecture. 'That is all very well,' he said; 'but how are we to grow rich, except on the turf, or at cards, or something? And you are just as likely, for that matter, to grow poorer than richer. They are having some music up there,' he said, turning decidedly in the direction of the music-room. Mr. Rich shook his head.

'You won't make much by music,' he said,—'at least, you amateurs don't. If I were Mrs. Severn I'd train that girl for the stage, or something. Why not? She must work for her living, poor thing! And do you take my advice, Mr. Frank,—don't waste your chances, or refuse a good thing when you may have it. Friends are all very well, but serve yourself first. You know the proverb,—"He who will not when he may, when he would he shall have nay."'

'If I should ever have any good things in my power I will recollect,' said Frank, laughing. But he was disturbed by this strange persistency. They had come at last, he thanked heaven, to the end of the walk; and it was on Mr. Rich's lips to propose another round. 'I think I'll go up-stairs and see what the young ladies are doing,' said Frank, hastily. Then Alf uttered a haw-haw under his moustache, and his father chorused loudly,—a liberty which the subject of this mirth somewhat resented.

'Ay, do,' said Mr. Rich; 'more natural than listening to an old fogey chattering, isn't it? Go to the young ladies,—I don't doubt you'll be very welcome; but nevertheless, Mr. Frank, don't forget that I have been giving you good advice,—and very good advice, too, you'll find it. Come along, Alf.'

Frank turned back to the house with a wonderful sense of relief, while the father and son resumed their walk. What could old Rich mean? What were the good things that might be coming his way that he was to be careful not to refuse? The question sent the blood to his face, and a thrill, for which it was difficult to account, through his whole frame. Was it Nelly's fortune that was thus waiting his acceptance? Was it—— He quickened his pace, and felt his temples throb, and something buzz in his ears. He had put aside the idea. He had resolved in his own mind that it was Laurie who was to face this question; but Laurie was gone, and, so far as he could see, everybody was agreed in thrusting it on his own notice. Was it necessary that he should go over all the arguments once more? 'Serve yourself first and then your friends,' old Rich had said, as if he had divined the intention of the young soldier to transfer this possible piece of good fortune to his brother,—as if he had any right to transfer Nelly Rich to any one! All this time she might be, and probably was, quite unconscious of the whole business. A girl might flirt a little with a man without ever thinking of him after. He was the only fellow at present with whom she could flirt. His face grew hotter and hotter as he went up-stairs. 'Don't waste your chances, or refuse a good thing when you may have it,' old Rich had said. After all, Frank himself was but a younger son. However matters turned out, he could not come in to a great fortune; and here was competence, comfort, security, before him. Frank had never been brought up to be anything but a young man of the world, and he did not know indeed how far it was right for him to put aside this chance. It was not a temptation he had to set his face against,—it was a reasonable, sensible prospect which probably he would be a fool not to seize upon. His freedom, after all, was but a poor thing to set against all that he would gain by such a marriage,—freedom for the mess, and the club, and the monotonies of a young man's life! For gaiety is as monotonous in its way as dulness; and Frank was man enough to feel that the kind of existence he was leading was not so good or so delightful as to be held fast at all costs. He would not be rendered miserable by being withdrawn from the mess. It would be no unendurable bondage to have a bright little companion to go everywhere with him! His mind dwelt for a moment on that thought with a softening sense of tenderness and gratified vanity. Then he pulled himself up, as it were, with a start. Was that Nelly, that sudden vision that had flitted before him? or was it—some one else? Breathless, not stopping to make any further investigation, he rushed up-stairs.

They were both there as usual;—Nelly in the low chair, with a book in her hand, talking to Alice, who stood leaning against the window, which was open. The sounds Frank had heard had been imaginary sounds. 'Come and talk,' Nelly had said, not caring at that moment for music. The soft air breathing through the window,—the sight of the budding trees and green of the park,—the sweetness of the flowers, were all music to Alice. How different it was from Fitzroy Square! The world, with which the child had as yet made so little acquaintance, breathed melodies to her from every corner. She was glad to play for anybody who asked her; but for herself, music was not so much a necessity there as at home. And she was very content to stand by the open casement with that sweetness which was sweeter even than the Lieder breathing about her, and the air rustling softly through her curls. Nelly was asking her all sorts of questions about home, and about Laurie Renton, who had at that moment an interest for her. Why had he gone away so suddenly? Had anything happened? 'You did not refuse him, did you?' she had asked, just as Frank entered the house.

'I,—refuse him? What do you mean?' cried Alice, opening her brown eyes.

'I mean what everybody means,' cried Nelly. 'Alice, my dear, you are a perfect baby. Did you never hear of a girl refusing a man before? Then you must have been very badly brought up. Perhaps you think we are to give in to them whenever they ask us; but that would never suit me.'

'I have not thought anything about it,' said Alice, with a sudden blush on her innocent cheeks.

'And yet you are sixteen,' said Nelly. 'I had not only thought about it, but done it, before I was your age. But then I have money. In this house we think a great deal of money. It seems quite right and natural to them all that men should ask me, and pretend to be in love with me, because papa is rich. Did you hear Frank Renton say last night he would never marry for that? Young men are all so frightfully prudent now-a-days; they laugh, and smirk, and say, 'Oh yes, of course,' and look at me as if I was something into the bargain that had to be taken with my fortune. I wish I had been an artist's daughter, like you. Then I could have taken up my father's profession, and nobody would have thought it strange. If I married that Laurie Renton now——' said Nelly, with meditative calm. Alice's blush grew deeper and deeper, and she turned away her face. She was a fanciful child, full of ideas which most people would think overstrained; and it made her cheeks flame, though she had nothing to do with it, to hear Nelly's philosophical peradventures. And then she remembered how suddenly Mr. Frank Renton had come in upon them last night. If he should by chance hear anything of a conversation like this!

'I don't know what you mean. I—can't—understand how you can—speak so,' said Alice.

'That is because you have been kept in the nursery, and never heard anything,' said Nelly; 'and much the best thing too. But it is long enough since I have been in the nursery, and there are always heaps of people about the house who do not care a straw for us. Why shouldn't I have married Laurie Renton? It would have been a very good thing for him, and he is living just as I should like to live. Ah! you have heard a great deal about love, and all that nonsense,' said Nelly, with a sigh.

'I have never heard anything about it. Why should people talk of such things?' cried the indignant Alice.

'Why shouldn't you talk of anything you think about?' said her companion; 'for of course you have thought about it, and read about it, and believe in it. But one comes not to believe. I don't care a straw for Laurie Renton. I don't know him. I have seen him once, and most likely I shall never see him again. But he and I might have made what you may call a reasonable match. He would have been a great deal the better of my money; and I should have been much the better of having him to go about with me, and take care of me, and tell me what to do. It would have been the very thing for us both.' And Nelly sighed again, having thus oddly brought herself just to the same point to which Frank's deliberations had brought him. But the sigh was not for Laurie; indeed, as she admitted, she did not know Laurie. If Frank had been like his brother, perhaps—— But he was not like his brother, nor was he like herself.

He was Frank, a young Guardsman and butterfly, like the rest; one of the men who had seized upon her own faulty sketch, and taken no notice of Suffolk's beautiful picture; a young fellow,—she said to herself,—without two ideas in his head; and yet——; 'I suppose you don't know much about his brother?' she said to Alice, leaning her arm upon the broad ledge of the window, and her head on that. The two girls were in this attitude, the one looking up to the other, when Frank himself arrived at the door.

This time he was very modest and discreet. He knocked, which startled them much, and then he asked, 'May I come in?' and entered softly after a pause. 'I was told I might come,' said Frank, folding his hands. 'I hope I have not done anything wrong.'

And Nelly looked up at him with a sudden blush. He was handsome, and young, and full of that splendid freedom and independence of movement which girls, being excluded from it, admire so intensely. Why should he insist on coming, and stand thus suppliant, with his hands folded, unless—— And last night he had knelt,—he had gone down on his knees as men are not in the habit of doing out of novels; and he was not like the other men. He was not exactly like them, at least, as they were like each other. And—— Nelly extended her hand, which was unnecessary. 'When a man has made up his mind in this determined way to effect an entrance, of course he must do it,' said Nelly. 'Come in, since you will come. Come and talk: we were talking of you, and you can give us all the information we want.'

'Talking of me?—that is too much happiness,' said Frank.

'That is, of your brother, which comes to about the same thing,' said Nelly, carelessly. 'Please give us a full account of all you have ever done, and your motives for doing it. I am full of curiosity to-day. It is Sunday, and one has nothing else to do. You had better begin at Eton, and tell us all about it,' cried the girl, laying back her head upon her high-backed chair, and looking full at him, with that calm observation in her face which is so exasperating to ordinary mortals. Frank was not exasperated, however, for there was a certain trace of nervousness in Nelly's audacity. As for Alice, she was horror-stricken.

'Oh, Nelly! how can you speak so?' she cried. To Alice, Frank Renton was a paladin,—too fine a being to approach with freedom at all, much less with candid questioning. Tell them everything he ever did! He would be angry, Alice thought. 'Oh, Nelly! how dare you?' she cried. And Frank was as much touched by the sound of that soft little exclamation as if her utterances had been those of the highest wisdom.

'Begin with Eton?' he said. 'It is so long ago I forget; and besides, I have always been so good, and gentle, and well behaved, that there is nothing to tell about me. I will tell you about Laurie, if you like. He was always an unlucky fellow,—too late for everything, and never quite sure whether he was right or wrong;—but the best fellow that ever was born. You would have liked Laurie if you had known him. And I wanted you to know him,' continued Frank. 'You would have suited each other so well.'

'Should we?' said Nelly, still looking up, and leaning back her head against the high back of her chair. 'Alice, please go and play us something. If you cannot manage the organ, there is the piano. Mr. Renton, tell me why you wanted me to know your brother, and why you thought he would have particularly suited me.' The question brought the guilty blood to Frank's face. What a little inquisitor she was! What strange, outspoken people were the entire family! 'Why did you think he would have suited me?—tell me,' she asked, looking fixedly into his face.

'Oh, I only thought,—I don't know that I had any motive;—I suppose because you are both fond of pictures, and both.'—here Frank paused to take breath,—'both,—why both artists, you know, in a way,' he said, with confusion; and during this broken utterance Nelly never once removed from him her brilliant eyes.

'I see,' she said quietly, while Frank looked out at the window, and saw Mr. Rich and Alf leisurely turning down towards the woods, and wished he were with them after all. Being advised for his good was bad enough, but to have his secrets thus demanded of him, and himself looked through and through, was worse. Confound it! what did she see? that he had been thinking of handing her over to Laurie? that he had been ready to traffic with her, presuming on the notice she had taken of him, and coolly planning to get her money for his brother? Was this what she saw, the little sorceress? Just then Alice, who had been sent away not to disturb the investigation, began to strike some plaintive chords on the piano. Ah, there was a creature who would never gaze at a man with such disdainful, suspicious scrutiny—a consolatory being, that would sweeten and smooth life, and make its sorrows bearable, instead of adding distraction to distraction! Frank felt sure that she had heard what was passing, and struck in at the most difficult moment to relieve his embarrassment and tranquillise his mind. Bless her! and of the other he had said, in his perplexity, Confound her! While he stood silent, looking out, the music stole about his heart and caressed and soothed him. He felt as if it had not been the music but the musician who did so; but of course that was nonsense. It freed him from the necessity of making Nelly any further answer, or asking what it was she saw, as a man strong in conscious right might have done. But all Frank's consciousness was of wrong.

It was Nelly who was the first to speak. She changed her position rapidly, and with it her manner and all that was objectionable in her looks. She leaned forward to him with her arm on the ledge of the window. 'I am impertinent,' she said; 'yes, I know you think so; but you must not be angry, Mr. Renton, as Alice says.'

'Angry!' cried Frank.

'Yes, angry; you might be, for I have been very disagreeable. I can't help being disagreeable now and then. You are very fond of your brother, and you wanted me to know him. It was a great compliment; and before you came I was saying to Alice how I wished I could have gone with him, and lived just as he did. But I can't, you know. A girl never can do anything she wants to do. That is what makes us envy you so, and admire your independence and your freedom,' said Nelly, looking up with different eyes,—with eyes as plaintive and insinuating as the music,—into Frank's face.

What could he do? He was mollified in spite of himself. 'Not so very independent, after all,' he said. 'A subaltern cannot boast of much in that way. I have to come and go as I am told, and ask leave before I can get away to see my friends.'

'And have a hard life altogether,' said Nelly. 'That is very sad; but if I were to ask leave ever so they would not let me go to Rome as your brother has done. I wish he had been my brother, and then I might have gone with him; but our poor boys don't understand that sort of thing. George knows about the money market and all that. And when Harry comes home he will probably be able to talk of indigo. Isn't it indigo? And Alf,—what should you say Alf knows most about, Mr. Renton?' said Nelly, with fun dancing in her eyes.

Poor Alf! Frank could not but laugh, though he was conscious of not being particularly clever himself. And it was impossible not to look down upon the sparkling face that gazed up at him. The music plucked at his heart and called him to attention; but he could not be so rude as to turn from Nelly. And then something might still be done in Laurie's interest. 'If you go to Italy next winter you will meet my brother,' he said; 'at least I hope so. I should like to be able to tell him to look out for you, if I knew when you were going;—I am sure he could be of use.'

'Next winter!' said Nelly, 'that is a long time off yet. No one can tell what may have happened before next winter. Do you expect to be gone from here that you speak in that uncertain way about where we are going?'

'I expect to be in India by that time,' said Frank.

'In India? Oh, yes, I remember; so you said,' said Nelly, and made a pause; then she asked suddenly, with a hurried glance at him, 'And you think there is nothing that could happen that would make you change your mind?'

'I don't know what could happen that would change my mind,' said Frank. He faltered as he spoke, knowing that there was one thing,—and that her very self,—which might alter all his plans; and yet feeling no desire to have his plans altered; but a more energetic determination, on the contrary, to carry them out. But what could a girl possibly mean by such a question? Not that, surely, of all things in the world! The pause that ensued was full of embarrassment. And the music swept in again suddenly and filled the whole place, and the rustling, palpitating silence between them. Nelly spoke no more. She let her head drop upon one hand, and with the fingers of her other beat time softly on the little table. The subject of the conversation was nothing to her; that was the inference in her change of attitude. 'Listen; how lovely that is!' were the first words she spoke; and yet she admitted that she did not care for music. Frank stood and leaned upon the open casement, with his eyes vacantly fixed upon the green world without; and though there was still the vibration in the air caused by the strange, secret, unacknowledged duel which had been going on between Nelly and himself, the sweet sounds once more entered into and possessed him. The strain took him upon its growing current like a toy, and flooded him, as it were, with changed sensations and a curious quietness. It soothed, and cheered, and stilled him all in a moment. And strangely enough, though he was a young man who should have known better, all these results seemed to him to have been produced not by the music but by the musician. It was to Frank as if Alice herself had whispered a soft 'Never mind' into his ear, and had charmed him instantly into such dreams as put away from him all recollection of the former embarrassment. He stood thus till long after Nelly had ceased to beat with her fingers on the table, and till she had almost grown tired of wondering at his absorbed countenance. She had suffered the music to end that particular conversation, feeling that it could go no further; but she had naturally expected that another conversation should begin after a proper interval. But such an idea did not occur to Frank. He was really absorbed in the music,— a thing which bewildered Nelly. She sat and beat time for five minutes, and then she stopped and looked at the Guardsman and at Alice with a look of wonder in her face. But Frank did not even observe her look. When she could no longer refrain herself, she burst into sudden speech.

'I do not understand music,' she said. 'Do you know what that means, you two? You are both so absorbed you have lost sight of everything else. Does it mean anything? Pray tell me what it is?'

'What it means?' said Frank; and Alice, though she had but half heard the question, paused as by instinct, the chords still vibrating under her fingers.

She had been perfectly passive, taking no part in the talk, not even knowing what was said; yet suddenly she too felt as Frank did, that they were engaged in opposite armies, two against one. Nelly affronted, a little hurt, angry without meaning to be angry, stood on one side—and on the other, the performer and the listener stood together, having forgotten everything. Alice felt this by instinct, with a quick pang of sorrow, yet of satisfaction. He and she were on the same side. It was pleasant not to stand alone.

'You look moon-struck,' said Nelly, more and more indignant, 'and it is still broad daylight. Yes; tell me what it means. What wailing spirit is in the keys? I cannot make it out. I have been listening and wondering for ten minutes. I know what books mean, and pictures; but I can't understand music. Tell me, you two, who are fond of it, what it is all about?'

Then Frank turned round upon Alice, and a look of mutual appeal passed between them. Mean? It was part of a mass; but Frank, for his part at least, did not know the solemn words to which the music was wedded; and he wanted no meaning that could be put into words. He felt what it was, instinctively. It was the only poetry of which his mind was susceptible. Alice was more fanciful, more imaginative, perhaps more intellectual than the young Guardsman; but yet the question was to her much what the question, What did 'In Memoriam' mean? would have been to a mind of different inclinations. The two looked at each other in a momentary wondering consultation. They were the two against one, connected by a secret bond. In a moment the colour flamed from one young face to the other. A sensation of happiness, tenderness, exquisite satisfaction and contentment, came over them both. Neither could explain, and yet both knew, felt, and felt together. And were ashamed!—Surely a more innocent bond could not have been. As for Nelly, with her quick eyes she saw the glance, and understood, and flamed up also, all over, with resentment and indignation, and a mortified sense of being superseded.

'Yes.' she said, with a hard little laugh, 'consult each other! I have asked heaps of musical people the same question; but they never could tell me. What is it about? Is there a story in it, or any meaning? Have a consultation; two heads are better than one. And please, when you make it out, tell me,' she cried, rising from her seat. 'I will go and get a book that I can understand.'

And before they could either of them say a word she was gone out of the room. The movement was so sudden, that they were both taken by surprise. 'What is the matter? Is she affronted?' said Frank, with a secret sense that he himself was the sinner. As for Alice, she was struck with consternation. 'What have we done?' she said, faltering, and then recollected herself, and blushed more deeply than ever. And there was a pause of dismay, during which the two strangers listened and waited for the return of the daughter of the house. Then Alice rose with tears in her eyes.

'Mr. Renton, I am so sorry,' she said. 'Miss Hadley always tells me musical people are so selfish, thinking everybody must like it. I will go and beg Nelly's pardon. I did not mean any harm.'

'Harm?' said Frank with indignation; but before he could add another word he found himself alone.

CHAPTER XIV.

FRANK'S PERPLEXITIES.

IT will be perceived, from all that has been said, that Nelly Rich used more freedom in the expression of her sentiments than is generally expected from girls of her age. A well brought-up young woman is not supposed to go off affronted when her admirer, real or supposed, shows a sudden interest in music, or anything else, independent of herself. The modern code of manners exacts that she should, if not grin, at least smile and bear it, with as much courage and as little of the air either of offence or resignation, as possible. Nelly betrayed her less exalted origin in this, that she allowed her real sentiments to escape her. There can be no doubt that she had given Frank intimations of her readiness to look favourably upon him which a more reticent girl would have blushed to give, and on which was built much that would else have seemed coxcombical in his behaviour. When a young woman asks if there is no possible chance that would induce a young man to change his mind about going to India or elsewhere, she is either beguiling and deluding that young man, or she is exhibiting, as far as she can, 'intentions' which are generally supposed to originate on the other side. And then her abrupt exit was a startling thing. When he was left alone in the music-room with the open piano, and Nelly's book lying on the table, Frank did not feel comfortable. He was left, as it were, master of the field. But it cannot be said that it is a pleasant thing to rout your friends so completely in their own house, and find yourself in solitary possession of their usual haunts. The evening passed, however, less unpleasantly than this scene would have led a looker-on to suppose. Alice, learning wisdom from experience, excused herself on the plea of being tired from playing; and Frank made his peace with Nelly, saying no more about his brother, and talking of the Beauchamps, and Mary Westbury, and his own home. The Renton woods were an unfailing subject,—as were also his own boyish adventures, into the history of which he was drawn by Mrs. Rich, whose inquiries were manifold. A man, especially if he is still a boy, has always a certain pleasure in uttering such reminiscences to sympathetic ears. The ladies laughed at his Eton scrapes, and were edified by his adventures on the river, and listened with ready interest, and smiles, and wanderings, to all his schoolboy tales. He felt himself of importance as he turned from one to another, and it pleased him to see Nelly seriously inclined to listen. She was interested,—it was no make-believe,—interested in Frank in the first place, and after that, like a true woman, interested in every detail about him. She liked to know how he had distinguished, and how he had committed, himself. It seemed to give her something to do with him; and Frank, too, felt the charm of confidence. She had put aside her waywardness, and listened with bright eyes of interest, with an eager ear, with smiles and exclamations. She made him describe Renton to her over and over again, and those points of view which people went to see.

'I could row you over,' he said, 'any day. From Cookesley to Renton is an easy pull. Let us make up a party and do it. The river is lovely, and if you have not seen it before——'

'I have never been higher up than Cookesley,' said Nelly; and thus it was arranged, though Mrs. Rich shook her head.

'We shall see when the time comes,' that wise mother said; and Frank perceived that it was only in case his mother should make up her mind to be civil that this little expedition would be permitted.

He made himself very agreeable to Nelly that evening, undismayed by the events of the afternoon. Alice was out of the way. She was at the other end of the room, looking over engravings, and resisting Alf's entreaties that she should play something. 'Nelly would not like it,' she said to herself; 'she is talking, and she likes that better.' And Alice felt herself somewhat silent and wistful, and wished herself back in Fitzroy Square. That evening it appeared to her that she was not enjoying her visit as she had expected to do. She missed her mother, and she missed the children, and Miss Hadley, and her usual duties, and perhaps something else too, though she did not know what was in her own thoughts. Sometimes she cast a wistful glance across the room at Nelly smiling and softened, with that look of absorbed attention in her brilliant eyes. Alice had been shocked by her friend's freedom of speech, but, as was so natural, impressed by it also. Unconsciously she herself began to speculate about Nelly. Could there be—as girls say—anything between her and Frank Renton? Was that why she was cross, and was it not the music? Alice felt herself to be pushed aside, and it was not a cheerful feeling; but fortunately the only form it took was a longing for home. She had home to fall back upon whatever might befall her here. If any vague discontent came down upon her heart, happiness and peace, as of old, dwelt and waited for her in the Square. This was her feeling, as she sat in the distant corner looking over the photographs. Alf had settled down sulkily when she refused to play to him, on a sofa near, and Mr. Rich slept the sleep of the just, the Sunday evening crown of the week's exertion, in an easy chair midway between her and the table, with a lamp burning brilliantly upon it, round which were grouped Mrs. Rich and Nelly and the young visitor. When Alice saw them laughing and talking, she felt that she would have liked to be there too, and have a part in the fun. But they did not call her, and she was too shy to go unasked, and she found the evening a little long.

When Frank Renton left Richmont the next morning it was with a mind by no means settled or at rest. He had received the warmest invitations to return from the parent pair, and Nelly was not slow to intimate that she looked for him soon. 'Come over here when Lord Edgbaston's refined society palls upon you,' Nelly said. 'Indeed, Edgbaston is a very good fellow,' Frank answered, apologetically. 'I know he is a lord,' was Nelly's reply. She did not care for a lord, nor had she given so much of her society or conversation to any one of her followers, though many of them were much more eligible in every way than Frank. This compliment went to the bottom of his heart. No doubt she was full of intelligence and discrimination, and could see the difference between one man and another; and she was, when she liked, the brightest little sympathetic creature, and awfully clever,—clever enough to make up a man's deficiencies in that way; but yet——! These were the young man's thoughts as he walked down to Cookesley to get his boat. He was going to the Manor, after all, to see his mother; and on the way he turned everything over again in his mind. Nelly was very nice, when she pleased; and though her connexions were nothing to brag of, still that was not a thing which people took into severe consideration when a man married money, especially when the money was young and pretty. And yet——! Frank could not but ask himself how it was that the girl who took a fellow's fancy—the one he would really have gone after had he been able to choose for himself— should never be the one who had the fifty thousand pounds. It was a curious spite of fortune. When he directed his mind to the serious consideration of this grand question—the first great social problem he had ever tackled on his own account—a singular dissipating influence always arrested him. Stray notes of music would float across his mind,—a bit of a melody which compelled him to hum it,—a perplexing bar which would separate from everything else, and echo in his ear. And when he returned to the consideration of Nelly Rich, another little agile figure stepped in before her, the one shadow jostling the other out of the way with a curious reality. It was not he who did it, nor had his will any share in the matter. They did it themselves, independent of any influence of his. So that the more he thought it over the more perplexed he became; and yet it was not a matter which could be suffered to run on and be decided any time. It must be settled, and that at once.

With his head full of these thoughts, he walked down across the cheerful, blooming country to Cookesley. The day was quite bright enough for the expedition he had proposed to Nelly; and when the recollection of this proposed expedition came back to his mind, Frank fell into pondering whether his mother would call. Why should she not call? It was quite true that she was an invalid; and also true that she was in the deepest of mourning; but still, the carriage, with Mary in it, and a card, would do. Mere civility! he said to himself. And if it should be for Laurie's interest,—or even for his own! Instead of going to India. Frank knew that his mother would have visited anybody in the country on that inducement. And it might come to that. He stepped into his boat with so serious a countenance that the men at the wharf took note of it. 'Them Rentons, they ain't up to no good,' one said to another. 'The eldest gentleman, as was here the other day, was awful changed, and this one, as is the swellest of all, looks as black as if he was a-carrying of the world on his shoulders.' This chance observation Frank overheard as he glided his boat through the maze of skiffs into clear water. It made him smile when he was fairly afloat and out of reach of observation. He had more than the world on his shoulders. What would the mere world have been, or any superficial weight, compared to the task of deciding what his whole life was to be? According as he made up his mind now would be the direction and colour of his existence. No wonder he looked black. But how was it that the eldest gentleman had so changed? And Laurie was gone without giving any reason. It was hard to think that it was their father's fault,—the father who had been so good to them. Seven months before they had all looked up to him with the undoubting, affectionate confidence of sons who had never known anything but kindness; and now they were all scattered to the different corners of the world, separated from each other, broken up, and set adrift. Frank was more a man of the world than either of his brothers, though he was so young. He could not but ask himself,—Was not old Rich right? Mr. Renton's mind must have been touched. He could not have been guilty of such an injury to them all had he been in full possession of his reason. Thus, if he did not look black, he looked at least very grave, as he pulled up the river, unlike the light-hearted young Guardsman who had so often made the banks ring with his laughter and boyish nonsense. He was approaching his twenty-first birthday, and he was having the grand problem submitted to his decision. It was not pleasure and virtue, certainly, which stood before him offering; him the irrevocable choice. There was no particular sin in adopting either course, and no unspeakable delight; nothing infinitely seductive to move his senses, or loftily excellent to restrain them. If he were to marry Nelly and stay at home, he would be to all intents and purposes as good and as honest as if he went to India. And if he went to India he would be sufficiently well off, and quite as happy,—perhaps happier than if he stayed at home. The question was a fine modern one between two neutral shades of well-doing, and not a primitive alternative between black and white, salvation and ruin. You will say that to marry a girl he did not love would have been a sin; but Frank did not see it in that light. If he did marry her, no doubt they would get on very well together. Nelly was not, as we have already said, a temptation to be resisted, but, most probably, a sober duty which he ought not to neglect. He was not passionate, like Ben, nor was he meditative, like his brother Laurie. He was the practical man of the family. If it had been decided to be right, no doubt he would have done it like a man, and been quite comfortable ever after. The difficulty was that there was too much neutral tint about the whole question. It was possible that he might do quite as well for himself in India as by marrying money. The chances were too equal, the gain too uncertain, to make the decision easy.

Mrs. Renton received him as usual in her dim room with the blinds down, a bottle of medicine on the table, and her arrowroot in the background. It was a different atmosphere, certainly, from that of Richmont. His mother wept a few tears as Frank kissed her. She was apt to do so now-a-days when one of her sons appeared. And Ben's farewell visit had been but a few days before, and had shaken her more than anything that had happened since her husband's death. She could do nothing but talk of him. 'He was looking quite well, Frank, quite well,' she said, over and over again, 'though I am sure living shut up in London all winter would have killed any one else. And he is to sail on Friday,' Mrs. Renton added with a sigh. As for Mary Westbury, she, too, bore traces of having been moved by Ben's visit. 'Oh, he is quite in good spirits about going,' she interposed. 'I think he likes the idea.' Frank, with his new-born experience, felt at once that something must have happened, and that all was not merely simple, straightforward, cousinly friendship between Mary and Ben.

'I suppose that was why you did not send for me,' he said; 'but, mamma, you must take the consequences. Instead of only dining at Richmont, I have passed the Sunday there, and I hope you will be so polite as to call. They are very good sort of people, and they have been very kind to me.'

'Those new people!' said Mrs. Renton. 'What a house for you to spend Sunday in! Your note never came till yesterday, when the servants came back from church; and I thought of course you must have gone back to Royalborough. Mary will tell you all about it, and how we consulted what to do.'

'But, mother, I want you to call on Mrs. Rich,' repeated Frank.

'My dear!' said Mrs. Renton, sitting up on her sofa.

But Frank was aware that she must not be allowed to stand up for herself, and confirm her own resolution by talk. 'They are friends of Laurie's,' he said, making a little gulp at the fib; 'they are fond of him, and they may have it in their power to be kind to him, too. They are going to Italy next year.'

'My poor Laurie!' cried Mrs. Renton. 'He has written me such a nice letter. He says he could not come to say good-bye; that it would have been too much for him. So he says; but I am sure he was afraid to come to let me see how pale he was looking. You don't think it is anything about his lungs which has taken him to Italy? He might confide in you.'

'Why it is for his pictures, not his lungs,' said Frank, with the cheerful confidence of ignorance. 'Those Riches are friends of his. I am sure it would be good for him if you could make up your mind to call. Don't you think he is the sort of man who ought to marry money?' Frank added, with a little embarrassment, after a pause.

'To marry money! Is he thinking of marrying?—and he has nothing!' cried Mrs. Renton, with consternation.

'But if she had a good deal?' said Frank. 'He will never make any way for himself. Don't you see, he is too good-natured and kind for that. So I think a nice little fortune that would keep him comfortable would be the very finest thing for Laurie. And I wish you would call at Richmont.'

'Is it Miss Rich that is to supply the little fortune?' asked Mary, with a smile.

'Miss Rich is very nice,' said Frank, with some indignation. Though he spoke thus of Laurie, it was not with any particular hope in respect to him. But if he himself should marry Nelly,—which seemed much more likely,—he would not drop any word which could be brought up against her. 'She is very accomplished, and draws beautifully; but unless you can get my mother to attend to ordinary civility, they can't be expected to like it. And it may be the worse for both Laurie and me.'

'Neither Laurie nor you should have anything to do with such people,' said Mrs. Renton; and then she stopped short, and a new current of thinking rose up in her mind. 'I do not like such things to be spoken of, Frank,' she said. 'It is disgusting to hear some people talk of marrying money. Has the young lady a great fortune? Did you say she was nice? Sometimes the children of those vulgar people are wonderfully well brought up. They get all that money can buy, of course. And did you say they were fond of Laurie? He has never mentioned them in any of his letters. Poor Laurie! Will his pictures ever bring him in any money, I wonder? And he never can go travelling about on his allowance,—that is impossible. Did you say Miss Rich had a very large fortune, Frank?'

'Enough to be comfortable upon,' said the Guardsman. 'They would be immensely pleased if you would call.'

'Oh, my dear, I am not strong enough, nor in spirits to call anywhere,' said Mrs. Renton, sinking back on her pillows. But the seed had been dropped in the soil. Mary Westbury's opinion, when she and Frank were alone, was that she would go. Frank, for his part, found himself a great deal more anxious about it than he had the least idea he was. Perhaps because of Nelly; perhaps only because of the difficulty,—he could scarcely say.

'I shall feel very small if she does not go,' he confided to Mary; 'and really, you know, I had not the least claim upon them, and they were very kind to me.'

'I thought you said they were friends of Laurie's,' said Mary. 'He never mentioned them in any way; but people have begun to gossip about you, Frank. I nearly laughed when you were talking so wisely of Laurie. It never occurred to you that other people might be behind the scenes and know better. Everybody says it is you.'

'What is me?' said Frank, with some heat. 'I did not think you were the sort of girl to repeat such folly. Because Nelly Rich is a nice bright little thing, and would be the very thing for Laurie——'

'Laurie again!' cried Mary, laughing. 'You are the strangest figure for a match-maker! They say, Frank, that these good people have quite made up their mind to have a gentleman of Berks for their daughter: and that is why they have always been so interested about us. And then they came to know you,—the very thing they want. I don't know if it is true, but that is what they say.'

'They say a great deal of nonsense,' said Frank. 'But, Mary, I have never had an opportunity to ask you anything. How about Ben?'

And now it was Mary's turn to change countenance. 'I don't think there is much to tell about Ben,' she said, with unusual curtness of expression. 'He is going to America, you know.'

'But there is something more than that,' said Frank. 'I can read it in your face.'

'Then you know more than I do,' said Mary Westbury, cooling down into that dogmatic obduracy and calmness which is a gift of woman. 'I am sure Ben did not confide in me.'

No—and wild horses would not have drawn anything further from her, that was evident. Mary, who was always so open, and candid, and straightforward, closed up in a moment, put shutters to all her windows, sealed her lips as if hermetically. If there had been nothing this would not have been necessary; but Frank had not time to go fully into the question. He gave her a keen, scrutinising glance, and then was silent. No doubt Ben had got into some scrape or other; but that his brother was not to know anything about it was equally clear.

'It is dreadful that you should all be going off at once,' said Mary. 'Ben did come to bid us good-bye, but Laurie has disappeared without even so much as that. I wish you would tell me something about Laurie, Frank. He must have known somebody better than the Riches surely;—some of those artist people. When you went to see him in town did you never see any of his friends?'

'Laurie's friends?' said the Guardsman, and it is undeniable that certain confusion stole over him. It was a kind of duel that was taking place between his cousin and himself. They were both of clearer sight than usual, enlightened by experience,—both anxious to find out something they did not know, and conceal something they did. 'Oh, yes,' Frank went on carelessly, 'I have seen several of his friends;—Suffolk, the painter,—though I don't suppose you ever heard of him; and there is a Mrs. Severn, in Fitzroy Square,—I think he was most intimate there.'

'Tell me about her,' cried Mary. 'It is so odd of Laurie to go away without coming home; something must have happened to him. It might not be anything of that kind, of course; but tell me,—were there daughters? or any one?'

Frank cleared his throat, nor could he keep a certain glow of colour from mounting to his temples,—most foolish and uncalled for, it was no doubt,—for Mrs. Severn's household was not, and never could be, anything to him. Either it was Mary's eyes looking at him so keenly, or simply a little excitement hanging about himself. Or he must have taken cold somehow on the river.

'Daughters?' he said. 'Oh,—well,—children, that's all; there is one little girl that plays charmingly,' Frank added, with easy candour; 'but Laurie never cared for music. I don't think there's anything in that.'

'And it could not be Miss Rich?' said Mary, fixing her eyes more keenly than ever on the young fellow's face.

Then his countenance cleared. He was himself unaware of the change of expression, but Mary saw it, and perceived at once that Nelly, though he talked of her so much, was not dangerous ground to Frank. 'No; frankly, I don't think it could be Miss Rich,' he said, with a laugh. 'I think it would be a capital thing for both; but I cannot say that I believe either of them have thought of it for themselves.'

'But this Mrs. Severn———?' insisted Mary, and she was aware of an immediate gleam of intelligence and embarrassment in his eyes.

'She is a painter' said Frank, 'and a widow, and a very nice woman,—at least I suppose so. To hear Laurie chattering to her you would think he found her so. I cannot say I remarked it particularly myself.'

'And young?' said Mary, breathless with her discovery.

'Oh dear, no,' said Frank, 'not at all young;—not old either, I suppose. A certain age, you know; that sort of thing. But really, if you are interested about her, you must apply to Miss Rich. I did not observe her much. Her little girl,' Frank continued, with again that soft drop of the eyelids, and gleam of sudden light from beneath them,—'she I told you of, who plays so charmingly,—is at Richmont now.'

'Oh!' said Mary. And Frank turned away to the window as if the conversation had come to a natural end. And as for his cousin, she seemed suddenly to have made a discovery; and yet, when she thought it over, could not make out what the discovery was. The little girl who played could not surely have anything to do with Laurie; or was it Frank himself who was moved by her music,—or,—. Mary was left as much in the dark as at the beginning. 'The boys' had all gone off on their separate courses; they had escaped out of the hands of their old confidante and unfailing sympathiser; and the idea grieved her. She would have given a great deal to have been able to read the meaning of that look in her young cousin's eyes. She would have liked in all sisterly tenderness and faithfulness to fathom Laurie's secret,—for a secret Mary felt there must be. As for Ben, that was different. She felt that the secret in his case was somehow her own.

'Old Sargent ought to be looked after, really,' said Frank. 'It is all very well to have a gardener who is a character; but those flower-beds are disgraceful, Mary. You should see the garden at Richmont. I suppose my mother does not mind; but, at least, you might look after it. I shall give the old beggar a piece of my mind if he comes across me to-day.'

'Are the gardens really so wonderful at Richmont?' said Mary; 'altogether it must be an extraordinary place. I have met Miss Rich once, and I thought her pretty; of course, I should like to know her, if—— But, Frank, you might tell me—— If that is really what you are thinking of——'

'If what is really what I am thinking of?' said Frank, with a laugh. Mary had laid her hand on his shoulder, and was looking at him anxiously. His face had changed once more,—the gleam under the eyelash, the softened droop of the lid, had disappeared: but the colour rose again to his face, though with a difference. 'Don't inquire too much,' he said, turning away from her. 'I can't tell you myself. No one can say what may happen. Don't ask me any more questions, there's a dear.'

'But Frank, only one thing;—is she really so very nice?' said Mary, with another effort to catch his eye.

'Oh, yes; she's very nice?' answered Frank, with a little impatience in his tone.

'And if,—that were to happen—you would not require to go to India?' said Mary, dropping her voice.

'No.'

'And,—only one word;—are you really, really fond of her, Frank?'

The young soldier shook her hand off his shoulder, and turned away with an impatient exclamation. 'Good heavens! what an inquisitor you are! Can't you let a fellow alone? As if a man can go and make a talk about everything like a set of girls!' he cried, and stepped out of the open window on to the lawn, where old Sargent was visible in the distance. Frank went straight to the old gardener, and began to give him that piece of his mind he had promised, using considerable action, and pointing indignantly to the flower-beds, while Mary stood and watched, feeling that old Sargent was suffering the penalty of her own curiosity. Her cousins had always been as brothers to Mary,—at least the two younger ones had been brothers; and it vexed her beyond description to find how they had both glided out of her knowledge upon their different paths. She was a good girl, and very sensible, everybody allowed; but still she was young, not in reality any older than Frank, and the first idea of love was sacred to her mind. The almost admission he had made struck her dumb. To think of a girl,—in that way,—and yet not be fond of her! Mary shrank from the idea as if she had received a blow. Of course, she had heard of marrying money, as everybody else has, and, like everybody else, had seen people who were said to have married money, and got on together as well as the rest of the world. It was a thing acknowledged in the society she was acquainted with to be a duty incumbent upon some people, and creditable to all. But yet,—one of the boys! Instinct carried the day over principle as inculcated everywhere around her. "With other people it might be well enough,—but one of us! Mary stood in great consternation, looking on while Frank delivered his lecture to the gardener. She wanted to say something more to him, and did not know how. Had not he better, far better, go to India, after all? It would be sad to have none of the boys at home, but not so sad as this. And then Mary cast a half-angry, half-pitying thought at Nelly Rich, poor wealthy girl, the 'money' whom Frank was trying to bring himself to marry. She was angry, like a woman, at this creature for so much as existing, and yet,—'Oh!' said Mary to herself, 'what a fate for a girl,—to be married as money! And how frightful, for Frank! and how base of him! and yet, oh, what a fate! poor, poor fellow!' This is how her thoughts went on as she stood gazing after him, with consternation, and sympathy, and horror, and indignation. Everybody would say it was quite right; even Mrs. Renton would go and call, for this reason, though for no other, and smile upon them for their wealth. Mary grew sick as she thought of it. Ben was infatuated, and blind, and foolish. He was going to be miserable in a different way, for the creature he loved was not good enough for him. But it was not so bad as this.

In the meantime Frank was very bitter upon old Sargent about those flower-beds. He upbraided the gardener with taking advantage of his mother's illness and her indifference to external things. He was so solemn about such a breach of trust that the old man was struck dumb, and had not a word to say for himself. It was a satisfaction to the mind of the young master, who had been stung by Mary's injudicious question, more than he could have avowed. Frank had to take a long walk, and do an immense deal of thinking, before he could bring himself back to his former easy sense of duty. Fond of her! Of course, if he married her he should grow fond of Nelly. He liked her very well now, or he never would think of it. Girls were such foolish creatures, and could not understand all the breadth of a man's motives. A pretty thing the world would be if it were built only upon what they called love. Love! It was very well in its way, but society wanted a firmer, more practical basis; but yet, notwithstanding all these reasonings, Frank was more shaken than he had yet been by the surprise and the pain that had come into Mary Westbury's face.

CHAPTER XV.

PROGRESS.

BEFORE Frank returned to his quarters, he had received his mother's promise that she would call at Richmont. 'I have given up all that sort of thing on my own account,' Mrs. Renton had said. 'I will never go into society again. All that is over for me; and I hope your friends understand so. I can't entertain people, you know; but anything that is for my boy's interests,' the mother said, magnanimously, sitting up among her pillows,—that was quite a different matter. Fifty thousand pounds going a-begging, so to speak, when such a small affair as her own card, or, at the worst, ten minutes' talk, might determine the house to which it should come! There could be no doubt about a mother's duty in such circumstances. Laurie, it was true, was out of the way; but there was no reason why Frank should not take advantage of such a windfall. Mrs. Renton's mind was not troubled by any of the scruples that moved Mary Westbury. Perhaps,—it was so long since it had come in her way,—love had lost its importance in her eyes. Perhaps she had never felt its necessity in any very urgent way. Mr. Renton had been the best of husbands, but yet it could not be said that there had been much sentiment, not to say passion, in their union. But Mrs. Renton, like every other sensible woman, understood the value of fifty thousand pounds. She had already made a calculation in her own mind as to the income it would produce. 'It can't possibly be at less interest than five per cent,—with a father to manage it who knows all about money,' she said. 'Five per cent on fifty thousand makes twenty-five hundred. They might take Cookesley Lodge and live very comfortably on that; and I should have them always near me.' This reflection made Mrs. Renton not only willing, but anxious, to pay the promised visit. She questioned her son a great deal about Nelly before he left her. What she was like, and the colour of her hair, and her height, and a hundred other details. 'If she is pretty it is so much the better,' she said, with maternal indulgence for a young man's weakness. 'I do not say anything, Frank,' she told him, as she bade him good-bye, 'for I see you are turning it over in your mind. And you know I am not mercenary, nor given to think about money. Alas! there are many things that money cannot do! It can't buy health when one has lost it. But it has always been my opinion that to marry young was the very best thing for a man. And, my dear boy, if it is in your power to secure your own happiness, and other things as well, I hope you will be guided for the best.' She meant that she hoped he would be guided to the fifty thousand pounds. And Frank understood what she meant as well as if she had said it. Mrs. Renton had never been poor in her life, and yet she appreciated money; whereas Mary Westbury, who had been brought up in a very limited household, and by a very prudent mother, felt in this present instance a scorn for it which no words could express. When she went out to the door in the starlight to see her cousin off, her mind was full of thoughts half contemptuous, half bitter. There was no moon, but a soft visionary light in the skies, partly of the stars, partly that lingering reflection of light which makes a summer evening so beautiful. Mary stood in the dark shadow of the doorway and watched Frank getting into the dog-cart. She said her good-night with a certain plaintive tone. 'Good-night! but you don't say good luck, Mary,' cried Frank, as he lighted his cigar. She came out upon the steps, and looked up wistfully at him as he spoke. The shadows of the trees hung dark all round, swallowing up in gloom the road by which he was going; and in the opening, out of the shadow, Mary looked at him, and thought he looked half-defiant, half-deprecating, as he struck a light, which made his form visible for a moment. The horse was fresh, and stood with impatience waiting the signal to start. 'Good-night,' Mary repeated; 'I don't know about the good luck:' and then he was suddenly whirled away into the darkness. The dog-cart was audible going down the long line of avenue to the gate which opened on the highroad, and now and then appeared for a moment out of the shadow where the trees separated. She felt melancholy to see the boy thus dashing forth, doubting and unguided, into the world. She was very little older than he was, and yet Mary kindly felt the insufficiency of Frank's youth to keep him in the straight way, much more keenly than he felt it himself. He was going, and nobody could tell what he was going to. And there was nobody to stand in his way and advise him. Thus Frank went out of sight, and the two ladies stopped behind with their different thoughts. Mary was not alone in her knowledge of his intentions; the entire household was soon pervaded by a sense of the coming event. Mrs. Renton, as she took her arrowroot, could not but give a hint of what she supposed to be going on to her confidential maid, and that trusted creature was not reticent. 'Mr. Frank's going to marry a lady as has made a terrible fuss about him,' the butler said, 'as rich,—as rich——! I hope, when he comes into his fortune, he'll have something done to keep us a-going here. It's hawful is this quiet,—and us as always had so much visiting.' 'He'll beat the old ones all to sticks,' said the cook; 'but I always said Mr. Frank was the one.' Thus it will be seen that he left a universal excitement behind him, and that of a favourable character. A wedding in prospect is always pleasant to everybody, and the servants' hall was as much impressed by the duty of marrying money as was their mistress. Only Mary in her heart, and one small housemaid, were sensible of the other side of the question. From Mrs. Renton, down to the boy who blacked the shoes, the feeling, with these two exceptions, was general. To have married for any other reason might have produced as many criticisms as congratulations. Frank would have been set down as too young,—a foolish boy; but to marry money was a thing so reasonable, that nobody could but applaud.

And Frank himself felt all its reasonableness as he returned to his quarters. He took the train at Cookesley Station for Royalborough; and when he had to change carriages at Slowley junction, stood and kicked his heels on the platform, so absorbed in his thoughts that he had not leisure to be impatient. In every way it was the most reasonable, the most natural, the most feasible thing. He cast his eye round the county, as it were, as he stood waiting for the down-train. For a man who was going to settle down, no county could be better than Berks. It was his own county, in the first place, where his family were known and considered,——and then it had a hundred advantages. It was so near town that a man could run up for a day as often as it pleased him; a good hunting county, with pleasant society, and the garrison at Royalborough, in which there are always sure to be some of his regiment, within reach. He cast his eye metaphorically over the district, and recollected that Cookesley Lodge was to let, and also that pretty house near St. Leonard's. Either of them, he thought, would do very well for a small establishment. So far as this his thoughts had advanced. He settled a great many things as he stood on the platform at the Slowley junction, and paced up and down with echoing feet, neither fuming nor fretting, absorbed in his own thoughts. The station-master kept out of Frank's way, in fear of being called to account for the lateness of the train; but he was too much occupied even to think of the train. To be sure, he could afford a good hunter or two without interfering with the other needs of the *ménage* in respect of horses. He thought of everything,—from the little brougham and the pony-carriage, and the cart for his private use, down even to the dogs which should bark about the place, and hail him when he came home. He thought of everything, except of the central figure who would bring all these luxuries in her hand. Certainly, he did not think of her. A chorus of barking terriers, pointers, mastiffs,—I know not how many kinds of dogs,—seemed already in his thoughts to bid him welcome as he drew near the imaginary house. But there was no representation in his mind of any sweeter welcome. He imagined the terriers, but not the wife running to the door to meet him. That he left out, and he was not even aware of the omission. On the whole, it grew pleasant to the eye,—this imaginary house. A Renton was sure of a good reception in the county which had known the family for hundreds of years; and if he wanted occupation, there was the Manor estate, left in the lawyer's hands only during the seven years' interregnum, which he could always keep an eye on; and his mother's interests, and her own property, which she would be so glad to have him at hand to see after. Cookesley, on the whole, would be the best. It was near the Manor, and not quite so near Richmont; and then there would be the river for the amusement of idle hours. It was a pleasant prospect enough. Youth, health, a good hunter, a pretty house, a pleasantly-assured position, and,—say at the least,—two thousand five hundred pounds a-year! A man should have no call to mope who had all these good things. Something, it is true, he left out from the calculation, but there was enough to fill any man with very comfortable sensations in what remained.

Thus it happened that he had almost made up his mind when he got back to Royalborough. He had weighed all the arguments in favour of such a step, and had found them unanswerable. The arguments against,—what were they? It is, indeed, impossible to formalise them or set such weak pleas against the solid, sturdy weight of reason which lay on the other side. Indeed, there was nothing that could be called an argument,—certain wandering notes of music that now and then stole with a bewildering effect upon his ear,—faint, momentary visions of a face which was not Nelly's. But what then? To be fond of music is no reproach to a man, even if the future partner of his bosom does not play; and as for the face, why any face may spring up in your memory, and glance at you now and then by times without any blame of yours. Some people, as is well known, are haunted for days by a face in a picture; and what did it matter to anybody if Frank's imagination, too, were momentarily haunted by the picture which he had made of a certain sweet countenance?

He felt that he had quite made up his mind when he went to bed; but the morning brought back a certain uncertainty. What a pity that Laurie could not have been got to do it,—Laurie, for whom it would have been so completely suitable! leaving Frank free to go to India! He could not but feel that this was indeed a spite of fortune. Laurie, poor fellow! could not go to India,—he never would make his own way anywhere,—he would only moon about the world and make himself of use to other people; and, so far as his own interests were concerned, would end just where he began. Whereas Frank felt confident that he himself could have made his way. And Laurie wanted somebody to take care of him, to give a practical turn to his dreamings, to keep him comfortable in his wanderings to and fro. If he could only be sent for from Italy even yet! What could have tempted him to go to Italy at this time of the year, which everybody knew was the very worst time,—bad for health, and impossible for work? Frank shook his head in his youthful prudence at the vagaries of those artist-folk. They never could be relied upon one way or another. They were continually doing things which nobody else did,—going away when they were wanted at home,—staying when they should go away. It must have been some demon which had put it into Laurie's head to take himself off at this particular moment, leaving to his conscientious brother the task of dealing with that fifty thousand pounds. Indeed, the morning light brought home to Frank more and more clearly the sense that this step he was contemplating was duty. The evening had had certain softening effects. The pretty little house, and the hunters, and the terriers, and all the pleasant country-gentleman occupations to which the young man had been born, came clearly before him at that pleasant hour. But, by daylight, it was the duty involved which was most apparent to Frank. He had no right to allow such an opportunity to slip through his fingers. If he did so, he might never have such a chance again. To neglect it was foolish,—wrong,—even sinful. He gave a little half-suppressed sigh as he sat down to breakfast, feeling strongly that high principle involved some inevitable pangs. But should he be the man to turn his back upon an evident duty because it cost him something? No! Ben might take the bit in his teeth and go out to America to make his fortune, like the head-strong fellow he was; and Laurie might prefer his own foolish devices to every substantial advantage under heaven; but Frank was not the man to run away. He could see what the exigencies of his position demanded, and he was not one to shirk his duty. And then, poor boy! he rounded his deliberations by humming very dolefully a bar or two of a certain plaintive melody, and ended all by a sigh.

'Sighing like a furnace,' said Edgbaston, who came in unceremoniously, followed by Frank's servant with the kidneys,—for his thoughts did not much affect his appetite,—and his letters. 'My dear fellow, that's serious. Ah, I see you have a card for the grand fête. We are all invited, I think.'

'What grand fête?' said Frank.

'There it is,' said his friend, turning over the letters, and producing an enormous square envelope ornamented with a prodigious coat-of-arms in crimson and gold. 'These are something like armorial bearings, you know. By Jove! people ought to pay double who go in for heraldry to that extent. Mine is not as big as a threepenny bit. It's a case of swindling the Exchequer. The arms of the great house of Rich, my boy. Don't you know?'

'There are Riches who are as good gentlefolks as we are,' said Frank, already feeling that this scoff affected his own credit.

'Oh, better,' cried Edgbaston. 'We are only Brummagem,—I confess it,—with a pinchbeck coronet. But I doubt if our friends are of the old stock. Open and read, Frank; this day fortnight. Archery fête,—everything that is most alluring,—croquet, good luncheon, dance to wind up with. We're all going. Hallo! there's a note enclosed for you!'

'And why shouldn't there be a note enclosed?' said Frank, colouring high, and thrusting the small epistle under his other letters. 'I suppose all of you had the same?'

'The card was thought enough for me,' said Edgbaston. 'Well, well, I don't repine. But I say, Frank, if you are going in for that in earnest, I see no use in carrying on about India. And I came to tell you of a fellow in the 200th who wants to get off going. Montague,—he's to be heard of at Cox's. You can do what you like about it of course, but you can't go in for both.'

'For both?' said Frank; 'what do you mean? I don't know anything else I am going in for. Did you say Montague of the 200th? Going to Calcutta, are they? Thanks, Edgbaston. I'll think it over. Of course one can't make one's mind up all at once.'

'I advise you to think it well over,' said his friend; 'and the other thing, too. You may look as unconscious as you please, but you can't conceal that you are the favourite, Frank. And, by Jove, it shows her sense. She's as jolly a little thing as ever I saw, and there's no end to the tin. If I were in your place, I'd see India scuttled first. I don't know a fellow who might be more comfortable; and I can tell you, you'll be an awful fool, my dear boy, if you let her slip through your hands.'

'Stuff!' cried Frank. 'I wish you'd let a man eat his breakfast in peace, without all this rubbish. Archery fête, is it? I didn't know anybody went in for archery now-a-days; and, as for croquet, I am sick of it. I don't think I shall go. What sort of a fellow is Montague? The best thing would be to run up to town, and have a talk with him at once.'

'If that is what you have determined on,' said Edgbaston; 'but, Frank, if I were you, with such a chance——'

'Oh, confound the chance!' said Frank; and the rest of the conversation was based on the idea that his heart was set on the proposed exchange, on the prospects of the 200th, and his own immediate banishment. He thought he had done it very cleverly, when at last he got rid of his comrade. But Edgbaston was not the man to be so easily deceived. He explained the whole matter confidentially to the first group of men he encountered. 'Look here, you fellows,' he said; 'mind how you talk of little Rich to Frank Renton. He has made up his mind to go in for Nelly, and he's awfully thin-skinned about it, and sets up all sorts of pretences. Frank's the favourite, I always told you; I'll give you five to one they are married in six months.'

Thus Frank's affairs were discussed, though he flattered himself he had so skilfully blinded his critic. When Edgbaston was gone, he drew the little note from beneath the other papers. It was from Nelly, as he thought, and there was not much in it,—but yet,—

'DEAR MR. RENTON,—Mamma bids me say that she forgot, when you were here, to tell you of the little party to which the enclosed card is an invitation. They were all put up on Saturday, before you came, and we forgot them. And I open your envelope only lest you should think it strange that we never said anything about it. I hope you had a pleasant walk to Cookesley. The river must have been lovely.

'The fête is in my poor little honour, so I hope you will come. It happens to be my birthday;—not that anybody except my own people can be supposed to care for that; but you, who are so fond of your family, will excuse poor papa and mamma for making a fuss. You know I am the only girl they have; though I am only

'NELLY.'

'*Richmont*, '*Monday morning.*'

Only,—Nelly! It was a tantalising, seductive little note, which tempted a young fellow to answer, even when he had nothing to say. She must have written it as soon as he was gone. She must have been thinking of him quite as much, at least, as he had been thinking of her. Something of the natural complacency and agreeable excitement which, even when there is nothing more serious in hand, moves a young man in his correspondence with a girl, breathed about Frank as he wrote his reply. He told her he could perfectly understand the fuss that would be made, and that it was astonishing how many follies other people, who could not claim such a tender right of relationship, might be tempted to do for the sake of a little personage who was only,—Nelly. And then he begged pardon on his knees for the familiarity. Thus it will be seen that things were making considerable progress in every way. This snatch of letter-writing did more for the sentimental side of the question than half-a-dozen interviews. The pretty little note with Nelly's little cipher on it, the suggestions of the conclusion, the humility which asserted a subtle claim on his discrimination as a man fond of his own family,—all this moved Frank, who was not used to such clever little suggestive correspondences. For the first time it occurred to him that Nelly was a sweet little name, and that it would be pleasant to have its little owner rush to meet him when he went home. For one moment the hunters and the terriers fell into the background. Thus it will be seen that the affair made admirable progress in every possible way.

CHAPTER XVI.

MRS. RENTON'S CALL.

AND it was not later than the Wednesday after when Mrs. Renton, moved to the pitch of heroism by the possible advantages to her boy, and fortified by a large cupful of arrowroot, with some sherry in it, got into her carriage and called at Richmont. Mary accompanied her, full of curiosity and opposition. Mary herself had thought Nelly Rich 'nice' when she met her and had no particular call to be interested in her; but now her feelings were much less amiable. A little sprite of evil tempting Frank to do what he ought not to do,—this was the idea which now entered Mary's mind as to her little neighbour. But, nevertheless, of course she accompanied her aunt merely to smile and say polite things to everybody. She could not help it; it was the duty which life exacted of a well-bred maiden. It was a very fine day, and both the ladies sallied forth with the hope, common to people who pay morning visits, of finding that the Riches were out, and that a card would serve all purposes of civility. 'They are sure to be out such a beautiful day,' said Mrs. Renton. 'I hope you put some cards in my case, Mary; and write your name on one, my dear, that they may see we have both called, should like to pay every attention, in case of anything——' Mary made a little wry face, but scribbled her name all the same, without any remark. But when they drew up before the door at Richmont their delusions were all scattered to the winds. Everybody was in,—Mr. Rich, Mrs. Rich, Miss Rich; and Mrs. Renton, not without an effort, got out of her carriage. She was much impressed by the beautiful footmen who stood about the hall. 'Poor old Beecham!' she said in her niece's ear; 'it never was kept up as it ought to be in their time,—poor things!' and her heart melted towards the people who had everything in such order. 'It would be a lesson to Sargent to see that garden,' she said; 'only to see it. Oh, my dear, what money can do!' So went in, with her mind prepared to be friendly. Mrs. Rich received her in a considerable flutter. She was the first county lady of any importance who had done her so much honour. Finer people than Mrs. Renton, indeed, had come down from town to the Riches' parties, and taken the good of all that was going, and laughed at the hosts for their pains; but no leader of the county had yet presented herself. Mrs. Renton was, as the maids say, *passée*, but, nevertheless, her countenance was as good as any one's for a beginning. She might have withdrawn from the world, but so much the mere was the world likely to be impressed by her example. It was the first ray of the sunshine of local grandeur in which it was the desire of Mrs. Rich's heart to bask.

'This is so kind,—so very kind,' she said in her flutter. 'You must let me send for my daughter. She is in her favourite room, with her pictures and her books; but she would not miss you for the world. This is the most comfortable corner, with no draughts. Some tea, Baker; let Miss Rich know Mrs. Renton is here.'

'Pray, don't disturb yourself,' Mrs. Renton said. 'I scarcely ever go out; but it is such a lovely day.'

'And so kind of you!' repeated the lady of the house. 'I had heard so much of your family,—such nice young men, and everything so charming, that I confess I have been longing for you to call. And I have the pleasure of knowing two of your sons, Mrs. Renton,—Mr. Frank, and the one next to him,—Mr. Laurence, I think,—delightful young men. I hope Mr. Frank does not really mean to go to India. It would be such a loss to the neighbourhood. I was telling him he ought to marry an heiress, and settle down in the county, and make himself comfortable. I told him I should have you on my side. And such a good son as he seems to be,—so fond of you. He surely cannot mean to go away.'

'I am sure,' said Mrs. Renton, 'I should be very thankful if any strong inducement fell in his way to keep him at home.' And just at this moment Nelly came in, in a white gown, with her favourite scarlet ribbons. The dress was not of flimsy materials, but dead, solid white, relieved by the red; and there was a flush upon her dark, clear cheek, and unusual brilliancy in her eyes. Frank's mother stopped short with these words on her lips, and looked at Nelly. Was she the strong inducement? She was a little agitated, and the nervousness and excitement made her almost beautiful. Mary Westbury stared at her too, open-mouthed, thinking, after all, Frank might have other motives. Nelly came in with a touch of shyness, very unusual to her. The nearest female relations of one who, perhaps———. If she had been even more agitated than she was, it would have been natural enough.

'This is my daughter Nelly,' said Mrs. Rich; 'my only daughter. She can tell you more about it than I can. We are to have a little fête for her on Monday week,—archery and croquet, and that sort of thing, and a dance in the evening. It would give us all the greatest pleasure if Miss Westbury would come. Nelly, you must try and persuade Miss Westbury. Indeed, I assure you, I spoke to Mr. Frank quite seriously,' Mrs. Rich added, sinking into a confidential tone, as she changed her seat to one close to her much-prized visitor. 'And he is so fond of you. I am sure he will not go if he can help it. How nice he is! and how popular among the gentlemen! We were delighted with the chance which kept him here all Sunday. Sunday in the country is such a nice domestic sort of day. There is nothing like it for making people acquainted with each other. I was so glad when I heard the hours pass and no sound of wheels. I think before he left us that he got really to feel that we were his friends.'

'He was very grateful to you for your kindness, I am sure,' said Mrs. Renton, who, though she could talk herself upon occasions, was fairly overflooded and carried away by this flowing current of speech.

'Oh, grateful,—no!; said Mrs. Rich; 'that word would be quite misapplied. It is we who should be grateful to him,—a young man accustomed to the best society,—for putting up with a family party. And your other son, Mrs. Renton, is delightful too. We met him in town. He took us to a friend of his, Mr. Suffolk, the painter, where Mr. Rich bought a most lovely picture. I should ask you to go up to the music-room and look at it but for the stairs. It is a trial going up so many stairs. Yes, we have done a great deal to the house. It must be strange to you, coming to call at a house you once knew so well. But, as Mr. Rich says, it is not our fault. We gave a very good price for it; and, if we had not bought it, some one else would. My husband has laid out a great deal of money upon it. He has excellent taste, everybody says; and, of course, being well off, he does not need to consider every penny, as, unfortunately, so many excellent people have to do. You would be pleased if you saw the music-room,—quite a fine domestic chapel they tell us. We have hung Mr. Suffolk's picture there. If you are fond of pictures——'

'Oh, thanks! but I am not able to move about and look at things as I used to be,' cried Mrs. Renton, in alarm.

'To be sure,' said her anxious hostess; 'I ought to have thought of that. You will take a cup of tea? It is so refreshing after a long drive. Your son is quite a painter, I know, and so is my daughter. I tell her I cannot tell where she has got it, for we neither of us could draw a line to save our lives, neither her father nor me.'

Thus Mrs. Rich fluttered on, more fluent than ever, probably in consequence of her agitation. She was anxious to show herself at her best to her visitor, and the consequence was that Mrs. Renton went away sadly fatigued, and with a sensation of pity for Frank. 'I never could get a word in,' she said, indignantly, when she found herself safely ensconced once more in the corner of the carriage. 'Mary, have you some eau-de-Cologne? I feel as if I were good for nothing but to go to sleep.'

'Then go to sleep, dear godmamma,' said Mary, soothingly; 'don't mind me; I have plenty to think about, and I am sure you are tired. But Miss Rich is not so heavy as her mother,' she added, conscientiously. Her heart compelled her to do justice to Nelly, but it was against the grain.

'I don't know much about Miss Rich,' said Mrs. Renton, sighing in her fatigue. And she closed her eyes, lying back in her corner, and dozed, or appeared to doze. As for Mary, she had, as she said, a great deal to think about, and indulged herself accordingly, having perfect leisure. But Mary's thoughts had more of a sting in them than her aunt's. She was thinking somewhat bitterly of the difference between hope and reality. How hopeful, how promising had been all those young men, her cousins! She herself, feeling herself as a woman as old as the eldest, though she was in fact the same age as the youngest, had thought of them in the exalted way common to young women. Something better than usual, she had felt, must fall to their fate. And yet so soon, so suddenly, what a miserable end had come to her dreams! Ben, for whose express benefit some unimaginable creature had always been invented in Mary's thoughts, had allowed himself to be taken captive by the first beautiful face, unaccompanied by anything better. He had set a creature on the supremest pedestal who was not worthy to be his servant, Mary thought. He had been beguiled and taken in by mere beauty,—not beauty even in which there was any soul. And Frank was going to marry money! She did not know about Laurie. Perhaps had she been aware how far he had erred on the other side, and how his admiration for the soul and heart had led him away, she might have been still more horror-stricken. The difference between fact and expectation made her heart sink. Was this all that hope was good for? was this all that men were good for? to be deceived or to deceive; to fall victims to a little art and a pair of bright eyes; or to affect a love which they did not feel? Mary's heart sank within her, as she thought it all over. But her thoughts were interrupted by Mrs. Renton, who stirred uneasily every five minutes and said something to her.

'I never saw Beecham look the least like what it does now,' Mrs. Renton murmured, and then closed her eyes again. 'I wonder what they are really worth,' she would say next, drowsily, with her eyes shut, 'when they can afford to spend so much on setting the house to rights. But the woman is insupportable,' Mrs. Renton added, with much energy.

Thus they went home again over Cookesley bridge and across the smiling country.

'I am sorry you did not speak to Miss Rich, godmamma,' said Mary, as they approached the gate of the Manor; 'she is very nice, and just as well bred as other people. I never could have told the difference.' A sentiment which, forced as it was from her by pure conscientiousness, made Mrs. Renton shake her head,—

'Ah, my dear, I never could have been deceived,' she said. 'When I saw her sitting by you, I said to myself in a moment, How easy it is to see which is the gentlewoman! But she is not so bad as her mother,—I can understand that.'

'She is not bad at all,' said Mary; 'and if that is really what is going to happen,—though I hope not with all my heart——'

'Why should you hope not? 'Mrs. Renton cried, sitting bolt upright, and opening her eyes wide. 'How unkind of you, Mary! Don't you see the poor boy may never have such a chance again? If we had her entirely in our own hands we might make a difference. I must speak to Frank to begin from the beginning, keeping her as much as possible away from her own family. I wonder what the father looks like? The family are so objectionable,' said Mrs. Renton, seriously, 'that such an arrangement would be indispensable,—at least if he ever hoped to make his way in society. I don't think I ever was so tired of any call in my life.'

'But her family may be fond of her,' said Mary, 'all the same.'

'Fond of her, my dear!' cried Mrs. Renton, with energy; 'what does that matter? You would not have a young man like Frank give up the society of his equals on account of his wife's family. It would be absurd. Besides, it will be the very best thing he could do for her to bring her away from such an influence; nobody would ever visit her there.'

'But, dear godmamma,' said Mary, persisting with the unreasonableness of youth, 'if that is the case, would it not be better for Frank to withdraw from it altogether? For nothing seems to be settled yet, and I think he might still withdraw.'

Mrs. Renton gave a cry of horror and alarm. 'I can't think where you have got such foolish notions,' she said. 'Why should he withdraw? I tell you I think it is very doubtful if he ever has such a chance again. Weak as I am, you see what an effort I have made to-day on his behalf. I am frightened by that woman, but I would do it again rather than anything should come in his way. I would actually do it again!' said the devoted mother; and after such an heroic decision what could any one say?

As for Mrs. Rich and her daughter, they were quite unconscious of the feelings which moved Mrs. Renton. When the carriage disappeared down the avenue Mrs. Rich drew Nelly to her, and gave her a soft, maternal kiss. 'If you ever have anything to do with that old lady,' she said, 'you will not find her difficult to manage, my dear. I was thinking of that all the time she was here. "My Nelly will turn you round her little finger," I said to myself. She is not one of your hard, fine ladies, that are as easy to be moved as the living rock.'

'I don't see that it matters to me,' Nelly said, impatiently. 'Mamma, I wish you would not go on thinking that every new person we meet——. It is quite ridiculous. Why should I have anything to do with her? And I don't think she would be easy to manage. She gave me a look as I came in, and lifted her eyebrows while you were speaking,——'

'She was as sweet as sugar to me,' said Mrs. Rich, 'and I hope I can see through people as fast as any one; and it is you who are ridiculous, my dear. As if you did not know as well as I do that Frank Renton does not come here without a reason. He is a young man who knows quite well what he is about; and, of course, it is he that has sent his mother. That Miss Westbury did not look half pleased, Nelly. I should not wonder if she wanted to keep her cousin for herself.'

'Mamma, you are too bad; you are always saying things about people,' said Nelly. 'She may have all the Rentons in the world for me. What do I care for her cousin? And why cannot you let me alone as I am? I am much happier here than I should be anywhere else. I hate all those silly young men.'

'Ah! my dear, I know what nonsense girls talk,' said Mrs. Rich; 'but I hope I know better than to pay any attention. I should be glad to keep you always at home, Nelly; but I am not a fool, and that can't be. And isn't it better to fix upon somebody that is nice, and will be fond of you, and will not take you away from us? That has always been my idea for you. I made up my mind from your cradle, Nelly, that I would choose some one for you. Many people in our position, as well off as your papa is, would want a title for their only daughter; but I want somebody to make you happy, my pet, and that will not be too grand, and take you away from your father and me.'

'That you may be sure no man shall ever do,' said Nelly, returning her mother's kiss.

If Mrs. Rich had but heard what the other mother was saying as she drove home,—'I will speak to Frank to keep her as much away from her own family as possible!' Or if she had been aware of the calculation in Frank's mind about the houses which were to be had in the county, and his decision in favour of Cookesley Lodge as being farther off from Richmont! Thus the two sets of people went on in their parallel lines, never coming within sight of each other. After all, it was poor Nelly for whom the question was most important. She went away across the park in her white gown, with her pretty waving ribbons, and a sketch-book under her arm, after this talk with her mother. Nelly had not attained the highest type of maidenly refinement. She had adopted something of that exalted code of manners which entitles a young princess to signify her preference. She was rich and petted, and set upon a pedestal, a kind of little princess in her way; and she had perhaps permitted Frank to see that his attentions would be acceptable to her in a more distinct manner than is quite usual. She was even conscious that she had done so, but the consciousness did not disturb her much. Communing with herself vaguely as she sat down under a tree, and arranged her materials for sketching, Nelly came to some very sensible conclusions about the matter. Yes; she liked Frank; he was nice, and he was very suitable. Her eye had singled him out instinctively from the little crowd of Guardsmen the first time she had seen him. Perhaps he was not clever,—not so clever as could have been wished; but he was very good-looking, and he was nice. And then, perhaps, he was younger than she quite liked him to be; but Nelly told herself philosophically that you could not expect to have everything. Her own ideal had been different. He had been thirty at least, a man of experience, with a story and unknown depths in his life; and he had been a man of splendid intellect, and looked up to by everybody; and he had been dark, with wonderful eyes, and a face full of expression. Whereas Frank Renton was fair, with eyes just like other people's, very young, and not intellectual at all. But he was nice,—that was the point to which Nelly's reflections always came back. And he was a gentleman of a family very well known in Berks, and would please papa and mamma by settling near them. And Nelly in her heart secretly believed, though even in her thoughts she did not express it, that Frank, though he might please papa and mamma by settling down, would in the meantime please herself by taking her all over the world. His ideal of the hunters and the terriers was very different from her ideal, though the latter was quite as distinct in its way. No doubt a young couple moving about wherever they pleased, dancing through the world here and there, over mountains and valleys, stopping where they liked, rushing about wherever the spirit moved them,—would be a very different thing from the caravanserai progress through Italy contemplated by papa and mamma and all their dependants. This was Nelly's ideal, very clearly drawn, and most seductive to her mind. Two people can go anywhere;—a young woman need not mind where she goes, nor how she travels, so long as her husband is with her. Even Mrs. Severn had told her stories of the early wanderings of the poor, joyous young painter-pair, which had filled Nelly's heart with longing. To be sure he was no artist; but still his presence would throw everything open to his young wife, and make every kind of pleasant adventure possible. No longer would there be necessity for pausing to reflect,—Was this proper? was it correct to do so and so? 'You may go anywhere with your husband,' was a sentiment that Nelly had been in the way of hearing all her life.

Thus it will be seen that Nelly Rich was not so much to be pitied as Mary Westbury thought. This marriage,—if it came to a marriage,—was an affair involving mingled motives on her part as well as Frank's. Yet, as she sat under the tree with her bright face shadowed by the leaves, and her white dress blazing in the sunshine, she might have been a little lady of romance, with the flowers all breathing fragrance around her, and above the tenderest blue of summer skies.

CHAPTER XVII.

A STEP THE WRONG WAY.

WHEN Frank Renton had sent off his note to Nelly, accepting the invitation for the birthday fête, and adding such little compliments as have been recorded, a kind of sensation of having gone too far came over him. He had not yet by any means made up his mind finally, and he had no desire to commit himself. It seemed necessary, by way of holding the balance even, to take a step in the other direction. So he set about making very vigorous inquiries concerning the 200th, their destination, and the character of the officers, and all the other points of information most likely to be interesting. And the result of his inquiries was a resolution to go up to town and see Montague, who did not want to go to India. Edgbaston and the rest might laugh, but Frank said to himself that he was far from having made up his mind, and that it was very important for him to acquaint himself with all the circumstances. It was on a June day when he went up to town in pursuance of this resolution, hot enough to dissuade any man from business, and especially from business connected with India. 'If it is like this in Pall Mall, what will it be in Calcutta?' Frank asked himself; but, nevertheless, he was not to be dissuaded. Montague, however, though certified on all sides to be at home, was not to be found. Frank sought him at his rooms, at one club after another, at the agent's,—everywhere he could think of,—but was unsuccessful. To be sure he got all the necessary information, which answered his purpose almost as well; but the ineffectual search tired him out. He was so thoroughly sick of it, and the day was so hot, that none of his usual haunts or occupations attracted him as it happened. After he had fortified himself with sherry and biscuits, he went rambling forth to spend his time in some misanthropical way till it should be time to return to Royalborough; but the best way that occurred to him for doing that was to take a walk. The Row was deserted; so, of course, it would have been foolish to go there; and he did not feel disposed to make calls; and lounging about the club,—or, indeed, anywhere where he should meet men and be questioned on all hands about himself and his brothers,—was a trial he was not equal to in his present frame of mind. So he went out to walk, which was a curious expedient. And of all places in the world to go to, turned his steps in the direction of the Regent's Park, which, as everybody knows, is close to Fitzroy Square.

I have never been able to understand what was Frank's motive in setting out upon this walk. He knew very well,—none better,—that it was entirely out of the world. What a Guardsman could have to do in such a neighbourhood, except, indeed, to visit a wayward brother, nobody could have imagined; and now the wayward brother was gone. He said to himself that he did not mind where he went, so long as it was quite out of the way of meeting anybody; and yet on ordinary occasions Frank had no objection to meeting people. He went up Harley Street, scowling at those scowling houses, and then he went into the smiling, plebeian park, among all the nursery-maids. How funny it was, he said to himself, to notice the difference between this and the other parks, and persuaded himself that he was studying life on its humdrum side. He looked into the steady little broughams meandering round and round the dull terraces. Was it any pleasure to the old ladies to drive about thus, each in her box? And then he walked down the centre walk, where all the children were playing. The children were just as pretty as if they had been in Kensington Gardens. Mrs. Suffolk's babies trotted past, with signs of old Rich's two hundred and fifty pounds in their little summer garments, though Frank knew nothing of them,—and he kept stumbling over two pretty boys, who recalled to him some face he knew, and to whom he seemed an object of lively curiosity. They held close conversations, whispering with their heads together, and discussing him, as he could see, and turned up wherever he went, hanging about his path. 'I tell you it ain't Laurie's ghost,' one of them said audibly, at length. 'He's twice as tall, and he's Laurie's brother.' 'Hallo!' Frank said, turning round upon them; 'you are the little Severns, to be sure.' No doubt it was the first time the idea had occurred to him. He must be close to Fitzroy Square, and being so, and Mrs. Severn having been such a friend of Laurie's, it was his duty to call. Clearly it was his duty to call. She was a friend of the Riches, too. There was thus a kind of connexion on two sides; and to be near and not to call would be very uncivil. Frank made friends with the boys without any difficulty, and took the opportunity of making them perfectly happy by a purchase of canes and whips from a passing merchant of such commodities, and set off for the Square under their guidance. It would not have mattered if Mrs. Severn had not known that he was in the neighbourhood; but of course the boys would hasten home and tell. And to be uncivil to so great a friend of Laurie's was a sin Frank would not have been guilty of for the world. Thus it will be seen that it was in the simplest, most unpremeditated way that he was led to call at the Square.

The scene he saw when he went in was a scene of which Laurie had once made a little drawing. Though it was so hot and blazing out of doors, the great window of Mrs. Severn's dining-room, which looked into her garden, was by this time of the afternoon, overshadowed by the projecting ends of her neighbours' houses, and admitted only a softened light. Alice sat full in the midst of this colourless day with her curls hanging about her shoulders, and her delicate face, with all its soft bright tints, like a flower a little bent upon its stem. The door of the dining-room was ajar; and this was how Frank managed to catch a passing glimpse as he was being ushered into the decorum of the great vacant drawing-room; for to be sure he was a stranger, and had no right to go as familiar visitors did, and tap at the padrona's studio-door. He saw as he passed Alice sitting by the window, her hands full of work, and her face full of contentment and sweet peace. And at her feet, like a rose-bud, sat little Edith, in all a child's carelessness of attitude, her little white frock tucked about her shapely, rosy limbs, her little feet crossed. Miss Hadley was in the shadow, and Frank did not see her. He thought Alice and her little sister were alone, and that he was in luck. He paused at the open door, though the maid led the way to the other. 'May I come in?' he said. Perhaps the tone was too much like that in which he had asked permission to enter the music-room at Richmont. Alice gave a great start at the sound of his voice, and dropped her work on the floor. 'Oh, Mr. Laurie's brother!' cried Edith, who was quite unembarrassed. And Frank felt himself charmed out of all reason by the little start and the flutter of the white work as it fell. 'I feared you were still at Richmont,' he said, 'and that I should not see you.' And so he went lightly in and found himself in Miss Hadley's presence, with her sternest countenance on, a face enough to have driven out of his wits the most enterprising cavalier in the world.

'It is Mr. Frank Renton,' said Alice. 'Miss Hadley, Mr. Renton's brother;' and Miss Hadley made him a curtsey, and looked him through and through with her sharp eyes, for which Frank was so entirely unprepared. The thought of finding Alice all by herself had been so charming to him, and he had brightened into such genuine exultation, that the way in which his face fell was amusing to see.

'Your mamma will be very glad to see Mr. Renton's brother, I am sure,' said Miss Hadley. 'Run, my dear, and tell her; and ask if he shall go to the studio, or if she will come here.'

'Don't disturb Mrs. Severn, pray, for me,' said the discomfited Frank. 'I was in the neighbourhood, and by accident met the boys in the park. I could not be so near without calling; but pray don't disturb her for me.'

'She is sure to want to see you,' said Miss Hadley. 'Have you heard from your brother? It was so very unexpected to us all his going away. I hope it was not his health. But you young men think so little of travelling now-a-days. Is it you who are going to India, Mr. Renton? Your brother used to talk a great deal of you.'

'Yes, I think I am going to India,' said Frank. Alice was standing putting her work aside before she went to tell her mother of Frank's presence; but at these words she turned half round with an involuntary movement,—he could see it was involuntary, almost unconscious,—and gave him a soft look of inquiry and grief. 'Must you go away,—shall we never see you again?' said the eyes of Alice. The tears were ready to spring and the lips to quiver, and then she returned to the folding of her work, and blushed all over her pretty throat.

And Frank saw it, and his heart swelled within him. To think she should care! Nelly disappeared out of his thoughts like the merest shadow,—indeed, Nelly had not been in his thoughts since he left Royalborough. 'I have not quite made up my mind yet; but I fear I must go,' he continued, answering her look. And Miss Hadley, always sharp, noticed at once the changed direction of his eyes.

'Run, my dear, and tell your mother,' she said. 'I will put your work away for you, and Edie may go and play with the boys. Run out into the garden, children. We cannot have you all making a noise when people are here.'

'But I want to stay and talk to Mr. Laurie's brother,' cried Edith. 'I love Laurie; there is nobody so nice ever comes now. And Alice loves him too,' said the little traitor, 'and tells me such stories when she is putting me to bed, about Richmont.'

'But, you silly child, it was Mr. Frank Renton who was at Richmont,' said Miss Hadley. Upon which the child nodded her head a great many times, and repeated, 'I know, I know.'

'Your brother was such a favourite with them all,' said Miss Hadley, apologetically, 'they get confused to know which Mr. Renton it is. He is very nice. Is he just wandering about on the face of the earth, or has he settled down anywhere? I don't think Mrs. Severn has heard; and that is strange too.'

'We don't know exactly what route he has taken,' said Frank, 'He is not much of a letter-writer. Of course my mother hears. And I don't think it is anything about his health. There is such pleasure to a fellow like Laurie, who never thinks of anything, in the mere fact of travelling about.'

'I always thought he considered everybody before himself,' said Miss Hadley.

'He never pays the slightest attention to his own affairs,' said Frank, 'which comes to very nearly the same thing; and yet he is the best fellow that ever was born.'

Having thus exhausted the only subject which they had in common, he and Miss Hadley sat and gazed at each other for some time in silence. The governess was very well aware that Laurie had not gone away for his health,—indeed, she had a shrewd suspicion what it was that had driven him away,—and she could not but look at Frank with watchful, suspicious eyes, feeling that there was something in his uncalled-for visit, in his embarrassment, and Alice's start and look of interest, more than met the eye. There might have been no harm in that, had he been staying at home. But a young man on the eve of starting for India! It would break her mother's heart, Miss Hadley said to herself; and though she was sometimes troublesome, and almost intrusive in her vigilance, the governess loved her friend with that intense affection of one woman to another,—generally of a lonely woman to one more fortunate than herself,—which is so seldom appreciated and so little understood, but which sometimes rises to the height of passion. Jane Hadley made herself disagreeable by times to the padrona, but would have been cut in pieces for her,—would have lain down to be trampled over,—could she have done any good by such an act to the being she held highest in the world. Therefore it immediately occurred to her that her first duty was to discourage and snub this new visitor. Going away to India, and yet trying to make himself agreeable in the eyes of Alice, was a sin of the deepest dye.

'You were going to change into another regiment, your brother said,' remarked Miss Hadley. 'When do you leave? I should think, on the whole, it would be pleasanter to change the monotony of your leisure for a more active life.'

'It is not settled yet,' said Frank. 'But I suppose I'll go. Yes; it is rather monotonous doing garrison work at home.'

'And what part of India are you going to?' Miss Hadley continued. Frank began to get irritated by the questions. Confound India! he did not want to think of it,—or, indeed, to trouble his mind with anything at that moment. He wanted Alice to come back again, to look at him, to speak to him, to play for him. He kept his eyes on the door, and felt that the place was empty till she came. Here it was he had seen her first. There, under the curtains in the doorway, she had stood lighting up the darkness with her face; there she had sat making the tea;—how clearly every little incident dwelt on his mind! As for Nelly Rich, he had not the slightest recollection where he saw her first, nor what the circumstances were. He was never restless for her return when she was out of the room; but at that moment he did not even pay Nelly Rich the compliment of contrasting his feelings in respect to her with his feelings to Alice Severn. He simply forgot her existence, and watched the door, and stammered what reply he could to the inquisitor who sat opposite to him,—like an old cat he said,—watching him with her keen eyes.

And when the door opened at last it was only Mrs. Severn who came in. Frank absolutely changed colour, and grew pale and green with disappointment. Laurie had thought her a type of everything most perfect in woman; but to Frank she was a sober personage, comely and middle-aged, and Alice's mother, which indeed was her real appearance in the world. She came in with a gleam of interest in her eyes, and a little eagerness in her manner. She had not taken off her painting-dress, but she had put aside her brushes and her palette, and sat down by him without any fuss about abandoning her work. With her intimates she worked on without intermission, but to strangers the padrona ignored the constant labour which filled her life.

'Have you brought us some news of your brother, Mr. Renton?' she said. 'I shall be so glad to hear he is safe in Rome. He should not have gone so late in the year.'

'No, I have no particular news,' said Frank. 'His going took us all by surprise. My mother has had two or three little notes, I believe. I was in the neighbourhood,' he added in an explanatory, apologetic way, 'and thought I would call.'

'I am very glad to see you,' said the padrona; 'Laurie Renton's brother can never be but welcome here. I have known him so long,—since he was a boy,' she added, with a little colour rising on her cheek, seeking in her turn to excuse the warmth with which she spoke; but the blush was for Jane Hadley quietly seated in the background seeing everything, and not for the unconscious Frank.

'Oh, thanks,' said Frank. 'Laurie was always speaking of you. I met Miss Severn the other day at Richmont. She might tell you, perhaps. How she plays! I don't think I ever heard anything like it. It draws the heart out of one's breast.'

'Ah, yes, Alice plays very well,' said Mrs. Severn, with placid complacency. 'She is doing something for me in the studio. She is as clever with her needle as she is with her music,' she added, calmly. Clever! and to compare her needlework with her music! This speech went a long way to prove that the padrona was a very ordinary, commonplace personage in Frank's eyes. That, however, did not matter so much. What was a great deal more important was that Alice did not return.

'I hope she liked Richmont,' he said; 'they are kind people, and the country is lovely just now. You don't know Renton, Mrs. Severn? My mother, I am sure, would be charmed to see you, and Laurie must have told you of our woods. My mother is a great invalid. She has always been so as long as I can recollect, but she would be delighted to see you. I wish I could persuade you and Miss Severn to come down for a day; I could row you up from Cookesley,' said Frank, eagerly. Alice came in just in time to hear these last words, and gazed at her mother with a longing look. She had not heard the previous part of the proposal, but to be rowed up the river from Cookesley! The words flushed her young imagination with every kind of delight.

'It is very tempting,' Mrs. Severn said, 'but I fear we must not think of it. Alice, you must go and make some music for Mr. Renton; he likes your playing. Are you in town only for the day?'

'Only for the day,' said Frank; and then he paused and put on his suppliant look. 'When I was here with Laurie I was allowed to stay to tea.'

'And so you shall stay to tea if you like it,' said the padrona, laughing. And Alice gave him a momentary glance and a soft little smile of content. A paradisiacal sense of well-being and happiness glided over Frank he could not tell how. It was something quite new and strange to him. He had been happy most part of his life,—not being yet quite one-and-twenty, poor fellow!—happy for no particular reason,—because he was alive, because he was Frank Renton, because he had got something he wanted; but this was a totally different sort of happiness. It seemed to float him away from all mean and indifferent things; he was mounted up on a pinnacle from the heights of which he contemplated the rest of the world with a tender pity; he was enveloped in an atmosphere of blessedness. This intoxicating yet subduing delight seemed to him the natural air of the place in which he was. They must breathe it all day long these happy people; even the governess who sat grim over her knitting and watched him with keen eyes. It was the air of the place, though the place was Fitzroy Square, in the heart of London, on the way to the City; for never in the summer woods, never at home in his hereditary house, never amid the luxuries and delights of society, had he breathed anything like it. He did his best to make himself agreeable to Mrs. Severn, but it cannot be asserted that he was sorry when she left the room, which she did after a while. True, Miss Hadley was there, more watchful than a dozen padronas; but the watchfulness seemed appropriate somehow and was harmonised by the atmosphere, just as summer air harmonises all out-door noises. The children rushed to the garden, getting tired of the quiet, and Alice went into the other room and began to play. I have said it was the only poetry of which Frank was susceptible. All the poets in one could not have moved him as these sweet, inarticulate floods of sound did, making the atmosphere more heavenly still, breathing a heart into it full of soft longings and a tender languor. The house, as we have said, was on the shady side of the Square— the great drawing-room felt like some cool, still, excluded place, in the midst of the hot and lingering afternoon. Frank threw himself into a chair at the other end of the room, from whence he could watch the musician without disconcerting her. There were the three great windows draped in white like tall ghosts ranged against the wall; and the chairs and tables all grouped in a mysterious way as if there were whispering spectators who marked all; and the cool grey-green walls with here and there the frame of a picture catching the light; and Alice in her fresh muslin gown, white, with lines and specks of blue, with blue ribbons tied among her curls, and her bright eyes intent and her white hands rippling among the ivory keys. The only thing that had ever made a painter of Frank was his meeting with Alice. His mind was becoming a kind of picture-gallery hung with sketches of her. He remembered every look, almost every dress she had ever worn,—the dark neutral-tinted one that night, the white at Richmont, and now the glimmer of blue ribbons among the curls,——

After a time Miss Hadley, who sat there patient with her knitting, like a cat watching a mouse, was called away for something and had to leave them reluctantly. And then it is undeniable that Frank took advantage of her absence and stole a little closer to the piano. He even interrupted Alice ruthlessly in the midst of her sonata.

'Play me this,' he said, humming the bars that haunted him. He was even so bold as to approach his hand to the piano and run over the notes. 'It was the first thing I had ever heard you play,' the young man added; 'I have done nothing but sing it ever since. Ah, forgive me for stopping you! Let me hear it again.'

'It is very lovely,' faltered Alice, stooping her head over the keys; and then by chance their eyes met and they knew—— What? Neither said another word. Alice's fingers flew at the keys with the precipitancy of haste and fear. She spoiled the air, her heart beating so loud as to drown both tune and time. As the notes rushed out headlong after each other, an indifferent looker-on would have concluded poor Alice to be a school-girl in the fullest musical sense of the word. But Frank, though he was a connoisseur, never found it out. He sat down behind her listening with a perfect imbecility of admiration. It might have been St. Cecilia, it might have been the angels playing in heaven whom Cecilia heard. To him it was a strain divine. To think that he had not known of Alice's existence when he heard these notes first! He began to babble in the midst of the music, quite unconscious of doing anything amiss.

'When I heard you play that first I had never seen you,' he said, and though Alice was at the crisis of the melody her hand slackened and lightened to listen. 'I could not think who it could be. I thought you must be the sick one of the family or something. And then, when your mother called you and you came and stood in the door——'

Alice now stopped altogether and did her best to laugh. 'What a very good memory you must have,' she said. 'I am sure I could not have remembered all that.'

'Yes; I have a good memory,—for some things,' said Frank, while she half unconsciously kept running on with one hand among the treble keys, half drowning his voice, half making an accompaniment to it. 'Your mother spoke of you in such a tone—I understand it now, but it bewildered me at the time, I thought you must be ill—or—sickly—or something. And then she called Alice, and you appeared under the curtains; I can see it all as plain as if it had happened yesterday. Laurie chattering enough for six with his back turned, and you standing in the doorway like——'

Alice made a great crash on the piano and burst at once into a grand symphony. Instinct told her to play, and it was just as well she had done so, for one minute after Miss Hadley appeared with her perpetual knitting in her hand. She gave Frank a look when she perceived his change of position and herself approached the piano. A young fellow who was going to India! That was his sole and unique description to Miss Hadley,—and she was deeply indignant at his presumption. The symphony was a long one, but Alice was restored to herself. Safety had come in place of danger. She had not wanted Miss Hadley to return, and yet under shelter of Miss Hadley her faculties came back to her. There was a good deal of crash and execution in what she was now playing, and it suited her feelings. It was a kind of music which Frank would have scorned at from any other player, but oddly enough it chimed in with his feelings now. They were both tingling all over with soft emotion and that first excitement of early love, in which it is the man's object to say as much as he may under covert of commonplace observations, and the woman's to receive it as if it meant nothing and to escape from all appearance of comprehension. And yet if by chance they looked at each other both knew, not what they were aiming at certainly, but in some darkened, vague degree that there was a meaning, and a very decided one underneath.

Then Mrs. Severn appeared again in her black silk gown, and the tea was set upon the table, and Alice made it as she had done before. It was like the same scene repeated, and yet it was not the same. Alice who had been to him but a fairy vision was now—— What was she now? Frank made a sudden jump from that side of the question, and felt his cheeks flush and a delicious glow come over his heart. But, not to speak of Alice, he himself was no longer an accidental guest received for his brother's sake; but if not a friend, at least an acquaintance received for his own. To Alice at least he was more than an acquaintance. 'I have lived in the same house with Miss Severn, and I feel as if we were old friends,' he said, and Alice, with a soft blush and smile, did not reject the claim. 'How pretty it was at Richmont!' she said, with a soft, little sigh. And if it had not been for that dreadful old governess, who broke in, in the most abrupt way, with something about India! What was India to her? What had she to do with it? If a man wanted for the moment to forget everything that was disagreeable, what business had Miss Hadley to interfere? Frank as nearly turned his back upon her when she made her second interpellation on the subject as good-breeding would allow. Was it her business? He was very wroth with the meddler, but very soft and benignant with every one else, talking to Edith—to the child's immense delight—as if she were grown up, and discussing games with the boys, and making himself very generally agreeable. He stayed long enough to watch the people beginning to arrive on their evening calls, and accepted all the circumstances of the house with the profoundest satisfaction and sense of fitness. But he could not find any more private opportunities of making known his recollections or his fancies to Alice, and went away at last when he had but time for his train, with a sense of intoxication and absorption in he knew not what golden dreams. India!—but soft—India, when a man came to think of it, might for anything he knew, involve brighter possibilities than he had yet contemplated. Speak low; whisper low. When this thought occurred to Frank he ran and took his leave with a sensation as if a whole hive of bees had set to buzzing in his head. As I have said it intoxicated him. He had need to go away, to get himself into the morose solitude of the train to think it over. The sudden light that had burst upon his path took all power of vision from his dazzled eyes.

CHAPTER XVIII.

WAVERING.

It has been seen that Frank Renton was not, in any sense of the words, a model young man. He was not offensive nor disagreeable, but as a pure matter of fact, the centre of his own world, as, indeed, we all are more or less. When it had been placed so very clearly before him that it was to his advantage to marry money, he had acquiesced, with a little struggle, feeling that the advantage was so great as to create a duty; but now, after this bewildering day, another prospect altogether opened before his eyes. He had forgotten Nelly. For the moment she passed from his mind, as if she had never been, and Alice had risen upon him like the sun. He could perceive now that from the first moment his heart had claimed her. Happiness, companionship, the very light of life, seemed to be concentrated for him in that simple youthful creature, ignorant of the world, innocent as a child, sweet with the earliest freshness of existence. He had no need to reason about it, to say to himself that it was she whom he wanted, she whom he had unconsciously been groping for; he knew it; it was clear as daylight; he seemed to himself to have been aware of it all along, from the earliest moment. A voice from heaven had spoken to him, as to Adam, crying, 'This is she.' Such was the thought that filled his mind as he went down to Royalborough in the dark and damp loneliness of the railway carriage. He had so much thinking to do that he had warned the guard that he must have a compartment to himself; and there he lay back in his corner with a very black shadow thrown on him from the dim lamp, and floated forth upon this Elysian sea of thought. But it was only for the first two minutes that it was Elysian. All at once he sat bolt upright, and remembered that he had forgotten something. Nelly! This recollection rushed at him like another railway train in the darkness, so that there was a sharp and violent collision. After the first shock Frank began to consider anxiously how far he had gone on that other side, what words he might have spoken, what inferences had been made. Only yesterday, it must be allowed, he was making very decided way towards Nelly. He had been softened, and brought nearer to her personally, and the house and the hunters had held a very high place in his thoughts. He had persuaded his mother to call, and written a note which was not at all unlike the first beginning of love-making. And yet, to-day, he had forgotten Nelly's existence. When he recollected all this, he grew suddenly very hot, and very uncomfortable. Love, even when it is unfortunate, has something sweet in it; but the thought of Nelly's little indignant face was not sweet. He had never loved her; he had never, even to himself, pretended to be fond of her. He had represented to himself that if they were married, no doubt the time would come when he should be fond of his wife. But while he was thus deciding in cold blood, the other had but to give a glance, and all was over with Nelly. When this terrible complication became apparent, Frank no longer found that there was anything Elysian in his circumstances; for this discovery suddenly revealed to him the entire circumstances of the case. Nelly was marriageable, for she was very rich; but Alice was poor. If the wealth of the one out-balanced the objections against her in respect to birth and breeding, there was no such saving clause in respect to the other. Even Mr. Rich patronised Mrs. Severn. The artist's family was of no rank, and had no such social standing whatever, not even that conferred by money. As for the distinction of art,—Frank was too much a man of the world not to know for how little that counted. Penniless, without connexions or prospects, or blood, or anything,—a creature who was only herself, and possessed only the qualities of her own mind and heart! To make such a marriage, Frank was aware, would be sheer madness. Nelly was different. Nelly meant Cookesley Lodge, with all its accompaniments and a certain sum a-year. Alice meant nothing but her simple self. No wonder the moisture stood heavy on his forehead. He had been a fool, in suffering himself to be thus moved out of all sense and prudence. And yet when he tried to turn to other thoughts his heart grew sick. He—almost—made a vow never to think of anybody, never to look at any one more. Why was fate always so spiteful? Why was it that Alice had not Nelly's fortune, or Nelly Alice's charms? It was not that he was mercenary. Money, except for what it brought, was not important to Frank; but there is a difference between being mercenary and being an idiot. And he knew so well what the world would say if, instead of marrying money, he married a girl who had nothing,—neither money nor any other substantial recommendation. He would be laughed at, and she would be snubbed,—and who could wonder at it? Thus Frank reasoned with himself, and groaned in his heart. And then he thought of India, and the world stood still for a moment that he might look that possibility in the face.

India! In the first place, it was out of the world, and the ridicule attending his fiasco would not, in India, be so overwhelming; but at the same time, the world is a very small place, and news would travel faster than by telegraph to everybody who was anybody. In India the pay was double, which was a very great matter; but then, on the other hand, would not the expenses be greater too? Not, of course, in proportion to Cookesley Lodge and the hunters, which, alas! it was no use thinking any more about, but in proportion to the tiny *ménage* which a young soldier with two hundred a-year, besides his pay, might venture on at home. And here, once more, Frank drew himself up, with a sensation of misery. Two hundred a-year and his pay barely sufficed for himself. To marry upon it would be simple madness, neither more nor less. And to wait seven years—— No! India was the only chance. It was the most usual thing in the world for a young fellow going out there to marry before he went;—therefore it must be practicable. There would be no society nor expensive habits,—as he supposed, in his ignorance,—and there was the chance of appointments, which was always worth taking into account. Frank contemplated the question all round, but it was a very dreary horizon which encircled him on every side. Poverty, the renunciation of most things which had made life agreeable—a struggle with care and the burdens of serious life,—instead of Cookesley and the hunters and terriers, and the country gentleman's existence, for which he had evidently been created! There was so much good in the young man however, that though he could not but contrast the two existences which thus seemed to be set before him, he could not and did not contrast the two through whose hands their different threads must run. He made no comparison there. Nelly had been swept out of his sky the moment Alice appeared.

One thing was quite clear to him at this crisis of excitement and emotion, while the image of Alice still danced before his eyes with all her soft looks and words;—Cookesley and its delights,—meaning Nelly and her fortune,—were impossible,—quite impossible; altogether out of the question. He had been capable in the abstract of doing a duty to himself and the world, and securing,—in default of Laurie, for whom he always acknowledged the position would have been so much more suitable,—all those advantages which seemed to be held out to him in Nelly Rich's hand. He liked her very well, and no doubt would have grown fond of her in time. That he could have done. His own interests, and the unanimous voice of his friends, and the appeal of the world in general, had all but decided the question. But Frank, notwithstanding the prudent and practical character of his understanding, was true and honest at bottom. And as soon as he discovered beyond question that he was in love with one woman, it became impossible for him to marry another, whatever the advantages might be which she brought with her. He was not capable of that. It was indispensable to him to be true, if not to Alice, who knew nothing about his sentiments, at least to Nelly. She had a right to it. He could have married her yesterday, but he could not deceive her to-day. What could he do? The clouds closed in upon him, swallowed him up, the more he thought it over. Do! Nothing but trudge forth to India, leaving his hopes of every description behind him,—a saddened and a solitary man. Neither one thing nor another, neither love nor wealth were practicable.

'I must never see her again,' Frank said to himself, as he got out of the train; 'I must never see her again!' Perhaps it was because of the very practicality and matter-of-fact character of his mind that he felt it dangerous to permit himself such an indulgence. He could not go and gaze and moon about her, as other men might, without anything coming of it. The only safeguard would be to keep away altogether. But it was not a cheerful thought; and,

- 153 -

consequently, when he emerged from the station with his hat down over his brows, a certain air of tragedy and misery was about the poor fellow. And if the reader of this sober history should at any time encounter on the railway between London and Royalborough an unfortunate and melancholy Guardsman, well thrown back into the shadow of the lamp, gnawing his moustache as he chews the cud of fancy, let him remember the miserable perplexities of poor Frank Renton, and pity the man. The impulse of the mature spectator's mind is so invariably to vituperate the military butterfly, that it is the duty of the benevolent moralist to turn the tide of sympathy towards that beautiful, frivolous, yet sometimes suffering creature, when he has the opportunity. After all, Guardsmen are men.

Frank kept his resolution for a week. He gave himself a fair trial. To describe the cogitations which passed through his mind during that time, would only weary the reader without bringing him any nearer to the issue of the conflict; for, to be sure, it does not matter so very much what conclusion a young man may arrive at in such a contest, after even weeks of thought. Five minutes may destroy the entire fabric at any time;—a sudden meeting,—three words,—all unpremeditated on either side,—a chance look,—even a few notes of music played unawares by strange hands,—will suffice to undo the finest piece of reasoning ever put together. Nor is it at all unusual in Frank's circumstances for a young man to make an absolute determination against marriage one day, and go and lay himself at the feet of the lady of his affections on the next. Many times, it must be allowed, Cookesley Lodge would burst like a sudden revelation upon the young man's soul. He could hear the hunters rattling up the avenue, and the dogs yelping a chorus of welcome; and then this charming home-scene would give place to a misty conception of an Indian bungalow,—whatever that might be,—and the fierce delights of a jungle-hunt. The question was not Alice or Nelly,—that would have horrified him;—but Cookesley with all possible comforts and indulgences, and India with none;—question enough to make a man ponder. Four or five days after his visit to London, though it seemed four or five years from the multiplicity of his thoughts, he rode over to Richmont, on an unacknowledged mission to prove to himself whether that image of Alice, which he had been trying hard to banish, would disappear before the close realisation of all the good things on the other side. He had tried to forget her, or rather he had tried to shut her out from his thoughts; to divert his mind to anything else in the world rather than allow it to dwell upon her. And he was now going to test what success he had had. Nelly Rich was sketching under the trees, as we have before seen her, when he rode up to the door; and instead of going in to pay his respects to her mother, Frank,—with a strong sense of duty,—crossed the lawn to where the white figure, with sketching-block on her lap, and bright ribbons fluttering about her, sat in the shadow of the soft limes. A prettier picture could not have been desired. The dead white of the dress blazed out in the sunshine, lying in crisp folds upon the soft grass. The silken lime-leaves made a flutter and chequer of light and shade upon the pretty drooping head. Nelly was older, more piquant, more expressive, indeed, to any unprejudiced eye more beautiful, than Alice Severn; not, as Frank said to himself hotly, that he ever had made such a profane comparison. But yet it was impossible thus to approach the one without thinking of the other. There was a technicality and a pretension, he thought, about all this paraphernalia of the artist. When Alice went softly to her piano, you never could have told, until you heard her, that she was anything but a school-girl. And no one seemed to give her any particular glory for her music. She was a little girl to all of them. Whereas Nelly was the mistress of everything, more mistress in the house than was her mother, and getting credit for all sorts of talent and cleverness. In his heart Frank took up a position of defence for the absent, whom, indeed, no one dreamt of attacking. No doubt he would have to talk of the sketch, and admire it as if it had been something very fine. At Fitzroy Square the mother had smiled and had just admitted that Alice played well;—and that she was as clever at her needle as at her music. How strange was the difference!

'Is it you, Mr. Renton?' said Nelly; and she put down her sketching-block hastily as he approached. 'I could not make you out till you came quite close. Did you not find mamma?'

'I confess I did not ask,' said Frank; and the consciousness that he was paying a compliment which he did not mean embarrassed him in his peculiar circumstances; 'I saw you here——' and then he stopped, the unfortunate youth giving double meaning to his words.

Nelly blushed. It was very natural she should after such an address; and her change of colour told upon Frank as the most terrible reproach. 'I thought Mrs. Rich would be with you,' he added, hurriedly; 'it is so pleasant out-of-doors on such a day. You were sketching, I am sure, and I have stopped your work.'

'Oh, it does not matter,' said Nelly. 'I want to draw the house, and I cannot get it just as I want it. I must have in the window of the music-room. You know I live there. I don't care for all the rest of the house in comparison with that one room.'

'Yes,' said Frank, with a sudden relapse, 'with such music as we had there the other day, the place was like paradise.'

'You liked little Alice Severn's playing,' said Nelly. 'Ah! yes, I remember. She plays very well. For myself I am not fanatical about music. I don't understand it. I want to know what it says, and it says nothing. And these musical people are so exclusively musical, they never seem to have brains for anything else.'

'But that could not be the case with—Miss Severn, I should think,' said Frank, taking a foolish pleasure in speaking of her, and making a little pause before her name like a worshipper. Nelly gave him a quick glance, and answered carelessly.

'Oh, Alice! She is a good little thing enough; but I don't think she has much brains,—few girls have,—or men either for that matter. I don't expect anything of the kind from people who come to this house.'

'You are not complimentary to your visitors,' said Frank, feeling mortified, and with a secret sense that something at least of this condemnation was intended for himself.

'Well, Mr. Renton, few of our visitors are complimentary to us,' said Nelly, with a flush on her face, which even Frank perceived was quite different from the soft blush which had greeted his first appearance. Probably her quick ear had caught some difference in his tone, though he was not himself aware of it. 'We are rich, and you come to us when we ask you, and are very civil; but I know you laugh at us behind our backs, and make very free with our names, and do not show us the respect you would to the most miserable creature who was of good family. And then you think we are taken in by it, and don't know——'

'Miss Rich, you must allow me to say that personally you are doing me a great injustice,' said Frank, colouring high. 'I cannot undertake to be responsible for everybody who comes here; but so far as myself and my friends are concerned——'

'Oh, I beg your pardon!' cried Nelly, turning her face towards him with sudden shame and penitence which made it beautiful. Her large brilliant eyes were full of tears, and the eloquent blood had rushed to her cheeks. She held out her hands to him in the fervour of her compunction. 'Oh, forgive me!—do forgive me! I was cross. I did not know what I was saying. I did not mean you.'

There was nothing that Frank could do but take the pretty, soft, appealing hands, and hold them in his own for a moment. He did not kiss them, as no doubt he would have done had he never paid that visit to the Square. 'There is nothing for me to forgive,' he said in softened tones. And then Nelly recovered herself, and took her hands away.

'But you must forgive me,' she said, 'for being cross to you, who, I am sure, did not deserve it. Your mother called on Wednesday, and mamma was so pleased. You know we are new people,—very new people—and it is a great thing for us to have Mrs. Renton calling. But because we are such spick-and-span new people we have always something happening to vex us. One hears bits of gossip about you officers,—how you laugh and discuss one, and take things in your head,' said Nelly, breaking off suddenly, and looking full in Frank's face. What did she mean? Whatever it was, it covered him with embarrassment and shame. This conversation at least was true. He had been taking things in his head, and he did not know how to meet her look, or give her any reply.

'I don't know to what you refer,' he faltered. 'I am sure, Miss Rich——' and then he broke off altogether, so great was his confusion under the steady light of her keen eyes. 'There is no doubt,' he went on, as soon as he recovered himself, 'that everything possible and impossible is talked about. It is the fashion everywhere now-a-days. You know it as well as I. But had anything that was less than respectful ever been breathed in my presence——'

'I was quite sure of that,' said Nelly, leaning towards him with glowing eyes and expressive face. The eyes were full of soft gratitude, and something that looked like a tender pride. 'I know that,' she repeated; 'you have always been so different!' The voice had fallen quite low, so that Frank had to lean forward to hear it. And there was encouragement in her look for anything he might have had to say, for anything he might have been moved to do, in the excitement of the moment. And Frank's heart was softened by compunction and the sense that he was not so blameless as he had claimed to be. The crisis of his fate had come.

THE END OF THE SECOND VOLUME.